THE SERPENT'S SIN

BOOKS BY KATHRYN ANN KINGSLEY

THE IRON CRYSTAL SERIES
To Charm a Dark Prince
To Bind a Dark Heart
To Break a Dark Cage
To Love a Dark Lord

THE MASKS OF UNDER SERIES
King of Flames
King of Shadows
Queen of Dreams
King of Blood
King of None
Queen of All

BLOODLINES SERIES
The Serpent's Bride

For a full list, visit www.kathrynkingsley.com

THE SERPENT'S SIN

KATHRYN ANN KINGSLEY

SECOND SKY

Published by Second Sky in 2026

An imprint of Storyfire Ltd.
Carmelite House
50 Victoria Embankment
London EC4Y 0DZ

www.secondskybooks.com

The authorised representative in the EEA is Hachette Ireland
8 Castlecourt Centre
Dublin 15 D15 XTP3
Ireland
(email: info@hbgi.ie)

ISBN: 978-1-80550-194-7
eBook ISBN: 978-1-80550-193-0

ONE

"If you help me murder my entire family."

Nadi couldn't process Raziel's words at first. They hung in the air between them as the wind whipped along the cliff and waves crashed against the rocks of the shore below the balcony.

What was *happening?*

Nadi blinked and took in the tableau before her. It would almost have been funny, if it weren't her problem to solve.

A small table, set for two—a white tablecloth underneath the delicate silverware and shining plates. Carefully prepared food, largely uneaten. A bottle of red wine. A pistol sitting beside it, pointed at her, placed there by her worst enemy.

Raziel Nostrom fit perfectly with the setting—the decaying and decrepit estate behind him, its stone walls crumbling beneath grasping vines, was his ancestral home, after all. It was past sunset, and the twilight sky cast shadows across his sharp features.

And then there was the corpse of Monica Valan—the woman Nadi was pretending to be—dead in a third chair next to them.

Nadi did the only thing that made sense in her head. The only thing that she could think of to do.

She laughed. *Hard.*

Raziel smiled faintly. Lacing his fingers together, in front of him, he sat back in his chair. "You don't believe me." A statement, not a question.

"You have everything." She gestured at him. "*Everything.* The metropolis—the *world*—at your fingertips. Money. Influence. Luxury. Good looks. Everyone and anything you could ever want. What possible goal could you be chasing that means you want them all dead? Is it just out of spite? You must see that you could never run their empire on your own."

Reaching out, Raziel poured himself another glass of wine. "Spite has nothing to do with it. Neither do jealousy or revenge. And you're quite right—Mael and Lana's underlings would never submit to my rule."

"So...?" Nadi eyed the gun on the table. She wondered if she could get to it first. Though, playing through the scene in her head—all the scenarios ended poorly. Even if she shapeshifted into someone else's form, Raziel was a vampire. He was faster, stronger, and tougher than she was in a face-to-face brawl.

She'd have to wait until she could catch him off guard.

Which was very unlikely at the moment.

The smile he paid her didn't reach his eyes. "I plan to throw all of the metropolis into chaos. And once I am done, I will rule over all vampires, humans, and fae alike—as my grandmother Lilivra once did."

Nadi stared at him blankly for a moment.

Then, she burst out laughing. Again.

And again.

This time, Raziel looked less entertained. He simply shrugged. "Mock me if you wish. I know my destiny."

She knew Raziel was *insane.* But she didn't know he was

delusional as well. This was his endgame? To destroy the Nostrom clan and to rule the metropolis? "How do you plan to destroy all the other vampire clans? Like the Rosovs, the Anotalis, the Molzars? Even the Toths would put up a fight."

He rolled his crimson eyes. "The Rosovs are the only true threat on that list. The others are annoyances. They will be useful servants in the new world I create. The Rosovs, however, will need to be dealt with. But only once my family is removed from the picture. One thing at a time."

"Right..." She paused. "And what happens if I say no?"

"I shoot you, and throw your corpse into the sacrificial crypt beneath the chapel. Along with the real Monica Valan." He smirked. "Seems only fitting that *both* my wives should be there, I suppose. Speaking of..." He reached for the gun and stood, pointing it across the table at Nadi. "Why don't we continue the conversation there. Seems more suitable. Besides. I'm sick of staring at her face."

Frowning, she stayed seated. "Pardon?"

"Get up, Nadi." He gestured with the gun. "I'd hate to have to shoot you."

She didn't know if he was serious, but she didn't particularly want to find out. Standing, she took a step back from the table and waited for more instructions.

Raziel walked over to Monica's corpse, and threw her over his shoulder as if she were a sack of potatoes. He motioned for Nadi to walk ahead of him. "You first, little murderer."

"I..." She hesitated.

His lips pulled into a thin line as he lifted the gun to point it straight at her forehead. "In. Now."

Yeah. All right. Fine. She walked into the estate. The sun had just finished setting, but her eyes adjusted quickly to the darkness inside the ruins. She liked the dark, honestly. A single bright moon gave her plenty of light to see by, casting dark and jagged shadows through the broken windowpanes of the building.

When she hit the first fork in the hallway, she paused. She had no idea where the chapel was. For all that she knew about Raziel, she knew nothing about his ancestral home. Why would she have ever bothered?

Raziel pressed the end of the gun to the spot between her shoulder blades. The cold metal sent an immediate shiver down her spine. "Left, beautiful."

Gritting her teeth, she turned left.

Buildings were a lot like bodies, in their own way. They had bones. Flesh. And now, with plumbing and electric lights—veins, of a sort. And just like bodies, when left to the mercy of nature, they would rot away.

Nadi had a theory when it came to buildings. That two places, built identically and put side by side, would age differently if one was lived in and the other was abandoned. She had no idea why. But a place like this—a place that had no life in it—was like a corpse left to decay in the ground.

Its doors were stuck in the positions they were left in centuries ago, never to open or close again. Wallpaper peeled and flaked like dried skin. The detritus crunched under her feet as she walked. She'd never had a chance to put her shoes back on. Whatever—once she had been used to walking barefoot through the Wild. This was nothing.

And the Wild was present here, as well. For wherever humanity and vampires weren't hard at work to destroy it, nature would be eager to fill the gaps. Vines and growth were pushing through the stones at every opportunity, finding every crack and gap.

The faint purple glow coming from the vines felt like home to Nadi. The smell of it was welcome—almost comforting, given the insanity she'd been through lately. Some of her kind were almost able to *talk* to the Wild. And there were legends of some fae who could command it—but she was very far removed from anything like that. Still, she could almost feel a low hum that called to her whenever she was close by. Like a song, resonating within her.

Finally, they reached an enormous set of arched double doors. There were symbols carved into their wooden surfaces, but they were faded and worn—whatever they might have depicted was now impossible to make out. At least to her untrained eye.

"Open them." Raziel was still behind her, pointing the gun at the back of her head.

Bristling a little at once more being commanded by him, she stepped up to the doors and gave them a tug. They were stuck.

Cracking her neck from one side to the other, Nadi shifted her form to the biggest, strongest man she knew. Ivan. Raziel's hulking bodyguard.

"Huh!" Raziel laughed. "Now *that* is quite something. Clothes and all. How does that work? You tore your stockings earlier."

She glanced over her shoulder at him. "Can we save the explanations for another time?" She answered him in a voice that was now very much not her own.

"Oh, that is bizarre." Raziel grimaced. "I suddenly realize how uncomfortable you could make a great many things for me. My imagination is suddenly running wild with all the ways you could use that ability to make things... deeply strange. Such as our sexual encounters. Please return to your truer shape as soon as you open the doors."

"I'm fucking *working* on it, asshole." She lowered her shoulder and put all Ivan's strength and weight into ramming herself into one of the doors, pushing it open a few feet.

"Although I'm sure Ivan would be flattered to know you thought of him." Raziel was still staring at her with a look that seemed to combine fascination and disgust.

Once she finished shoving one of the arched doors open far enough for them to pass through, she dropped Ivan's form. She wasn't particularly keen on continuing to wear it around either. Ivan's form was convenient to use, but being that big and lumbering just felt unnatural. Combing a hand back through her dark hair, she barely got a chance to even blink before Raziel was gesturing with his gun again for her to walk down the center aisle of the chapel.

Now that she could take a moment to see it, she let out a small, surprised and impressed whistle.

The wooden pews were carved from dark mahogany. Their surfaces were black at first glance, only glinting reddish-gold in the reflection of the moonlight where they hadn't been damaged by time and weather.

At the head of the room was a stone altar. It was *ancient*—weathered and worn by time. It looked even older than the rest of the estate, if she had to guess.

But along the walls, framed by the columns that held up the suffering structure of the chapel, were paintings. Friezes that revealed what the chapel was built to worship. Not the Mother or Father moon. Not even the older, darker gods. It was a chapel in service to—and in worship of—*vampires*.

Pale figures, ghostly things illuminated by the moonlight streaming in through holes in the roof, all were gathered in procession facing the altar, each one bowing their head in reverence, hands raised in supplication.

"How much do you know of the history of Runne?" Raziel asked the question from behind her. "What do they teach you fae in the underground?" His tone was free of any sort of accusation or judgment. In this moment at least, he seemed honestly curious. "You seem educated. But you spent most of your life in the metropolis, from what I can gather."

His voice echoed in the room. The ceiling was tall, soaring high above them. There were several holes through it, and the rest was damaged, revealing the beams of the ceiling like a ribcage.

"I know enough. Why?" She glanced behind her. He still had the gun pointed at the back of her head, and the corpse slung over his shoulder.

"I'm interested in your side of the story. I know what was taught to me." He briefly gestured with his gun toward the paintings on the walls.

"Which was?" Nadi walked down the aisle, tracing her hand along the curves of the pews as she did.

"A tale of *noble liberation*. Of *freeing the sheep from their oppressors*." Sarcasm was thick in his voice. "The beastly and terrible fae overran this world. They kept the vampires and humans in servitude, and their cruelty knew no bounds. Until our great savior appeared..."

When Nadi reached the end of the aisle, she could see what the painting behind the altar depicted. It was of a beautiful woman—one who was unmistakably a vampire. Her skin was almost the same color as her hair—pure white, flowing around her, like it was caught in the drift of a river. Her head was haloed by both the Mother and Father moons.

She was the vision of youthful beauty. Her lips were a bright red, and her fangs were bared not in a grimace of violence, but in an expression of rapture. Her arms were held out as if to embrace those who might approach her.

And at her feet were gathered humans and other vampires alike, kneeling in supplication to the goddess.

"Behold." His tone was flat and devoid of any reverence. "Grandmother Lilivra."

"Bullshit?" She arched her eyebrow, though he couldn't see her expression from where he was standing behind her.

"Bullshit."

"So... She isn't real?"

"Oh, she's real." He walked up to stand in front of the altar.

The gun was still aimed at her. "There's a rope over by the wall there. Pull it."

"Why?"

"Because I only have two hands, Nadi."

Rolling her eyes, she headed over to the only thing she could think he could possibly be referencing. A rope fed through a series of pulleys through the floor and again through the ceiling. It was the only thing that looked like it had been touched in the past hundred years.

With a shrug, she took hold of the rope and pulled.

It didn't budge.

"I suppose you'll have to put Ivan's back into it." Raziel grinned, clearly pleased at his cleverness.

"Very funny." She sighed. Deciding to not make it that easy for him, Nadi shifted into Raziel's shape, instead. She grinned back at him with a mirror of his own amusement.

Raziel's expression instantly fell. "I do *not* like that."

"Then, don't run your mouth," she replied in his voice. She grabbed the rope and pulled. In his form, it soon began to move.

"Is there a limit on how many times you can shift in a day?" He seemed once more honestly curious.

"Not an exact number. But I can get tired. What about your hypnotism?" It was bizarre to hear his voice coming out of her mouth. She wasn't a fan of it either, to be frank.

"Mm. Same. Too many times, and I'm liable to give myself a migraine."

As she pulled the rope, a section of the stone floor rumbled and began to hinge open.

Ah yes. The crypt. For the sacrifices. That would make sense. Once the lid was hinged all the way open, Nadi tied off the rope and shifted her form back to her own. She was also eager to turn the focus of conversation back to the painting of Lilivra and away from herself. She gestured to the image of the painted woman. "If she's real, then why is she bullshit?"

"Hm?" Raziel glanced over at it. "I mean, her whole *story* is bullshit. This? All this sacrifice nonsense? The story of the ancient vampire who made the original deal for a sacrificial human? All these old *rituals*. It's made up." He dropped the real Monica on the ground next to the hole with a *thud*. "Lies and stories told to keep people in line. It's about power. Nothing more. Nothing less."

"But... you've met her."

He took his hair out of the ribbon that kept the long black strands tied at the base of his neck and combed his hand through it for a moment before retying it. He suddenly seemed to be in a very unusual mood. Serious. Dour, almost. "In a manner of speaking. She was behind a sheer curtain, sitting in a bed. She is over a thousand years old. At this point, she probably looks less like that"—he gestured up at the radiant image in the painting—"and more like the corpses in there"—he gestured at the gaping black hole into the crypt below. "A withered old hag."

That was when it hit her. "You want to kill her too."

"Of course I do!" He grimaced. "Look at this place! If she were really some kind of all-powerful *vampiric savior*, would our home have been left to rot? Would we be forced to cower in a festering city packed with humans? No! We let a *human* mayor rule the *human* city and we abide by their *human* rules!"

Nadi couldn't help but stare at him in fascination. This was the real Raziel. This was what she was missing this entire time —the piece of him that she had never understood.

"We are fed this horseshit story of how we defeated the fae and beat back the Wild. Yet we cower from it behind our walls. We let it take our home from us. The metropolis shrinks more than it grows, year after year after year." Raziel looked down at Monica Valan's body. Then, he used his foot to push the corpse into the pit.

Nadi would have remarked at how callous the act was. But,

in fact, it was remarkably similar to the way she'd disposed of Raziel's other bodyguard, Hank, not even thirty-six hours ago.

Sure. Fine. Monica had been innocent. Hank had been a willing accomplice of a vampiric mass murderer. There were differences. But a life was a life.

There was a *crunch* as the body hit what sounded like a pile of dried sticks at the bottom of the hole. But Nadi knew it wasn't kindling Monica had broken upon landing. It was a pile of her predecessors.

Raziel was still in a dark mood, his muscles tense as he went back to the pulley that would lower the stone slab back over the crypt.

Nadi stayed where she was to watch, the only mourner at a sad excuse for a funeral.

The slab fell into place with a resounding thud that resonated through the room, shaking loose some plaster from one of the walls.

As the dust settled, Nadi broke the silence. "You want to... what? Reclaim Runne in the name of vampires?" She couldn't help but laugh a little. "Murder your family and raise an army and run this world the *right* way?"

Raziel's red eyes glinted in the moonlight. He shifted his gun to his other hand, still pointed at her, as he took a step toward her. "Yes."

She couldn't believe what she was hearing. "You're going to fail, you know. You're going to die. And even if you don't, even if you kill your family, you won't win in a war against *nature*."

"That's where you're wrong." He smirked, taking another slow, careful step toward her. His expensive shoes clicked on the stone floor, echoing between his words. "Because this world has never seen anything like me."

He really was serious.

Deathly serious.

"And now, my dear sweet murderer... you have a very important decision to make."

"You want me to swear I'll help you?"

The laugh that left him was soft. "No." With one long stride, he nearly closed the distance between them, forcing her to step back. "You would simply lie. You would even likely believe it. You would do anything to have another chance to kill me, to kill my family." Another step, and she was forced up the stairs toward the altar.

"Then what?" Before she realized what he'd done, she'd backed up the stairs and into the altar, bumping into it. "If my words can't convince you, I don't know wh—"

He was fast. Damn vampires. In a blink, he closed the distance between them. Her breath hitched as he was suddenly right there, the gun pressed up underneath her jaw, silencing her, tilting her head back.

The darkness in his eyes wasn't violence. It wasn't rage. It was *lust*. Pure hunger as he watched her with those crimson eyes of his. He pressed the length of his thigh against hers, pinning her to the cold stone of the altar.

She bit back every part of her that wanted to moan at the sensation. At the feeling of the power in him. It should be revolting. She should *hate* this. Being at his mercy.

"Look at you... my beautiful little fae. My assassin. My killer in the dark. Look at all that *hatred*, all that uncertainty in your eyes—and what eyes they are. Like cut gems, sparkling in the night..." His voice was dusky and deep as he tilted her head farther back with the gun. Pressing his other hand to the stone beside hers, he leaned in to kiss her throat, slowly, as if savoring the taste. "I need you to answer something truthfully, Nadi. I need you to look me in the eyes and vow to me that you aren't lying."

"And if I can't...?"

"Then you and I are done here." He scraped his fangs against her skin, causing her to jolt.

Her head reeled. *Fuck.* Her body felt like it was on fire. She wanted him. *Needed* him. Damn him to the pits.

"You'll kill me."

"No. You leave here alive. Return to the Wild, to the shadows, return to hunting me and my family. I don't care—I'll let you disappear." He slid his free hand, very lightly, up the bare skin of her arm. It gave her goosebumps. The tenderness of it in sharp contrast to the press of the muzzle of the gun up underneath her chin.

It made her want to scream.

"I want to make sure you understand what's at stake here first, my perfect little creature." He tilted his head to the side slightly as he studied her features. "I am going to ask you a yes or no question. You can answer truthfully... or you can choose not to answer."

When she stayed silent, staring up into his ruby eyes, he continued. "But if you refuse to answer..." His anger turned into something wicked. Something dangerous as his lips turned up in a vicious, hungry grin. "I will *force* a response out of you. And trust me... I can be"—his hand tilted her head just slightly farther back with the gun—"very convincing..."

That should have terrified her. Absolutely horrified her. But her heart was racing with something that wasn't fear. No, it was something far more dangerous for her than that—because she could handle fear. No, it was desire. And if he hadn't pressed her up against the altar, her damn knees would probably have given out.

What in the moons was *wrong* with her?

"Ask your *fucking* question, vampire."

He placed the gun down on the altar next to her with a click before cupping her cheek in his hand. He rested his thumb against the hollow of her chin, the point of his nail just pricking the skin of her lower lip. His cologne, all spices and roses, washed over her.

"All the time we've spent together... when we've fucked. When we've laughed. When we've touched. What we've *shared,* you and I. All that we've exchanged." He tilted his head to the side just slightly, studying her face.

With a slow, creeping and purely evil smile, the Serpent asked his question. "Tell me, little fae... how much of your heart belongs to me?"

TWO

It felt like the world itself had dropped away. Like Nadi was in free fall. But all too quickly, the world came rushing up to meet her and she was slammed unforgivingly into it.

"How *dare* you!" She slapped his hand away from her before using both palms to shove him back a step. Going for the gun, she aimed it at him and pulled the trigger.

It clicked. Harmlessly.

She pulled it three more times.

Nothing.

"*Fuck—*" It wasn't loaded. *It hadn't been loaded the whole time.*

The laugh that left Raziel was pure evil. He didn't need the gun anymore, did he? Maybe he never needed it at all. "You've come so far, Nadi. You killed Hank. You risked everything. You killed your own *uncle* for this. Would you really throw it all away now?"

With a snarl, she threw the gun to the side of the room. It clattered against the wall.

"That is not an answer, little fae. To either of my questions." He grinned in triumph. He'd laid a trap. Baited it. And she'd stepped right in. "Yes or no. Have you ever felt something *real* between us? Answer me truthfully."

Adrenaline rushed through her. The sort of panic that hit when she was suddenly caught red-handed sneaking through someone's house, preparing to murder them or their family member.

She could walk out the door. She could just leave. She could. She *should*. But that was admitting something, wasn't it? That was admitting that she *couldn't* give him an answer.

The trap he'd laid was brilliant. Simple. *Flawless*. And superbly, wonderfully cruel.

She couldn't answer "no."

It would be a lie, wouldn't it? And it hadn't occurred to her until right then and there. The little bit of rot, of mold, that had been growing in the corner of her soul since who knew when.

To her absolute horror... some of it *had* felt real.

But like *fuck* she was going to tell him "yes."

Like *fuck* she was going to give that smugly smiling piece of bloodsucking *shit* exactly what he wanted to hear.

So instead, she growled, and launched herself at him, intending to claw his face off with her fingernails if she had to. *"You fucking bastard!"*

Raziel laughed, seemingly delighted by her answer. "What's wrong? Hm? Why can't you give me an answer? Isn't it a simple question? You despise me and you want me dead more than anything in the world, don't you?" He grabbed her by the wrists, yanking her off balance, nearly sending her crashing to the ground.

He outclassed her as a fighter on a good day, and she was too angry, too upset to focus on strategy.

He'd won the fight before she'd even started.

She knew it.

And he knew it.

But that didn't mean she wasn't going to try to take a chunk out of him. "Shut the *fuck up!*" She stomped on his foot as hard as she could, using her heeled shoes to her advantage.

He snarled in pain, throwing her forward and away from him. Her back hit the altar hard enough that it knocked the wind out of her for a moment.

Before she could turn, his hand was at the back of her neck.

He slammed her down over the table, pinning her to the surface. "Now, little murderer, we come to the very important part of all this." His voice was a deep growl as he pressed his body against hers. "Remember what I said... if you can't answer, I will *make* you answer..."

She could feel every inch of him as he ground his hips into hers, a promise and a threat. It took everything in her not to moan in anticipation.

By the moons, she wanted him to make good on that threat. She wanted to feel him *take*. To feel his power.

But it was wrong. He'd killed her family. She'd vowed revenge on him. Snarling, she pushed up as hard as she could, struggling, but it was useless. He was too strong. "Get *off* me!"

"If I let you up, it will be because you're planning on walking out that door and never coming back. Is that what you want? For me to let you go?"

She froze.

Leaving meant losing the close proximity to her kill. All the hard work she'd done and everything she'd sacrificed to get there.

Leaving also meant losing... Raziel.

And that cinched something around her heart in a way that made her so extremely disgusted at herself that she wanted to rip out her soul and burn it.

"Believe me, I understand how difficult this must be for you." He slowly began to run his hand along her thigh, pulling up her dress to her waist before gliding his hand over the globe of her ass, then pressing his hips into her again with a low groan.

"You hate me. You want me dead. And here you are... *wanting* me. And if that were all it was, that would be fine. But it isn't just that, is it? There's something more buried deep inside."

"Shut *up*—" She felt like she couldn't breathe. He was touching her. *Her*. Not Monica. *Her*. Nadi. A fae. This wasn't a lie. This wasn't a game. This wasn't all for show.

This. This was *real*. She'd never felt more exposed in her life.

"When was the last time you had sex as yourself?" He squeezed her ass hard, digging his fingers into the skin.

It did anything but make her want him to stop. She pulled in a hiss through her teeth and snarled at him, slamming her hand on the table. "Let me *up*, you *son of a bitch!*"

"That is a fair statement. My mother *is* a massive bitch." He laughed. "Answer my question, Nadi. When?"

She twisted, trying to claw at him, anything—desperate to simply hurt him. Make him bleed. He'd ripped her heart out of her chest, it was only fair she got to do the same to him.

"Ah-ah." She heard a click, and there was a press of cold metal to the side of her neck. A knife. "Be still for a moment, Nadi."

"Don't you dare!" She froze. But by all the gods, the sensation of the edge of the blade as he dragged it down, ever so carefully over her skin, not cutting her, just *teasing her*, made her want him more than she could put into words.

Pressing her forehead to the table, she let out a cry of frustration.

"I know. I truly do." He began cutting her clothes off with the knife, easily slicing through the fabric. "But, trust me—love and hate are not mutually exclusive."

He left her in just her stockings and her underwear. "Can you answer me yet? Yes or no?"

She was shivering. Not because she was cold.

His hands slowly slid up and down her sides, stroking her

body. Touching her. Touching *her*. Not Monica. Every curve was his to explore. Every inch. And he seemed intent on doing exactly that.

"So beautiful in the moonlight... I suppose that was what you were designed for, siren. Can you sing?"

She could. Quite well, actually. In another life, that was probably supposed to be her calling—luring sailors to their deaths with her song. But like *fuck* was she going to tell him anything about it.

Leaning down, he kissed her shoulder. She tried to jerk away from his touch, and he only chuckled at the useless gesture. "You have every right to be angry. Stay angry. I want to feel you fight me. I want to feel the moment you surrender."

"Fuck. You."

He stroked his hand lower, stepping back from her a bit so he could cup the core of her body. Her underwear had been ripped to shreds when she had shown him her true form. It made it easy enough for him to delve a finger inside of her, discovering quickly how much her body was not nearly so conflicted as her mind was on the matter.

She expected him to taunt her. Mock her. Belittle her for how much she wanted him. Instead, he only moaned, and drove his finger deeper inside of her. "That's it, my beautiful fae... *yes, Nadi—*"

The words sent a shudder through her unexpectedly. Squeezing her eyes shut, she tried not to sob at the warring feelings battling for supremacy inside of her.

When a second finger joined the first, she couldn't take it anymore, and the choked, mewling sound of need escaped her. Not just for *sex*. But for *him*.

"Sshh..." He paused, moving to lie atop her. For a moment, the whole world was him—the smell of him, the sound of him, the feel of his body on hers as he kissed her cheek. He wiped away her tears and kissed the corner of her lips, slowly, tenderly.

"Let it go. Feel it all. Everything. Tonight, we break it all down... and see what's left when we're done."

Feel it all.

Break it all down.

She nodded, weakly, shutting her eyes.

He kissed her cheek again. His words were soft but insistent. Somehow tender but unyielding in the same moment. "Say the word *stop* and this all ends in an instant. Tell me *wait*, or *no*, or *I can't*, and I'll only push you harder. But *stop*, and you are free. Do you understand?"

With another weak nod, she kept her eyes shut.

"I need to hear you say it, little murderer... I need to hear you say 'I understand.' Can you do that for me?" It felt like he was trying to coax her off a ledge. And perhaps, in the strangest of ways, he was.

Let it go. Feel it all. Everything. Tonight, we break it all down.

That was what she needed.

In a nearly broken whisper, she answered, "I understand."

He smiled against her skin. "Then, let's begin..."

* * *

Perfect little creature. *His* perfect little creature. Nadi was trembling beneath him—in rage, in fear, in desire. Raziel understood. Tonight would change things forever between them, one way or another. Because he couldn't stand a single second more of this lie they'd built between them.

No. He needed to know if there was anything in her—anything at *all*—that felt any kind of compassion for the detestable monster she had sworn to destroy.

Even if he suspected that in his process of extracting what she was hiding and showing it to the light, he would damage it forever. It might die, bleeding out all over the floor.

The story of his life.

But he couldn't go on, not knowing where they stood. And neither could she.

She probably expected him to simply take her like she was now, bent on the altar and at his mercy. Simply wreak havoc on her until he met his end. But that wasn't the *point*.

Straightening up, he stroked his hands over her body. What a lithe creature she was. Curves in all the right places. But muscular—clearly a *predator*, like him.

Her skin was such a beautiful shade of pale sea green, it almost seemed to glow in the moonlight. Resting her cheek on the table, she kept her head tucked close to her shoulder, as if trying to hide in the dark veil of her blue-black hair.

Like he'd allow that. Unclasping his belt, he pulled it from around his waist. She went tense, probably expecting him to hit her with it. He chuckled.

Feeding the end of his belt through the buckle, he slipped the loop over her neck and pulled her hair out from underneath it.

Before she could yank her head out of the trap, he cinched it tight, holding the rest of the leather strap in his hand like a makeshift leash. "I've always wondered what it would be like to have a pet fae..."

"You *cock-sucking* son of a *bitch!*" Her hands went to her throat, grabbing at the leather strap.

Good. He wanted her mad. He wanted her to *fight*. He wanted her to work it all out. Yanking on the belt, he pulled her neck back, forcing her to arch her spine and restricting her air supply. She gagged, her words breaking off in a gasp as she struggled for breath. One of her hands had to press down on the stone altar to support her weight and keep it off her throat, the other threading fingers under the strap to try to make space for air.

In the same moment, he drove two fingers back into her

waiting heat, growling in pleasure at how eager she was for him. "By the moons, Nadi..."

He plundered her depths at a hard, relentless tempo, keeping the pressure on her throat with the leash until he felt her body tighten around him. She was on the verge of release. Grinning wickedly, he let up the pressure. She collapsed onto her elbow, gasping for air. He stilled his hand inside of her, but didn't remove it.

He watched as she lowered her head, her face veiled by her dark hair. Coughing, she swore at him in fae between breaths. He didn't need a translator to know that whatever she was saying, breathless and furious, was likely colorful, detailed, and violent.

Chuckling, he leaned down and kissed her shoulder. "I am not going to fuck you tonight unless you *ask*."

"*What?*" Oh, she was going to be apoplectic with him when all was said and done. And he couldn't wait.

"You heard me." He pulled back on the makeshift leash again, watching her body go taut beneath him as a shudder of pleasure wracked her body. Loving it. Hating it. Wanting to surrender. Wanting to fight. Wanting to be *taken*. Wanting *power*. Wanting to give it up.

Everything he could ask for.

He began to pump his fingers inside her, waiting and watching for the moment that she began to crest and—

Releasing the pressure on the leash, he let her collapse back to the altar.

She wailed in fury.

And he could only laugh. "Two."

* * *

"Six."

Nadi was going to lose her mind. She was going to *lose her moons-damned mind.* Everything was starting to blur together in a sea of rage, desire, and agony.

"Seven."

"I am going to *kill you,*" she ground out between her teeth. She had run out of all the swears she knew in both languages and had devolved into threats. "I am going to cut off your balls and make you eat them before I do—" Her words broke off into a gasp as Raziel pulled back on the leash. He was doing it a little harder each time, and this time she saw spots in her vision.

Maybe she'd pass out. That'd be a relief.

But he knew her better than she would have guessed. Because no matter how close she got—to oblivion or bliss—he never *quite* brought her either.

Air rushed back into her lungs. His fingers inside of her stilled.

"Eight."

She let out a sob and whacked her forehead on the altar. She'd given up punching the stone surface.

He chuckled. "Careful. Don't leave a bruise. Or would they even appear in your other form, anyway?"

"Fuck. You."

"That is what I'm waiting for you to say. Do you think I'm not *also* in misery?" He leaned over her, resting his arm on the altar near her as he nuzzled in close to her ear. "I have never wanted anyone so very badly as I want *you,* my little fae..."

She shuddered at his words. "Don't lie to me."

"Why would I?" His hand left her for a moment, only to be replaced by the pressure of his hips. She could feel the outline of him, every inch of him, desperate in his own obvious need. His voice was a thick, dark growl. "Something in me cries out for you, Nadi—your blood, your body—but it's evolved past that. I want *you.* I want *you* here, with me. Beside me. Don't you understand? I'm not offering you what I am because I don't have other options. Don't you get how much of a risk you are?"

He couldn't possibly mean what he was saying. He couldn't *possibly*.

"But that is a topic for another night." He chuckled, his tongue running along her cheek briefly before he continued. "Tonight, I want to fuck you in the moonlight. I want to desecrate this holy altar. Because no matter what—whether I succeed or fail—this moment will linger on. Just think, Nadi. You and I, right now, will have just a little bit of revenge on the rest of my family. The next time a Nostrom comes here to perform some sacred ritual, the ghost of our act will haunt them."

Nadi shuddered. What a mental image.

"Just say the words, little fae, and you can have as much of me as your sweet little body can handle. And we'll fuck like the animals we are, right here, with the painted faces of my ancestors looking on."

She wanted and needed him dead.

She wanted and needed him.

She hated him.

But it was more than that.

Wasn't it?

And that was what he was trying to prove to her.

A disappointed sigh left him. He was going to start up again. She couldn't—*just couldn't*—

It was only one word that left her. One, choked, desperate word—she couldn't even quite understand what she was trying to say with it. She could only hope that he knew.

"Raziel—"

* * *

Nadi whispered his name.

It was a broken, agonized word.

And it was the most amazing sound he had ever heard.

Gently, Raziel lifted her from the altar, and scooped her up in his arms. She looked startled. Good. That was what he wanted.

He wanted *her* to fuck *him*.

He could ravage her like a beast. But this was about what she wanted. About her surrender. About her admissions. He'd have his way with her plenty of nights to come. He sat her atop the altar before joining her, shifting her until she straddled his lap, facing him.

She sat there, watching him with uncertain eyes that were as dark as the night sky and yet flickering with every shade of color.

Slipping a hand into her hair at the base of her neck, he kissed her. Kissed the *real* her. Nadi. His little fae assassin. Who had infiltrated his home and crept into his bed.

Who could have killed him. A dozen times over.

And perhaps had done something far worse and far more cruel to him in the end.

A low purr began in his chest, and he felt her shudder. "You do love that sound."

Her gaze was suddenly hazy. "It's—it's cheating..."

He furrowed his brow. He forced it to stop. The dazed expression fled almost as quickly as it came. He'd never seen anyone react to the sound like that before. *Fascinating...*

Something to experiment with another time. He had other plans for her tonight.

He returned to devouring her lips with his. She tasted like the Wild—like the tang of plants and growth. But he found he... didn't hate it. Far from it. He found himself chasing more of it.

Grasping one of her breasts in his hand, he toyed with the dark nipple there, already pert and hard from her arousal. It was too tempting not to pinch it between his fingers, hearing her cry against his lips in protest.

He broke the kiss to watch her features, drinking in her expression as he repeated the action on the other side. She was flushed, her lips swollen and parted. Her hands were pressed against his chest, not quite grasping, not quite pushing him away.

He lay back on the altar, like he was some kind of sacrifice. How many times had he watched someone be sliced open on the stone, bled out like a lamb in the name of Lilivra? Now, his beautiful fae would ride him to oblivion on the same surface. *It was perfect.*

He reached between them and undid his fly, lowering his pants to finally, *finally* free himself from his trousers with a grunt of relief.

Nadi needed no instructions as to what to do. She sat up on her knees, one hand grasping his length, the other pressed against his chest.

What a perfect view. Reaching behind her, he wrapped a hand around the makeshift leash that still dangled from her neck with the other.

Her eyes slipped shut as he pulled on the leather, arching her back and tightening the loop just enough to apply pressure, but not enough to restrict her air. She'd need all that she could get.

"No. Look at me."

Those dark orbs met his.

He smirked. "Good little fae." He rested his head back against the stone surface. "Begin."

* * *

Nadi couldn't help but whimper as she bore down on him.

Raziel had asked her when the last time she'd had sex in her real form had been... Not since before he'd killed her family. So it was *tight*.

But at least she was ready.

As ready as she could be.

She tried to drop her head, tried to hide, tried to focus on the sensation of him at her core as the pressure built. But he pulled back on the leash every time she did, forcing her to arch her back.

"Keep your eyes on *me*, Nadi," he snarled. "I'm the one you're fucking. *I'm* the one you wanted. *I'm* the one you're here with."

Like she'd ever forget any of this, for better or worse. He was the one who had her body *screaming* not just in need, but in need for *him and only him.*

When finally the pressure was too much and her body gave way, a cry broke from her that was half pain and half bliss. And he caught it with his lips, suddenly sitting up to catch her in a kiss that almost made her weep with an emotion she couldn't name. Wouldn't name.

His hips rolled beneath her, a primal and instinctive motion that he clearly couldn't control. The fingers of one of his hands dug into her hips as he obviously struggled to keep himself still beneath her.

When he parted from the kiss, his words were once more little more than a growl. "Never felt anything—quite—" He lay back with a shudder. "You are forcing me to rethink my opinion of fae..."

"Shut... up." She could barely breathe. Barely think. All that existed was *him.* And the feeling of him. *Moons.* It hadn't ever felt like this before. She kept lowering herself on him, little by little, feeling him stretch and fill her.

It was so different in her true form. Not just the sensation of him. But she was truly exposed. Truly *herself.* There was no more hiding. No more avoiding him. No more evading what she'd been trying to keep from him—and herself—this entire time.

"Look at you…" His words were a breathless exhale. "Flawless creature…"

She couldn't take any more of him. The strain of him was a dull ache that was threatening to send her over the edge from just his presence inside of her alone. There was only one problem. There was still more of him left.

And she knew what he was going to do…

He gripped her hip hard with one hand, and shifted his other hand to her shoulder. Pressing down, he snapped his hips up toward her.

A sensation slammed through her that was beyond any ecstasy she had ever felt before. All the pent-up release from the torture he'd levied on her combined with the sudden violent impact had her seeing white and unable to even make a sound as he pressed her body down onto his with every ounce of his strength.

He wasn't being gentle with her anymore.

He was a vampire. And she was fae. She could take it and he knew it.

She couldn't cry out. Couldn't make a sound. Could only sit there, impaled on him, shivering in her ecstasy as her body clenched and released around in him in waves.

He wasn't immune from it either, lying there beneath her, his fangs extended as he grimaced, snarling as he clearly tried to maintain control.

When she could breathe again, she could only summon one word. "F—*fuck*…"

Raziel's eyes were blown out, almost black with how dilated they were. "Yes, indeed." He looked almost feral. "I suggest now… you begin to do exactly that, little fae… Or *I will do it for you.*"

It was clear that was a threat.

But despite what had just transpired, it seemed her own body wasn't sated either. The fire in her still ached for him.

Ached for what it felt, buried deep inside her. His grip changed, once more wrapping the leather strap around his hand behind her back.

"*Begin.*"

An order she was keen to obey, for once. She lifted her hips, feeling the glorious friction of him as he slid from her, before driving them back down, the deep pressure of him returning.

It was just as he had said. Perfect.

Each time she repeated the action, she gasped as she filled herself with him, loving it more and more. Every inch of him seemed fitted to her. Just a little too much in all the right ways.

He tightened the pressure on the leash and her body reacted in kind. It was wrong, but she *loved* how that felt. Loved the bizarre combination of helplessness and control as she set the tempo and fucked herself on top of him.

"That's it..." Raziel smoothed his hand over her stomach, his fingers splayed. "Good, my beautiful assassin. How does it feel? Soon, I'll take every part of your body as my own. Every ounce of you will be *mine* and *mine alone.*"

Yes. Moons, *yes*, that was what she wanted. She drove her body down on him faster, deeper, harder.

"Once you trust me, I have so many toys I want to show you... so many ways to make you sing my name in pleasure and agony..." His breath was beginning to hitch. "And perhaps, once all this is over, I will let you do the same to me..."

"I—*ah!*" Her words broke off as he bent his knees behind her, changing the angle abruptly. He had used the leverage to suddenly retake control, lifting his hips up into with a downward stroke.

He pulled the strap tighter, but didn't cut off her air. It was just about the pressure that arched her back. She rolled her hips against him as he met her strokes with his upward thrusts, violent, harsh, and desperate. Far more forceful than what she could muster on her own.

"Yes—fuck—*yes*—" Words were spilling from her lips without her even realizing it. Both her hands were on his chest, needing them for support. "Raziel, please—I—"

"Tell me you need me, little fae... say it's *me* you want..."

He already knew the truth. He'd seen it plain as day, even before she was willing to admit it to herself. Tears stung her eyes, but there wasn't any point in denying it. "Yes, Raziel, please—I need you—"

And damn her soul to oblivion.

She did.

But in this moment, damnation could wait.

"That's my sweet fae..." Raziel growled, keeping up the same violent tempo. "Let go. Let it all go. I'm here."

Her body shattered. Release hit her like an ocean wave and dragged her under. She might have cried out his name. But he was kissing her again, his tongue tangled with hers.

She felt him spasm deep inside her. He buried his head into her shoulder as he wrapped his arms around her, clutching her tight. He pulled her down onto him as hard as he could, as far as he would go, as he filled her and muffled the roar of his own ecstasy into her.

They were both shuddering when he finally lay back and brought her with him, her head resting on his chest.

She didn't know what to think. Or what to say.

"Nadi... I believe you'll get your wish." Raziel paused as he caught his breath. "Because one way or another? You will be the death of me..."

THREE

"How's this?"

"Mm... less green."

"Better?"

A chuckle. "No. It was closer before."

Nadi sighed. She was used to doing this with a mirror. Attempting to fashion herself a vampiric version of Monica with only Raziel for feedback was proving to be more difficult than she'd imagined.

But it at least gave her something to focus on. Something to think about that wasn't what they had just done. And what Raziel had just forced out of her.

It hung in the air between them. She knew they needed to *talk* about it. It was going to fester in her chest if they didn't. Whatever was going on between them, whatever he'd just wrenched out from the dark corners of her, couldn't go back into the hole she'd been storing it in.

All that would have to come later, though. It would wait until they were back aboard the yacht. If they stayed in the estate much longer, Ivan would get concerned, and he'd blunder into the abandoned building looking for them. And that was the *last* thing they needed.

So—*pragmatism*. At least shifting into Monica also gave her the appearance of false clothing, seeing as Raziel had ruined her real ones.

Cracking her neck to the side, she shifted her skin tone again. She could base herself off Raziel's well enough, but he'd pointed out she couldn't be a one-to-one match. Monica had been far more tanned than him. She would look unnaturally "dead," even for a vampire.

And so began the trial-and-error game in which they were currently engaged.

It also didn't help the fact that he clearly found this *extremely* amusing. "What's so funny?" She glared up at him.

"Nothing. I'm merely fascinated. I'm smiling because you're becoming flustered, which I find adorable." He tilted his head to the side slightly. "What's the problem?"

Despite everything they'd just done, it felt like trying on underwear in front of him. Which wasn't more personal, just a different kind of intimacy she wasn't sure she was comfortable with. Rolling her eyes, she paced away a few steps to put some distance between them. "Because you're putting way too much importance into this. No one is going to suspect that I'm secretly a fae shapeshifter masquerading as a vampiric Monica."

"I put together the puzzle well enough." He folded his arms over his chest. "My family will as well given enough time. And this game we will have to play with them will require time and patience. This masquerade of yours must be perfect."

"So, what happens when I'm expected to *do* something vampiric?" There was a major flaw with this plan. "You all have bizarre powers. I won't. Short of being able to summon fangs on command."

"You would be surprised." He smirked. "You would have been created by my blood—and I have a unique gift among our kind. Who is to say that you would not have a unique *mutation?* Vampires have been known to take the shape of mist, bats, wolves... It is perfectly believable that one of us might have the ability to mimic other humanoids."

With a dismissive shrug of his shoulders, he moved to one of the wooden pews and sat, putting his feet up on the back of the pew in front of him at an angle to accommodate his long legs. "I think it will play into our ruse. In fact, it will help ensure my family sees you as an asset and not a mistake to be quickly disposed of to save political face. My not sacrificing you goes against our ancient code, blah, blah, blah." He waved his hand in the air exhaustedly. "The bitch will see this as a slight and the other clans will see this as weakness. Unless we show them how useful you suddenly are, she's likely to finish what she thinks I couldn't."

He had a point. And Nadi hated it when he had a point. Otherwise, Raziel's mother, Volencia, was just as likely to have one of her men slit her throat and quietly dispose of her before word spread too far that "Monica" was still alive—well, undead. Whatever.

With a sigh, she ran a hand down over her face. "All right. But we'll have to pretend that my powers are erratic. That I have little control over them and that it'll be hard to maintain it for long. I don't want them *using* me."

"Deal." Reaching into his coat pocket, he produced his silver cigarette holder and pulled out one of his strange incense-smelling cigarettes and began to smoke it. She watched as the embers at the end glowed before the smoke curled up into the air around him. "Now. Less green. More yellow-pink. You aren't actually supposed to be a rotting corpse, dear."

It took several more tries, but she finally got to an appearance he was happy with. When it came to changing her eye color, however, she managed to get that right on the first try.

At least to something that he approved of. When she changed the color, he began to laugh.

"What?" She frowned. "What did I do wrong?"

"Nothing. They're perfect." He was standing closer to her at that point, the dim light of the room making it difficult to see color for the both of them. "Perhaps just a little more *magenta* than someone like you would prefer."

She despised the color pink and everything close to it. Judging by the look on her face, it showed. "Great."

He chuckled. "That is why I laughed." He leaned down to kiss her forehead.

She pulled back abruptly and out of his reach. "What are you *doing?*"

That seemed to surprise him briefly before his expression smoothed. "We will talk this through back in private, Nadi." He almost looked hurt. Almost. "Now. Let's get this over with. You will have to 'play dead' as it were, as we return to the yacht. I'm sure you can handle that."

She nodded. "How do you think this plays out when we get back?"

"Simple. Mother will be furious with me. I will be punished for disobeying orders." He winced. Clearly, he had suffered similarly in the past. "But I suspect it will blow over. Then, we can begin our work. Together. Now. Play dead like a good girl, will you? I'm eager to get out of this... miserable building."

The trip back to the yacht was awkward, to say the least. Going limp and pretending to be a corpse.

And Ivan wasn't thrilled, either, when he saw Raziel show up carrying her. "You're fucking kidding me."

"Just shut up and get us back to the yacht."

"But—"

"I don't pay you for your opinions, Ivan."

The rest of the ride on the skiff was spent in silence. Nadi was thrown over his shoulder, just as the real Monica had been, as he climbed aboard the yacht. It wasn't exactly dignified, but there wasn't really any other way for him to climb a ladder.

She supposed she'd forgive him.

For *that*, anyway.

Everyone on the yacht would have seen her. All of the staff who were loyal to other masters than simply Raziel would be eager to radio ahead word of what they had just seen. They'd have a bill to pay the moment they set foot ashore.

It wasn't until he laid her down on the silk comforter of the bed in the master suite of the yacht and threw the deadbolts with a loud series of clicks that he spoke to her. "You can move now."

"Thanks for not dropping me. Or smacking my head on anything." She opened her eyes and sat up, cracking her neck. Going limp for that long weirdly put a crick in her spine. After the time spent in the ruins of the estate, the luxury of the yacht was utterly jarring. It felt... wrong, somehow. Dishonest. Vampires didn't belong surrounded by soft velvet, glistening brass, and polished marble. Not in her opinion. But clearly, Raziel didn't agree with her.

Raziel pulled the heavy curtains to block the windows. Just in case. Probably a good plan.

Getting up, she went to the bathroom to look in the mirror. Her eyes were indeed a reddish-pink. Magenta. She hated them. But they'd do. And now she could memorize what color her skin was supposed to be in full light.

Raziel appeared in the reflection as he stepped up behind her, a black bathrobe in his hands. "Seemed to be the least I could do." He frowned at her reflection, wrinkling his nose. "Shed this face. I find it offensive, now that I know what you truly look like."

How oddly flattering. "Someone might come in and see me."

"The door is three-inch-thick steel with four deadbolts. Ivan can't get in, and not even Mael could bust it down. No. We won't be disturbed." His look of disgust deepened. "Drop the illusion."

It was a command, but it lacked any sort of weight. Seeing Monica's face on her seemed to truly bother him. Letting out a breath, she dropped the glamor. Once more fully naked and herself—though with legs, as her tail would be far too inconvenient—she watched his reflection in the mirror.

He draped the bathrobe over her shoulders. She tucked her arms through the sleeves and tied it around her waist, not bothering to thank him. He was the reason she was nude, after all.

"Come with me, Nadi." He took her hand, and led her to the bed. She resisted. "No, no. I am done with that for now."

"Then, what are you after?"

"Just come here, will you?" He kicked off his shoes, already in just a white button-down and his pants. He scooted farther onto the bed. "I want to talk. And... I want to see the real you, again."

"This is the real me." She climbed onto the bed, and sat on the covers, a few feet away.

"The rest of you." Reaching out, his hand trailed over her legs. "All of you."

"Why?" She arched an eyebrow at him.

"I haven't seen anything like you before." There was an almost troubled, confused look in his eyes. "And I find I want us to speak without all these lies between us... for once."

Glancing away briefly, she shut her eyes. Fine. He'd already seen what she looked like. She might as well let him have what he wanted. She let the rest of her glamor fall. She hated having to take her real form on dry land—it felt awkward and unnatural. She wasn't meant for it, after all. But it'd have to do. She let her tail drape over the cover, reaching all the way across the enormous bed and over the edge and onto the floor. "There."

His gaze trailed over her body, drinking in the sight. It was clear he was holding back from what he wanted to do—which was touch. Laughing, she lay down onto her stomach. "You're a fucking idiot. *Now* you're gentle?"

"This seems different." He reached out and ran a hand over her scales with a quiet *huh*. "Does it hurt you to shift?"

"No, thankfully. Unless I'm restrained when I do it. Handcuffs, ropes—something that makes me go from smaller to larger, that kind of thing." She shouldn't be giving away all of her secrets, but she'd never had anyone be honestly curious. Even her employers generally kept a *safer-not-to-know* mindset.

His fingers wandered to her fins, toying with the delicate, almost torn-lace material of them. "If I were to handcuff you, and you were to take Ivan's form—you would be injured by that, for example."

"Exactly. I could do it, but I'd be liable to break the bones of my wrist in the process. Worth it to escape, but not without cost." Folding her arms, she laid her cheek down on them. She suddenly felt tired from the whole day's ordeal. And his hand gently roaming over her tail was strangely calming.

"You never answered my question from before, Nadi. When was the last time you made love wearing your own face?" He shifted closer to her, his hand still running along her tail.

Taking in a breath, she held it, and let it out in a rush. What was the point in hiding anymore? "Since before you killed my family. I was a young woman. Barely little more than a girl. It doesn't really count."

"No, I suppose it doesn't." He lay down next to her, stroking her hair back and away from her face, watching her curiously with a frown etched into his perfect features.

It felt so odd to have him touch her. Not sexually—not in a *needy* way. But like she was something special. Something to be... cherished.

"Were there other fae in your family like you? Like this?"

"No. But that wasn't uncommon. I had a cousin who had

the legs of a goat. Only one in our clan like that." She rolled onto her back, mostly just to get a little more distance between them. She felt too warm. "We were all unique in our own way. Some fae would leave their clans in search of others like themselves."

"Did you ever feel that pull?"

"Yeah."

"And why didn't you go?"

When she didn't answer immediately, he let out a small, quiet laugh. "Ah. Your revenge. Me."

"Yeah. You."

"And now things between us have become complicated, haven't they, Nadi?" He wasn't going to let her escape him so easily, draping an arm over her. His face was only inches away now, those crimson eyes flicking between hers, drinking in her every expression.

This was what she was trying to avoid. The real peeling back of everything.

"I suppose." She wanted to roll away from him. To hide it all. To deny every ounce of it—every scrap of the truth. To look him straight in the eye and tell him that he was wrong, she felt *nothing*, and everything that had just passed between them had been a ploy.

Or to tell herself that she was playing him. That this was all still just a game. A game to ensure that she was properly positioned to get her revenge when she had her chance.

But it would be a lie.

"Nadi..."

"What do you want me to say, Raziel?" She tried to keep back the tears. "What more do you want to cut from me? I lost my *family* to you. I learned to kill for you. I killed my *uncle* for you. I—"

His lips crashed against hers, silencing her. And she couldn't have been more grateful. Because the demanding kiss pushed the encroaching pain from her thoughts. There was only him.

Only them.

When they parted, he rested his forehead against hers. "I know, Nadi. I know." His voice was quiet, barely more than a rumble of thunder in the distance.

He didn't apologize. And she didn't want him to. Hell, if he tried to, she'd probably knee him in the groin. It was the last thing she wanted. She made her choices. And she was *still* making her choices, when it came down to it.

Whatever this was that was growing roots.

Wherever it took them.

It was her choice to let it continue...

Or rip it out and let it die.

"Tomorrow is going to be a long day." Raziel pushed away from her, climbing from the bed to unbutton his shirt and shrug out of it. "Word will already have been sent ahead by the captain that I came aboard with a vampiric Monica."

"Yeah. I know." She shifted back into her legged form. Her tail was just too ungainly. She slid under the covers and the sheets. There was no reason to even fuss about who slept where at this point. "No way to stall your mother for a day?"

He huffed a laugh. "You've met her." He tossed his shirt aside. Undressing the rest of the way down to his boxers, he kicked his clothes carelessly into a pile. "What do you think?"

She laughed once as well. Yeah. She knew the answer to the question. Lying back against the pillow, her head swam with how tired she was. "I think we should kill her first."

The bed sagged as Raziel climbed in beside her. He pulled her in close to him, tucking her against his chest. She fought the urge to go rigid against him. It was instinctual.

"While I don't disagree, and I hate the bitch as much as you do, I have other plans." He kissed the back of her head. "But we'll discuss it another time."

Right.

Plans. *He* had plans. On how to kill his family. And now they were working *together*. No, worse than that. He assumed he was in charge, of course. That was a harsh and uncomfortable realization.

That, plus the horrible truth that some part of her was starting to *care* about this monster she was now about to sleep with.

It didn't matter how much she wanted him.

It didn't matter how much she cared about him.

She needed to find a way out.

She *had* to find a way to salvage this mess.

One way or another.

FOUR

"Are you *insane?*"

Raziel kept a faint smile on his face as he looked down at his sister Lana. He was used to this. It wasn't the first time he had received a dressing-down from her. Hopefully, it would be one of the last.

Because, if all went to plan, she would be dead soon.

He wondered who would be the one to get the kill on Lana. Him, or his new little murderer. Either way, he was going to watch.

Azazel was sprawled out on a sofa, looking entirely uninterested in the conversation, reading a book. Lana went nowhere without her favorite pet.

And Ivan was standing near Monica, looking as stern as ever. He had informed his bodyguard to keep watch over his newly vampiric wife. He could not trust his mother not to attempt to murder her over dinner.

"Stupid question." Lana placed her hands over her face as she paced back and forth over the carpet in front of him. "Of course you are. Of *course*."

He lit his cigarette, enjoying the taste of the incense and wood chips on his tongue. It was an odd habit he picked up decades ago, but one he found hard to shake. That, along with the coins he was constantly toying with. They gave him something to help ration his thoughts when his mind wanted to go faster than the rest of him.

Lana plucked the cigarette from his mouth and immediately tamped it out in a brass bowl that sat atop the elegant antique credenza against the wall. His mother's home was far more dated than his. She preferred the look of things from a bygone era—all deep lacquered wood, crimson drapes, and all so dimly lit that without their vampiric eyesight the family would have been constantly tripping over velvet footstools.

"You know Volencia hates it when you smoke," Lana hissed. "Are you trying to make this worse on yourself?"

Raziel rolled his eyes. "She smokes. This house reeks of *actual* cigarettes. I hate the smell of that hideous weed she rolls up and puts in those papers for some reason."

"Exactly! She says you smell like a bonfire. Always taking after your father, smoking woodchips." Lana went back to pacing with an angry sigh. "Bad enough you walk in with *that*." She gestured at the young woman standing nearby, close to the door, her hands tucked into the pockets of her dark coat.

Monica, to them. To him? *Nadi.* What a wonderful name. It was deeply amusing how attractive the rancher's daughter had been to him until he knew the truth—until he realized that so much of the fire and razor's edge that he had come to desire in the young "human" had actually belonged to the *fae assassin* who had come to murder him. The little bits of her own personality she had allowed to shine through the lie she had so carefully played were the parts he had adored, not the act she had worn.

And a brilliant job she had done in her lie, he had to give

her credit. To share his bed—his life—to slide into the Serpent's lair without notice. It was only because of her dreams of grandeur and desire to murder his entire family that he was still alive.

If she'd wanted him dead... he would be. Several times over. He had been at her mercy for *weeks*.

By the moons, that shouldn't make him want her as badly as it did.

Because now that he'd seen her true face—knew her true self? It would not stop haunting him. The image of Nadi atop him while holding a knife to his throat, cursing him with lust and hate in her eyes, kept waking him from sleep.

They were destined to destroy each other. One of them would end up dead. A duel to the death. And it was *delicious* to him. He would have it no other way.

There she was, hiding behind the veneer of Monica-turned-vampiress. As flawlessly as any actor upon a stage, with her slightly magenta eyes and her pale skin. Shy, but determined. Frightened, but like a cornered cat. Not afraid to lash out with her sharp claws.

"That is my wife, need I remind you." He pulled a coin from his pocket. If he couldn't smoke, he'd amuse himself in other ways. He began to walk the coin across the backs of his fingers, moving to stand by the window.

"You needn't remind me," Lana bit back. "But I apparently need to remind you that you were supposed to *kill her!*" The shrillness of her voice made Raziel wince.

"The plan changed." A simple fact. It did.

"And why? Why! That's what I don't understand." Lana was furious. It was always funny when she got all wound up. So pointless. Such a waste of time. "Sure, she's cute, but you've never been one to get—"

His patience, however, was running thin. "Show her, Monica."

"Are... are you sure?" Monica grimaced. Good girl, still flawlessly playing the part. "I haven't quite figured out the... whole... clothes... thing..."

Oh, very clever. Likely drawing off her experience mastering her skill when she was a young fae. The image of her accidentally tearing apart her clothing when shifting forms did nothing to help the low hum of desire that had been burning in him since their foray at the estate. "She's about your size. It'll be fine."

Lana was clearly unamused. "What are you two babbling ab—"

Monica shifted forms into one that flawlessly matched Lana, only wearing Monica's clothing. She smiled. "What are you two babbling about?" she parroted in a perfect imitation of Lana's voice and tone.

Lana staggered backward, falling into a chair.

Ivan jumped away from Monica as if he were suddenly an old woman who had spotted a mouse.

Azazel did a double-take, before snapping his book shut and sitting up on the sofa, his mouth agape.

Monica, wearing Lana, marched up to Raziel. "Are you *insane?* Stupid question. Of course you are. Of *course.*" She repeated the first half of the conversation to him flawlessly, even pacing around on the carpet, copying Lana's mannerisms with a *disturbing* degree of polish, even to his eye.

Raziel wondered idly how well she could copy his own personality. He had seen her take his form, but she hadn't been copying his mannerisms. Likely for his own comfort, he realized.

That was skill, *not* magic, that gave her that gift.

She grew so much more frightening to him in that moment.

And he wanted her *so much more* for it.

The form of Lana melted back into that of vampiric Monica, and she stepped to Raziel's side, wrapping her arms around his waist as if she were suddenly afraid of the world. She exhaled, seeming exhausted.

He draped his own arm around her, holding her close. "My blood had an interesting effect, you could say."

"What the fuck—what the *fuck—what the fuck—*" Lana was in a panic. "That—that's not—that's not possible—that's not—bats are *one thing*, but—"

"You remember cousin Mikhail, do you not?" Raziel kissed the top of Nadi's head. She rested her cheek against him. "He could take the shape of all manner of animals at will, not simply bats like we Nostroms can. Wolves. Rats. Even a camel for that one party." He chuckled. "Oliren can change his form into mist as well as bats. Is it such a stretch to imagine this? In some ways it's more natural, when you think about it."

Lana was numbly shaking her head. Azazel was still staring, agog.

Vampires sometimes had a singular gift that ran in their family. With the Nostroms, it was the gift of shifting into bats. With the Rosovs, they could speak to animals—though there were no animals in the metropolis and pets were illegal, so it was a rather useless gift.

Those vampires like Raziel or the ones he had mentioned like Mikhail or Oliren were considered powerful and rare muta-tions. Or, now, "Monica."

"So fucked up," was Ivan's simple, three-word addition to the conversation.

"Thank you for the summary, Ivan." Raziel smirked. He was very, very proud of himself in this moment. It wouldn't guarantee that he would come out of the evening unscathed. Hardly. But he was now quite convinced that "Monica" would be allowed to join the family.

Because such a skill was far too useful to destroy.

Lana stood from the chair finally, never taking her eyes off Monica like she was some kind of freak of nature—which to be fair, she was—just not for the reasons Lana might believe. She hurriedly left the room, likely to go tell their mother what she had just witnessed.

Good. It saved them both having to repeat the parlor trick.

"I don't want to die," Nadi murmured to him. Moons, she was *too good* at this.

"You won't. Not here. Not today." He tipped her head up to look at him. "Not if I have anything to say about it." Nadi might shy away from his touch. She might bare her little fae fangs and hiss at him like a feral cat. But Monica? Monica was *his*.

Leaning down, he kissed her. Kissed his murderous little fae. His wife. It was a cheap ploy to steal an embrace from her, he knew. And she would likely be furious with him later.

But he wanted a kiss.

And he knew she wouldn't break character.

Sure enough, when he pulled away, her eyes had drifted shut, and her hand was lightly clasping the lapel of his suit coat. There was peace and bliss on her face.

He wondered if that, too, was an act.

He wondered why that hurt him.

Lana stormed back into the room. "Dinner is served. Ahead of schedule."

It was time to face the music. He straightened his shoulders and released his little murderer. "Come, Monica. Let's get this over with."

* * *

Nadi sat rigid at the formal dining table, her eyes fixed on the plate before her. Maintaining the glamor of a newly turned Monica was a layered experience—she had to look pale, subtly different from the woman's human form, and keep the slightly magenta tint in her eyes.

But controlling her expression was proving to be the real challenge.

Volencia Nostrom sat at the head of the table, resplendent in a gown of midnight-blue velvet that seemed to absorb light rather than reflect it. Her silver-streaked black hair was piled atop her head in an elaborate arrangement secured with jeweled pins that glinted when she moved. Everything about her exuded power and control.

To her right sat Mael, uncharacteristically solemn, his massive frame somehow seeming smaller, hunched, as though he were trying to hide from the seriousness of the situation. To her left was Lana, who couldn't quite hide the smugness in her expression. Farther down the table, Azazel lounged with practiced indifference that didn't quite mask his interest in the proceedings.

And beside Nadi, unnervingly still, sat Raziel.

The silence stretched for what had seemed like an agonizing two minutes since they'd all been seated. No one touched the first course laid out before them. No one spoke. Nadi could feel the weight of Volencia's gaze like a physical thing, assessing, calculating.

"I suppose," Volencia finally said, her voice cool and precise, "we should discuss the hideous elephant in the room."

Nadi fought the urge to laugh. *Hideous. Nice.* She kept her posture demure, her shoulders slightly hunched—precisely how Monica would behave in such intimidating company.

"You've made quite a mess of things as usual, haven't you, Raziel?" Volencia continued, sipping from a crystal goblet filled with blood and wine. "The Valan arrangement was explicit. The girl was to be sacrificed according to tradition. Yet here she sits—not only alive but *turned*. You *abject fool*."

Raziel's face remained impassive. "Things change, Mother."

"Things change when I decide they change," Volencia snapped, setting down her glass with enough force that the bloodwine sloshed dangerously close to the rim. "Your disobedience has cost us dearly in political capital. The Rosovs are already making advances on our territory in the lower districts, citing our 'inability to honor traditional contracts' as justification. Even the Toths are acting out of line. The Toths! You have no honor. I sometimes wonder if you aren't somehow a bastard, after all."

Nadi caught the subtle way Raziel's jaw tightened, the only indication that his mother's words had landed. She found herself fighting the unexpected urge to reach for his hand under the table.

"However," Volencia continued, her gaze shifting to Nadi, "I understand your... wife... has manifested an unusual ability."

Nadi lowered her eyes, playing the role of the intimidated newborn vampire. "Yes, ma'am."

"Look at me when I address you, girl."

Nadi raised her eyes, meeting Volencia's cold stare. The matriarch studied her as one might study an insect under glass.

"Show me."

Taking a steadying breath, Nadi allowed her form to shimmer and change, adopting Volencia's appearance as precisely as possible—from the particular arch of her eyebrow to the way she held her shoulders. The transformation was perfect, in every detail.

"Fascinating," Volencia—the real one—murmured, leaning forward slightly. "This is not mere illusion. You've replicated my form exactly."

Nadi shifted back to Monica, allowing exhaustion to show on her face. "It... takes effort, ma'am."

"I imagine it does." Volencia sat back, tapping one long fingernail against the stem of her glass. "Well, this does change things. A shapeshifter in the family could prove useful. Particularly with the current political climate."

"Mother, surely you're not suggesting—" Lana began, but Volencia silenced her with a look.

"I'm suggesting nothing. I'm stating facts. Monica will be spared, not because she is Raziel's bride, but because her abilities now represent an asset to this family."

Mael cleared his throat. "The question remains of how we address the broken contract with the Valans."

"Yes," Volencia nodded. "Which is why I've called a full council meeting for tomorrow night. All branches of the Nostrom clan will be present, and we will determine the best course of action." Her eyes narrowed as she looked at Raziel. "You and your wife will attend and accept whatever assignment the council deems appropriate to restore our standing."

"Generous of you," Raziel said, his voice carefully neutral.

"Generous indeed," Volencia replied coolly. She gestured to the staff waiting by the walls. "You may serve the main course now."

The staff moved silently around them, replacing the untouched first course with platters of rare meat and goblets of fresh blood. Nadi's stomach turned at the sight, but she maintained her composure. Monica would be new to this diet, after all—some distaste would be expected.

"Before we begin," Volencia said once the staff had retreated, "there is the matter of discipline."

The tension in the room thickened.

"Mother," Mael began, his gaze flicking to who he believed to be Monica, "perhaps this could wait until—"

"It will not wait," Volencia cut him off. "Raziel's actions have undermined our authority and endangered our position. There must be consequences." She looked directly at Raziel. "Remove your clothing."

Nadi's head snapped up, certain she'd misheard.

"Mother—" Raziel started.

"Now." The word cracked like a whip.

For a moment, Nadi thought he would refuse. There was a flicker of something dangerous in his eyes—a glimpse of the Serpent beneath the controlled exterior. But then, slowly, methodically, he stood and began unbuttoning his shirt.

Nadi watched in disbelief as Raziel stripped, piece by piece, his movements deliberate and unhurried. His face remained a mask of indifference, though she could see a muscle twitching in his jaw. When he was completely naked, he stood still, making no attempt to cover himself.

"On the floor," Volencia commanded. "You'll take your meal like the animal you've proven yourself to be. Nothing more than a disloyal mutt."

Raziel's eyes flickered briefly to Nadi before he lowered himself to the floor beside his chair. One of the servants approached with his plate, setting it on the ground before him.

"No hands," Volencia added. "After all, dogs don't have hands, do they?"

A small, triumphant smile played at Lana's lips. Azazel watched with undisguised fascination. Mael's expression had grown stormy, his eyes fixed on his own plate.

And Nadi? Nadi felt something dark and vicious unfurl in her chest as she watched Raziel bend to eat from the plate like a dog. She should have been delighted by his humiliation.

She should be rejoicing.

This was the man who had murdered her family, who had haunted her nightmares for eighty years. His degradation should have been sweet as honey.

Instead... she found herself gripping her knife with white knuckles, imagining how it would feel to drive it through Volencia's eye socket. To wipe that smug smile off Lana's face.

The vampiress she was impersonating wouldn't dare show such rage.

She forced herself to relax her grip. Forced herself to breathe. Forced herself to relax. Nadi channeled it inward, letting the rage burn in her stomach as she swallowed down tiny bites of food that she couldn't taste.

"Monica," Volencia said suddenly. "You're barely eating. Is something wrong with your meal?"

Nadi swallowed hard. "No, ma'am. The taste is different, is all. Everything is just—just new to me still."

"Ah, yes. The transition can be difficult." Volencia's smile didn't reach her eyes. "But you'll adjust."

The rest of the meal passed in excruciating slowness. Nadi observed the family dynamics with careful attention. Volencia clearly ruled with an iron fist. Lana delighted in Raziel's degradation, occasionally making little comments that dripped with disdain.

Mael, interestingly, seemed increasingly uncomfortable, his gaze frequently straying to Nadi as if measuring her reactions.

Throughout it all, Raziel remained silent and composed, even as he was forced to lap at his plate like an animal. The dignity he maintained in such circumstances was remarkable—and somehow made the spectacle all the more grotesque.

When the meal finally concluded, Volencia dismissed them without ceremony. "Tomorrow night. Eight o'clock. Do not be late."

As they rose to leave, Nadi automatically reached for Raziel's clothes to hand them to him, but Volencia stopped her with a sharp "Leave them."

Nadi froze, conflicted.

"It's fine," Raziel said quietly. "Go."

She hesitated only a moment before following him out of the dining room, painfully aware of his naked form walking ahead of her. The staff they passed kept their eyes averted, clearly accustomed to the Nostrom family's particular brand of cruelty.

They had nearly reached the foyer when Mael's voice called after them.

"Monica? A moment."

Raziel stopped, his back stiffening. Nadi turned to see Mael approaching, his expression unreadable.

"Before the meeting tomorrow night." Mael had his gaze fixed on Nadi, ignoring Raziel almost pointedly. "I'd like to speak with you privately. There are matters concerning your new... position in the family that we should discuss."

Nadi felt Raziel bristle beside her. "Whatever you have to say to my wife, you can say to me," he said, his voice dangerously soft.

Mael's golden eyes flicked briefly to his brother before returning to Nadi. "May I... may I schedule a private meeting with Monica? She has been tugged in different directions enough of late. I wish to speak to her about what it's like to be a Nostrom. From perhaps a different perspective."

"Of course," Raziel echoed, the words dripping with venom. "Why would I ever not trust you, brother?"

Nadi placed a gentle hand on Raziel's arm—a gesture that would seem comforting to observers but was actually intended to restrain. "It's all right," she said softly.

Something passed between the brothers—a silent battle of wills that Nadi couldn't fully interpret.

"As you wish," Raziel finally said. "May I at least be allowed to know where and when?"

"The Blue Terrace. Noon tomorrow," Mael replied. "I'll send a car."

Nadi nodded, feeling under her hand tension vibrating in Raziel's body. "I'll be ready."

Mael inclined his head, then glanced at his naked brother with something that might have been regret before turning and walking back toward the dining room.

As they stepped out into the night air, a servant appeared with a long peacoat for Raziel, which he donned in silence. Their car waited at the end of the drive, Ivan at the wheel.

Neither of them spoke during the ride back to Raziel's estate. Nadi stared out the window, mind racing through the implications of everything she'd witnessed. She had expected to feel triumph at seeing Raziel brought low. Instead, she felt only a deepening of the complicated emotions that had been tangling inside her since the night at the estate.

It wasn't until they were alone in his bedroom, doors locked behind them, that Raziel finally broke the silence.

"Enjoy the show?" His voice was strained as he shrugged off the coat and headed for the bathroom.

Nadi hesitated, then followed him. "No," she admitted. "I didn't."

He paused, hand on the shower door, surprise flickering across his features before he masked it. "I would have thought my humiliation would be the highlight of your evening."

"I would have thought the same."

Their eyes met in the mirror, and for a moment, neither spoke.

"Why did you agree to meet with Mael?" he asked finally.

"Information." She shrugged. "The more I know about the dynamics between all of you, the better positioned we'll be to take them down. Besides. Don't you want to know what he's up to?"

Raziel studied her reflection, as if searching for deception. "And if he offers you a better deal than I have?"

Nadi considered her answer carefully. "Then, I'll weigh my options, just as you would in my position."

A slow smile spread across his face. "Fair enough, little murderer. Fair enough." He opened the shower door. "Get some rest. You'll need it for tomorrow's performance."

As she turned to leave, his voice stopped her one last time. "Nadi."

She looked back, meeting those unsettling red eyes.

"Remember who you're dealing with. He's not on your side. And remember whose side *you're* on."

That was the problem.

She was supposed to be on nobody's side but her own.

And now?

She didn't know if that was still the case.

FIVE

Nadi woke to an empty bed.

It took her a moment to orient herself—the silk sheets beneath her, the high ceiling above, the gentle whisper of drapes against the floor as they moved in the night breeze. Raziel's bedroom. She'd been sleeping here for weeks now, first while pretending to be his human wife, now as his unlikely conspirator.

The space beside her was cold. He'd been gone for some time.

Sitting up, she scanned the darkened room, her fae eyes easily adjusting to the low light. A sliver of whitish-blue moonlight spilled across the floor from the partially open balcony doors.

She found him there, standing at the railing, staring out over the metropolis. He was only wearing a pair of black silk pants, his long hair unbound, tendrils of it dancing in the breeze. His pale skin seemed almost to glow in the moonlight, the lean muscles of his back defined by shadow.

For a moment, she simply watched him. The creature who

had woken her up from her nightmares in a cold sweat for the past eighty years. The monster who had murdered her family. The man who had begun to stir something inside her that she didn't dare to name.

Wrapping herself in one of his dressing gowns—the one he'd given "Monica" was too flimsy for the cool night air—she approached the balcony. The stone was cold beneath her bare feet as she stepped out to join him.

"I think I already know the answer, but... are you all right?" She knew she shouldn't care.

Raziel didn't turn, didn't acknowledge her presence at all. His eyes remained fixed on the distant lights of the city, on the spires and towers of the metropolis that reached toward the Father moon like worshippers.

The silence stretched so long that Nadi thought he might not answer at all. When he finally spoke, his voice was distant, hollow.

"The first time my mother used me as her weapon, I was thirteen."

Nadi kept her eyes on the cityscape, giving him the privacy of her averted gaze.

"There was a human merchant who had offended her. I don't even remember how—refusing to sell her something she wanted. I remember even thinking as a child, it was trivial. Petty." He paused, his fingers curling around the railing. "She told me to make him eat his own fingers, one by one. And I did. Because I knew if I didn't, my punishment would be even worse. You can imagine how I had already learned that lesson."

A chill ran down Nadi's spine that had nothing to do with the night air.

"That's how it began. Small cruelties that grew more elaborate as I grew older. My brother and sister were trained for politics, for business. I was trained to be something that families like ours need but never speak of openly." His lips curled in a mirthless smile. "The monster in the closet. The shadow at the end of the hall. The serpent slipped into the sheets to poison you."

Nadi remained silent, sensing he needed to speak more than he needed her response.

"Mael was always the golden son. The heir. Lana, the precious daughter. And I was... the spare. The one they could afford to break." He ran a hand through his hair, pushing it back from his face. "Volencia would have me punished for the slightest infractions. Not by her own hand, of course—that would be beneath her. She'd have others do it. Usually, Mael. To 'toughen him up.'"

He turned then, leaning back against the railing to face her. The moonlight carved his features into sharp relief, throwing his eyes into shadow.

"Did you know vampires can starve for years without dying? We simply... waste away. Become living skeletons, mad with hunger. I spent my twenty-first birthday locked in a cell beneath our ancestral home, starving, because I had shown mercy to one of my mother's enemies."

Something twisted in Nadi's chest. "How long did she keep you there?"

"Six months." His voice was flat. "When she finally let me out, she brought me a girl. Human. Terrified. Said she was my birthday present." His jaw tightened. "I was so hungry... I drained her dry in minutes."

Nadi felt sick. She had known, intellectually, that the Nostroms were cruel. But this was beyond cruelty. This was systematic destruction.

"When I turned eighty, I was punished for no reason at all. Volencia simply wished to show me the depths to which she could make me suffer. Simply to remind me what I could be made to endure. I was chained to the bottom of the fountain in her garden." His tone was almost nonchalant. As if he were describing a trip to the store.

A deep coldness settled over her as the horror of his words dawned on her.

"Vampires cannot die by drowning. We simply continue to exist within that state of drowning in perpetuity. I was left there to watch while she held parties... I can still see their faces gazing down at me, smiling and laughing as they sipped their wine while I hung there in delirious agony."

Her hand tightened on the railing to keep from reaching out to him.

"Eventually, I became what she wanted," Raziel continued. "The perfect weapon. The merciless killer. The torturer who could make anyone do anything he wished with a single word." His eyes found hers in the darkness. "I learned to enjoy it, Nadi. That's the worst part. I *became* the monster she created, because it was the only way to survive. And I truly *do* enjoy it... on so many levels."

She could see it now—what had once been a frightened boy. The child who had been twisted and broken until he became something unrecognizable even to himself.

"Lana was always her favorite," he said, turning back to the city. "Even when she failed, she was forgiven. Mael was the heir, so he was protected, groomed for power. But me? I was expendable. Useful only as long as I was willing to get my hands dirty."

"Why didn't you leave?" Nadi asked, genuinely curious. "You're powerful in your own right. You could have gone anywhere. Gone to rule one of the outposts."

A bitter laugh escaped him. "Where would I go? The Nostroms are one of the oldest, most powerful vampire clans in Runne. There's nowhere they couldn't find me. And betrayal..." He shook his head. "What do you think the punishment for betrayal would be? Besides, they're still my family. Twisted as it is, there's love between us too."

Shutting her eyes, she let out a breath. She understood. She didn't want to. But she did.

"So you see, little murderer," he said, his voice taking on that familiar sardonic edge, "I'm using them exactly as they've used me all these years. The student has simply surpassed his teachers."

In that moment, Nadi understood him with terrible clarity. Every cruelty, every manipulation, every twisted game—they were the tools of a child who had never been shown any other way to interact with the world. He had been crafted into a weapon and never given the chance to be anything else.

They had turned him into a killer.

And he had turned her into one.

It didn't excuse what he'd done to her family. Nothing ever could. But for the first time, she saw the full tapestry of causes and effects that had led to that night, to the moment when her world had ended and her path of vengeance had begun.

"What about your father?" she asked. "Was he like her?"

Something dark flashed across Raziel's face. "My father was weak. He stood by and watched it all happen. His silence was as bad as her actions." He paused. "She had him killed when I was little more than a toddler. She staged a whole public trial for a false crime and had him executed—drawn and quartered. His organs were carved from his body like he was nothing but an animal, jarred, and scattered to the far ends of Runne to keep him from returning. But to us? His *children?* She proudly professed that he had grown weak. He had outlived his usefulness."

The brutality of it struck Nadi anew.

"Now you know," Raziel said, straightening from the railing. "The sad, pathetic history of the Serpent. Boohoo. You must be so disappointed."

"No," Nadi answered honestly. "I just understand some things better now."

He studied her face in the moonlight, searching for what, she wasn't sure. Pity, perhaps? Disgust? Whatever it was, he seemed satisfied with what he found—or didn't find.

"We should get some sleep," he said finally. "Tomorrow will be... complicated."

As they turned to go back inside, Nadi found herself speaking without planning to. "My mother used to sing to me when I couldn't sleep."

Raziel paused, looking back at her with an unreadable expression.

"She'd stroke my hair and hum this old fae melody," Nadi continued, not sure why she was sharing this, only knowing that she needed to offer something in return for what he had given her. "I still remember how it felt. Safe. Like nothing bad could touch me while she was there."

"Until I took her away."

Nadi met his gaze steadily. "Until you took her away."

The weight of eighty years of grief and rage and hatred hung between them, acknowledged but unchanged. Yet something else was there too now—a strange, tenuous thread of understanding.

"I can't undo what I did," Raziel said finally. "Even if I wanted to."

"I know." Nadi stepped past him into the bedroom. "I don't expect you to try."

She climbed back into bed, aware of him watching her from the doorway. When he finally joined her, keeping to his side of the bed, she felt the mattress dip beneath his weight. Neither spoke again.

But as Nadi drifted back toward sleep, she found herself facing an uncomfortable truth—the man beside her was no longer just the monster of her nightmares.

He was becoming something far more dangerous—someone real, someone complex, someone she might come to understand.

And understanding was only a breath away from forgiveness.

That thought terrified her more than anything else.

The Blue Terrace was aptly and uncreatively named—a sprawling teahouse with azure glass walls that caught the midday sun casting cool sapphire light across its patrons. It was the kind of establishment that existed solely for the vampire elite to conduct their business away from prying eyes, where the staff moved like ghosts and the private rooms offered complete discretion.

Nadi had done a few hits here in the past.

The maître d'—a sleek human with a silver streak in his otherwise jet-black hair—led her to a private alcove overlooking a courtyard where a fountain splashed musically. Mael was already waiting, rising as she approached.

"Monica," he greeted her, his voice a deep rumble that seemed at odds with the gentleness in his golden eyes. "Thank you for coming."

She gave a small, shy smile. "You sent a lot of um... friends." He hadn't just sent a driver with a car. He'd sent a driver and two armed guards.

Mael's mouth twitched. "My apologies. Security has been heightened since the attack on your wedding to Raziel. I'm sorry you are caught up in the middle of it. And now that he made the decision to turn you and bring you back alive? Everyone is walking on the edge of a knife. If any other family wishes to make a play for power, now will be the time. While we are all trying to find our footing."

"I'm sorry I'm the cause of it." No, she wasn't. But Monica would be.

"It isn't your fault. None of this is, from the beginning." He gestured for her to sit, then took his own seat across from her. He filled the chair completely, his broad shoulders nearly spanning its width. Where Raziel was lithe, predatory elegance, Mael was raw, imposing power.

"How are you feeling?" he asked, genuine concern in his voice. "The transition can be difficult."

Nadi lowered her eyes, playing her role. "It's... different. Everything is so intense. The sounds, the smells..." She glanced up through her lashes. He wasn't the first vampire she'd seduced... "The hunger."

Mael nodded sympathetically. "It will become manageable with time. Though I must say, you seem to be adapting remarkably well. Most newborns are quite... unstable. I do hope Raziel is feeding you."

A server approached with a silver tray bearing two crystal glasses filled with dark crimson liquid. Nadi's stomach twisted at the thought of drinking blood, but she maintained her composure as the glasses were placed before them. "He—he's doing his best, I think. The best that he's capable of."

When the server withdrew, Mael leaned forward slightly. "I wanted to speak with you privately because I'm concerned, Monica."

"Oh?" she asked, lifting her glass to her lips but not drinking. She'd have to, eventually. Mael would notice if the liquid didn't disappear. But she could get away with it at first.

"My brother." His expression darkened. "And what he might be doing to you."

Nadi set her glass down carefully. "Raziel has been... kind to me."

"Has he?" Mael's voice was soft, but there was steel beneath it. "I've known my brother for over two centuries, Monica. Kindness is not in his nature."

She let her eyes flicker down, as if uncertain. "He spared my life."

"For his own purposes, I assure you." Mael reached across the table, his massive hand stopping just short of touching hers. "I need you to understand something. The Raziel you think you know—the one who speaks softly, who shares your bed, who saved you from the sacrifice—is not the real Raziel."

"Then who is?" she asked, allowing vulnerability to creep into her voice.

"A monster," Mael said bluntly. "He has killed hundreds, maybe thousands, without remorse. You know what he did to the Iltanis. But that's not all. He has broken the minds and bodies of those who trusted him, those who cared for him." His eyes held hers intently. "Including his previous lovers."

She let fear flicker across her features—letting the truth of her own past inspire the emotion. She had seen Raziel's cruelty firsthand, after all. That was how she was taught to lie—to act—using pieces of the truth.

"I don't say this to frighten you," Mael continued. "But I need you to understand the danger you're in."

"But why? Why do I matter?" She kept her voice barely above a whisper.

Mael hesitated, then placed his hand over hers. His touch was warm, solid, and strangely comforting—a stark contrast to Raziel's that always held the promise of sudden violence.

"Because I see something in you," he said finally. "Something worth protecting. You've shown remarkable courage and adaptability. You've survived what would have broken most humans. And now..." His gaze traveled over her face with a warmth that made her unexpectedly warm. "Now, you might be exactly what this family needs to move forward."

"I don't understand."

Mael withdrew his hand, leaning back. "The family doesn't trust Raziel. To be truthful, we never have. But now? After his defiance with the sacrifice? Mother has tolerated his... eccentricities... for centuries because he's useful. But his latest act of rebellion has pushed her beyond patience."

That was interesting. Very interesting. "What does that mean?"

"It means that I believe Volencia may do something extreme. Or ensure that something extreme happens." Mael's voice dropped lower. "Tonight's council meeting isn't just about assigning you both a task to restore our standing. It's about deciding Raziel's fate."

She had to fight the urge to lean forward. This should be frightening to Monica. Terrifying, even. Instead, Mael was giving Nadi the answer to all her problems served up to her on a silver platter. This could rid her of Raziel—and her complicated feelings for him with it. "She would hurt her own son?"

A humorless smile crossed Mael's face. "You saw what she did to him last night. She's done far worse to him. Death would be a mercy in the long run."

Nadi looked down at her untouched blood, arranging her features into an expression of distress. "What can I do?"

"Align yourself with the winning side," Mael said simply. "I can protect you, Monica. I can ensure your place in the family, regardless of what happens to Raziel."

She raised her eyes to his, genuine confusion in them now. "But I still don't understand why you would do that for me? You hardly know me."

Something flickered in Mael's golden eyes then—something that had nothing to do with familial concern. His gaze dropped briefly to her lips before returning to her eyes.

"Let's just say I see potential in our... association."

Ah. The implication was clear. Nadi felt a strange pull toward him in that moment—not attraction. Sure, he was more than handsome, even if he wasn't exactly her type. But it was a recognition of an opportunity. Mael was offering her a second chance.

She could have another attempt at taking out the Nostroms from within. Without the Serpent around to muck things up. If her goal was simply to infiltrate and destroy the Nostroms, aligning with Mael would provide better access, better security, better chances of success.

So, why did the thought leave her feeling hollow?

"What would you have me do?" she asked, playing into his expectations.

Mael leaned forward again. "Watch my brother. Listen to what he says, especially when he thinks you're not paying attention. If he mentions the Rosovs, or anything about Mother's plans, I need to know." He paused. "And if he hurts you—if he even threatens to hurt you—you come to me immediately."

Nadi nodded her head. "I'm afraid of him sometimes." It was easy enough to play into the narrative. "The way he looks at me... like he's imagining all the ways he could tear me apart." It wasn't a lie either.

"That's because he is." His tone was grim. "My brother views everyone as either a tool or a toy. And both eventually break."

He reached for her hand again, and this time, she met him halfway. His thumb stroked across her knuckles in a gesture that was clearly meant to be more than just comforting.

"You don't have to face him alone, Monica," he murmured. "Not anymore."

The sincerity in his voice caught her off guard. Mael truly believed he was helping her, protecting her from his dangerous brother. And perhaps, in his own way, he was.

"Thank you," she said softly, squeezing his hand. "I don't know who to trust anymore."

"You can trust me," Mael said, his eyes never leaving hers. "I promise you that."

The meal continued on from there, drifting through other topics that were far less interesting. Discussions of her home—which she had to carefully make up on the fly. He told her all about how he used to go hunting for Wild creatures just outside the wall as a child. But, as the conversation went along, it meant she couldn't avoid something she'd been desperately hoping to this entire time. But now it was inevitable.

She had to do the deed of drinking the hideous glass of blood.

As they spoke, Nadi carefully extracted information while maintaining her vulnerable facade. Mael revealed that the council meeting would include distant branches of the Nostrom family rarely seen in the metropolis. That security would be heightened not just because of Raziel's defiance, but because of increasing tensions with the Rosov clan. That the task they would likely be assigned would involve infiltrating Rosov territory.

All valuable intelligence for her plan with Raziel.

If that was still her plan...

But as the meeting drew to a close and Mael escorted her back to his waiting car, Nadi found herself unsettled by how effectively he had managed to plant seeds of doubt. Not about Raziel's nature—she had no illusions about that—but about their alliance.

Was she backing the wrong Nostrom? Mael was clearly the more stable, more rational choice. The one who would give her greater access to the family's inner workings. The one less likely to snap and kill her on a whim.

But was Mael the one more likely to win?

And was Mael the one who would be easier to control?

As she settled into the plush leather seat of Mael's car, she caught him watching her with that same heated intensity.

"Tonight," he said, closing the door beside her, speaking

through the open window, "remember what I said. Whatever happens, I will keep you safe."

The car pulled away, leaving Mael standing on the curb, a mountain of a man whose golden eyes followed her until they turned the corner.

Nadi leaned back, closing her eyes and letting out a long breath. The meeting had gone exactly as she'd hoped—she'd gathered intelligence, established Mael's trust, positioned herself as a potential ally.

So, why did she feel like she'd just made a terrible mistake?

SIX

Nadi adjusted the crimson lace of her dress as the car pulled up to Volencia's estate. The deep red fabric clung to her body like a second skin. She had to admit, Raziel had good taste, even if the dress showed off more of Monica Valan's *assets* than the poor newly turned vampire would be comfortable with.

Her thoughts were a storm, debating between her paths ahead. But she had to focus on the task at hand. Tonight was going to be difficult to navigate as it was, without the new opportunity from Mael clearing the way ahead of her. Never mind the fact that she had to play the part of *vampire* in front of a room full of *vampires* on top of it.

"Remember," Raziel murmured, his lips close to her ear. "Not a word unless directly addressed. Most newly turned are still adjusting to their senses. You're overwhelmed. Lost. In awe."

"Oh, I'm sure." She rolled her eyes. "Helpless and naive. Trembling in the glow of your *sheer glory*, let alone that of a room full of Nostroms."

"Precisely. Play to their egos." His smile was thin. "It will make them underestimate you. I was quick enough to do just that, wasn't I? And look where it got me."

She really hated it when he made a good point.

"You wouldn't happen to have a huge bomb, would you? This would be the perfect opportunity," she muttered to him under her breath.

He chuckled. "If only it were so simple... many of them aren't so easy to kill."

"What about your gift? Does it work on them?"

"If it did, I would have slaughtered them all long ago."

Another good point. She sighed.

The car stopped at the foot of the grand marble staircase leading to Volencia's home. Unlike Raziel's mansion with its modern wood and sleek but brooding elegance, his mother's estate was all polished lacquered woods and detailed carved surfaces. But despite the velvet and twisting embroidered textures, the whole space felt cold. Heartless. Lethal. And it was far older than Raziel's. More antiquated.

Out of date.

Like a sculpture in a museum. Where Raziel seemed to be trying to keep up with the evolution of time, Volencia's home was frozen and locked in bygone era. And happily so.

Ivan opened the door, and Raziel stepped out first, offering his hand to help her. His palm was cool against hers—he hadn't fed recently. Another calculated move. He would appear weaker than he was. The dance of deception never ended in this family.

The doors to the council chamber swung open as they approached. Two guards in matching dark crimson suits stood at attention, their faces impassive. Nadi recognized one of them from Raziel's estate—a spy, then. She wondered who else in this sprawling dynasty had divided loyalties.

The chamber itself was a masterwork of intimidation. A horseshoe-shaped table dominated the space, elevated on a dais so those standing before it would be forced to look up. Twenty vampires sat around it, their faces ranging from ancient and wrinkled to youthfully smooth, but all bearing the same predatory stillness. Their visible ages were no indication of their years either. Vampires aged in strange ways—not predictably like the fae. Some aged faster, growing old in fewer years on the calendar. Some, like Volencia or Raziel's grandmother Lilivra, seemed to take centuries to age a decade.

Nadi suspected it had something to do with the strength of their bloodline, but it was only a suspicion on her part. She had no way of knowing for certain.

Behind the seated vampires were their attendants, guards, and other members of the extended Nostrom clan—at least forty more pairs of eyes watching their every move.

At the center sat Volencia, resplendent in a gown of the deepest red adorned with diamonds that glittered like cold stars. Mael lounged to her right, his massive frame somehow elegant in a charcoal suit. Lana sat to Volencia's left, her blonde hair elaborately styled and her magenta eyes bright with amusement.

The room fell silent as they entered. Not the natural quiet of anticipation, but the deliberate hush of a performance about to begin.

Raziel guided Nadi to the center of the open space, his hand on the small of her back. They stood together, which was strange enough for her as it was.

"Raziel," Volencia's voice cut through the silence. "And... Monica." The way she hesitated before saying the name made it clear she considered it disgusting.

"Nostrom council. Brothers and sisters. Lords and ladies of your regions. Elders." He paused. "Mother." Raziel inclined his head, just enough to acknowledge her without showing true submission. "We have come as commanded, to face judgment for *my* actions."

"Indeed." Volencia's lips curved into what might generously be called a smile. "How very dutiful of you. Especially after your catastrophic failure at the estate. You have embarrassed your family line. You have embarrassed all of us seated here, boy."

A murmur rippled through the assembled vampires. Nadi kept her gaze lowered, playing the part of the overwhelmed fledgling, while cataloging every exit, every potential weapon, every threat in the room.

But most of all, she was making note of every single one of the vampires in attendance. And who the biggest threats were, and in which order she'd have to kill them, if things went tits up.

"I would not characterize it as a failure, Mother." Raziel's voice remained perfectly measured. "Rather, a change in strategy."

"A change—" Volencia laughed, the sound like glass breaking. "A change in *strategy*? You were given explicit instructions. The sacrifice was non-negotiable. And now all of us who sit assembled have *our* power threatened and *our* political surety shaken because of *your* impudence."

"And yet..." Raziel gestured vaguely toward Nadi. "Here we are with a far more valuable asset than a momentary blood rite to some distant, upstart local gang lord with dreams of grandeur. This momentary upheaval from the Toths and the Rosovs can be dealt with in the same manner we always have, and you know it." He waved a hand dismissively. "By maneuvering or violence, they will fall in line. She is something far more rare and worth purchasing at any price."

Volencia's eyes narrowed, and Nadi felt the weight of her scrutiny like a physical pressure. "Step forward, girl."

Nadi moved one pace ahead of Raziel, lifting her gaze to meet Volencia's. She had practiced this moment in her mind— not too defiant, not too meek. A balance of respect and strength.

"You were human mere days ago," Volencia said. "Now you

stand before the Nostrom council as one of us. For the time being, at any rate. If we deem you unworthy, your severed head will be placed upon a stake as recompense for the broken rite of sacrifice. So I will begin with this question. How do you find your new existence?"

A direct question. Permission to speak.

"Overwhelming, Lady Volencia." Nadi's voice was soft but clear. "But I am... grateful and honored for the opportunity to serve the family in this new capacity."

The vampire matriarch studied her for a long moment. "And how exactly do you imagine you will serve us?"

"However I am directed, my lady." Nadi lowered her eyes again, with a gesture of submission that twisted a knife deep in her soul. Raziel might be the only one who understood what that sentence cost her. But even still, he might not.

Mael shifted in his seat, drawing attention. His golden eyes flicked over Nadi with an expression that might have been concern, might have been calculation. "She seems to have adjusted remarkably well. Most fledglings can barely form coherent sentences so soon after turning. If she has adapted so well this quickly... he may not be lying about her capabilities and strength."

Raziel's expression revealed nothing, but Nadi felt the tension in him ratchet higher. "Monica has always been exceptional. That was the reason I kept her."

"Exceptional," Lana repeated, her tone making the word an accusation. "Yes, we've noticed her... *exceptional* qualities."

Volencia raised a hand, silencing her daughter. "The council has not gathered to discuss the girl's physical appearance or the merits thereof. We are here to address the consequences of your actions, Raziel."

She stood, and the entire room seemed to hold its breath. Even Nadi felt the instinctive urge to freeze.

"The sacrifice at the ancestral estate is not merely tradition," Volencia continued. "It is a demonstration of power. A signal to all vampire clans that the Nostroms maintain the old ways and the strength they represent. The strength *we* represent."

She began to pace, her movements deliberate and graceful. "By failing to complete the sacrifice, you have significantly weakened our political standing. The Rosov family, in particular, has taken note."

"The Rosovs are opportunists," Raziel countered. "They've been looking for any excuse—"

"*Silence!*" Volencia snapped. "You do not interrupt me in my own council chamber. Not after what you've done."

Raziel's jaw tightened, but he bowed his head.

"The Rosovs control the eastern quarter of the metropolis," Volencia continued, addressing the entire council now. "They've been encroaching on our territory for decades, but this? This display of weakness has emboldened them. Braen Rosov has already reached out to three families that we once called allies, suggesting that perhaps the Nostroms no longer have the strength to protect their interests. If we do not act, *and act quickly*, we will lose a large portion of the city we control and be cut off from our supply of the drugs that we gather from below to fund our operations."

Murmuring filled the chamber, concerns passing from mouth to ear in a wave of disquiet.

"However," Volencia raised her voice slightly, silencing the whispers, "the situation is not beyond salvaging."

She nodded to Lana, who rose to stand beside her mother.

"My daughter has offered a solution." Volencia's pride was evident in the slight softening of her expression. "One that will not only repair the damage done but potentially strengthen our position beyond what it was before."

Lana stepped forward, her sequined dress catching the light with each movement. "I will marry Zabriel Rosov."

Gasps echoed through the chamber. Nadi kept her face carefully blank, but internally she was reassessing everything. This was no minor territory squabble—this was a major power shift in the metropolis.

"A marriage alliance?" One of the elder council members shook his head. "The Rosovs have refused such arrangements for centuries."

"Zabriel is more... progressive than his siblings," Lana replied, her smile enigmatic. "He understands that our families have more to gain from cooperation than conflict."

Nadi didn't miss the flash of calculation in Lana's eyes. There was more to this arrangement than she was revealing. Nadi tried to think what she knew about Zabriel Rosov. Only that he was the second of the four children. Braen was the eldest, followed by Zabriel, and then his two sisters, Nabrisi and Asha. Braen and Nabrisi both had reputations for being brutal and cruel in their own unique ways—for making people *disappear*. But there was little to nothing known about Zabriel and Asha. That in and of itself made them likely the more dangerous of the four siblings.

Panic started to buzz in the back of Nadi's mind. But she had too little to act on. There was nothing she could do to stop the trainwreck happening in front of her.

"This is a tremendous sacrifice on your part, Lana," another council member said, his tone reverent. "To willingly enter a political marriage for the good of the family..."

Lana lowered her eyes modestly. "We all serve the Nostrom legacy in our own ways."

Nadi had to admire the performance. If she hadn't spent time around Lana, hadn't seen how the Sweetheart Mistress operated, she might have believed this show of reluctant duty. No, this was all a shot directly at Raziel.

"There is, however, one obstacle to this arrangement," Volencia continued, her gaze shifting back to Raziel. "The eldest Rosov brother, Braen, opposes the union. He is notoriously unstable. Dangerous."

"He's a rabid dog," Mael interjected, his deep voice carrying to every corner of the room. "Unpredictable and vicious, even by the standards of his family."

Nadi didn't miss the pointed look he gave Raziel.

"For the wedding to proceed, Braen Rosov must be eliminated," Volencia said, her voice matter-of-fact, as if discussing the removal of an inconvenient piece of furniture. "Permanently."

"And Zabriel is aware of this?" another council member asked, his brow furrowed.

"It was his idea." Mael's expression was thin. "He knows Braen has grown too dangerous."

Volencia turned her cold gaze to Raziel. "And you, my son, will see to this task personally."

Raziel's expression didn't change, but Nadi, standing close enough to feel the slight shift in his posture, knew the command had struck home.

"Mother—" he began.

"This is not a negotiation." Volencia's voice was steel. "You created this situation. You will remedy it. And your... bride will assist you. It is clear she delights in such things."

Nadi felt the eyes of every vampire in the room fall on her, studying her reaction. She kept her expression neutral, though her mind was racing. They were being set up. This was no simple assassination—it was a test. Possibly a death sentence.

"Killing Braen Rosov will require more than brute force," one of the council members observed, an elderly vampire with silvered hair. "He is paranoid and well-protected. Previous attempts have failed. Spectacularly."

"Which is precisely why Raziel is the perfect choice for this task," Volencia said, her smile sharp. "His particular... talents are suited to the job."

Another council member leaned forward, his face deeply lined with age. "And the girl? What value does she bring to such a mission?"

Before Raziel could answer, Mael spoke up. "Monica has shown remarkable adaptability and quick thinking. Qualities that will complement my brother's more direct approach."

Nadi caught the slightly surprised look that flashed across Raziel's face. Mael was defending their partnership? Interesting.

"Indeed," Volencia agreed, though her expression suggested she was less than pleased with Mael's intervention. "The two of you will work together to remove this obstacle to our family's advancement." She returned to her seat at the center of the council table, the movement deliberate and theatrical. "You have two weeks. Lana's wedding is scheduled for the full moon of the Devourer. I expect Braen Rosov to be eliminated no later than seven days before the ceremony."

"And if we fail?" Raziel asked, his voice perfectly neutral.

The silence that followed was an almost palpable weight. Every vampire in the room stared, waiting for Volencia's response.

When it came, her voice was soft but carried to every corner of the chamber. "Then, the council will be forced to reconsider whether your continued existence serves the interests of the Nostrom family."

The threat hung in the air. Nadi felt a chill run down her spine. Not for herself—she had always known her hunger for revenge could end in her death—but for the implications of what Volencia was saying. The Nostrom matriarch would eliminate her own son without hesitation if he failed to serve her purposes.

Why had Nadi ever decided to come here in the first place?

She should have just let them tear themselves apart.

"I understand, Mother." Raziel's voice betrayed no emotion. "We will not fail."

"For your sake, I hope not." Volencia's gaze shifted to Nadi. "And for hers." She lit her cigarette, casting her face briefly in the glow of the flame. "It's of no loss to me, either way."

Nadi met the vampire's eyes, allowing just a hint of defiance to show. It was what Monica would do—not cowed, but still aware of her precarious position.

"The council is dismissed," Volencia announced. "Raziel, you will receive the intelligence we've gathered on Braen Rosov by nightfall. Study it carefully. This is not an opportunity for creativity."

As the vampires began to rise from their seats, conversations already breaking out among them, Nadi felt a presence at her side. Mael had descended from the dais and now stood close enough that she could feel unnatural heat radiating from his massive frame. He must have fed very recently.

"Be careful, Monica," he said, his voice pitched low so only she and Raziel could hear. "My brother's methods tend to be messy, as you've seen. And Braen Rosov is not to be underestimated."

"I appreciate your concern," Nadi replied carefully, "but I trust my husband's judgment."

Mael's golden eyes studied her face. "Do you? I wonder." He turned to Raziel. "Don't let your personal feelings interfere with this task, brother. We all remember what happened the last time you were assigned to deal with Braen."

Raziel's expression hardened. "Ancient history, Mael. I've learned from my mistakes."

"I sincerely hope so." Mael nodded to Nadi, then moved away to join a group of council members who were clearly waiting to speak with him.

As they exited the chamber, Nadi could feel Raziel's tension radiating from him like crackling electricity in the air.

His hand on her back guided her through the corridors of Volencia's estate and back to the waiting car, but his mind was clearly elsewhere.

Only when they were safely inside the vehicle, with Ivan at the wheel and the privacy screen raised, did Raziel finally speak. "Well." His voice tight with controlled fury. "That went about as well as expected."

"They're setting you up to fail." Nadi was watching the streets go by.

Raziel laughed, the sound thin and sarcastic. "Of course they are. The question is whether they want me dead, or merely humiliated."

"From what I saw in there, I'm betting on the former. Or both." She paused. "What was Mael insinuating when we left?"

He turned to look at her, his red eyes reflecting the light of the streetlamps in the dimness of the car. "Braen Rosov and I have... history. My mother knows that sending me to kill him is either a suicide mission or a test of my loyalty."

The raw honesty in his voice surprised her. "What kind of history?"

Raziel looked away, staring out at the passing cityscape. "The complicated kind."

She lowered her voice. The glass was up between them and Ivan, but she didn't trust that his bodyguard couldn't hear them. "If we're going to have any chance of succeeding—and surviving —I need to know what I'm walking into."

For a long moment, she thought he wouldn't answer. Then, so quietly she had to strain to hear him, he finally spoke. "He was once... the only person in this gods-forsaken city who showed me something resembling kindness."

The admission hung between them, heavy with implications. Nadi studied his profile, the sharp lines of his face cast in shadow.

"And now they want you to kill him."

Raziel nodded, his expression hard. "Welcome to the Nostrom family, darling. Where loyalty is always rewarded with torture and death."

The bitterness in his voice was palpable. For a moment—just a moment—Nadi felt a flicker of something dangerously close to sympathy.

She tamped it down viciously.

"We should focus on the mission." Desperately, she steered the conversation away from emotional territory. "Tell me everything you know about Braen Rosov."

Raziel's lips curved in a humorless smile. "Oh, I could tell you many things about Braen. But perhaps the most important is this—he's even more dangerous than my family believes, and twice as clever."

"Then, why hasn't he made a move against the Nostroms before now?"

"Who says he hasn't?" Raziel's eyes met hers. "Braen plays a very long game. If he's openly opposing this wedding, it's because he wants something we can't yet see."

Nadi considered this, turning the problem over in her mind. "So we're not just being sent to kill him. We're being used as pieces in whatever game he's playing with your family."

"Precisely." Raziel nodded, a spark of approval in his eyes. "And that, my sweet little murderer, is why we need to be even more careful than usual."

The car pulled up to Raziel's mansion, and Ivan came around to open the door. As they stepped out, Raziel leaned close, his lips brushing her ear.

"Trust no one," he whispered. "Not my family, not my guards. Everyone is playing their own game. And we're the pieces most likely to be sacrificed."

With that cheerful thought, he guided her into the house, his hand at the small of her back once more. To anyone watching, they would appear as a united front—the dangerous son and his new vampire bride.

But Nadi knew better. They were two predators circling the same prey, their alliance tenuous at best. And when the time came, she would have to decide where her true loyalties lay—with Raziel, with herself, or with the vengeance that had driven her for so long.

As they entered the house, a servant approached with a silver tray bearing a sealed envelope. Raziel took it, breaking the black wax seal with his thumb.

"It would seem," he said, scanning the contents, "that my mother is eager for us to begin. This contains their intelligence on Braen's movements and security."

He handed the pages to Nadi. "Take a look. We'll begin planning tomorrow morning."

The dossier was detailed and extensive—security rotations, known associates, properties, even preferred hunting grounds for feeding. Nadi was impressed. And, if she were *really* honest, she was jealous. It must be nice to have real money and connections. If she'd had these resources when she was an assassin, her job would have been so much easier. Someone had been watching Braen Kosov very closely for a very long time.

At the bottom of the last page was a handwritten note in elegant, flowing script:

Remember what happens to pets that bite the hand that feeds them, my son. Do not disappoint me again.

Nadi looked up to find Raziel watching her, his expression unreadable. "Your mother doesn't leave much room for interpretation, does she?"

"Volencia has never been one for subtlety." He sneered. "At least not when it comes to threats." Taking the papers back from her, his fingers brushed against hers. "Get some rest. We have much to discuss and I need you sharp."

As he turned to leave, Nadi called after him. "Raziel."

He paused, looking back at her with one eyebrow raised in question.

"If Braen cared about you, or you him"—pausing, she chose her words carefully—"are you certain you can go through with this?"

Something dark flickered across his face—pain. Or perhaps anger. Maybe both.

"My dear, sweet Monica," his voice was edged with steel, "caring for someone has never stopped me from killing them. If anything, it only inspires me to remove them from my life. You'd do well to remember that."

With that parting shot, he left her standing in the foyer, the warning hanging in the air between them like the blade of a guillotine, poised to fall.

SEVEN

"You can't be serious."

Nadi studied the elaborate floor plan spread across Raziel's desk, tracing its winding corridors with her finger. Braen's personal jazz club, The Poisoned Serpent, was a testament to both opulence and paranoia—four stories of gambling, entertainment, and private rooms for the metropolis's elite, all protected by no fewer than thirty armed guards.

While the Rosov family had many clubs in their portfolio, and most of them were managed by Braen himself, apparently *this one* was his personal favorite. He rented out a suite above it and spent most of his nights there, far away from the estate that was technically his family home.

Many of the private rooms in The Poisoned Serpent were meant for *discerning guests* and activities that they wished to engage in outside of the home but away from prying eyes.

"He named his club after you?" she remarked, raising an eyebrow at Raziel.

A shadow passed over his face. "Braen's idea of a joke."

Right. Either that, or their *complicated* friendship was perhaps more than a friendship.

"So I'm going in there just to observe? Learn his patterns, find his vulnerabilities?"

"For now." His voice gave nothing away. "I need to know what he's hiding. Specifically, what leverage we can use to draw him out for the kill."

"And how exactly do you propose I get past his security?" She went back to studying the map. They were alone, so she could at least speak freely about her abilities and their situation. "Even if I took the place of one of his men, they rotate in pairs. A lone guard would draw questions immediately."

Raziel leaned back in his chair, toying with one of his gold coins—flipping it over his knuckles in that mesmerizing pattern that had become so familiar to her but no less hypnotizing. "We don't go in as guards. In fact, I'm not going at all. And *you're* going in as the staff."

"Oh, joy. The help." Nadi frowned.

"No one notices the staff, after all." His smile was thin. "And your current face is becoming known in our circles."

He flipped the coin into the air, catching it with a snap of his wrist. "And you've proven to be quite adept at... blending in. I have no fear you will be quite fine on your own."

She was flattered. More than she should be. He actually was sending her out to do this on her own. Huh. "Bartender, cook, waitress, and so on."

Raziel got to his feet, moving to stand beside her at the desk. "Different forms, different times of day. We need to understand how Braen's operation works from the inside before we make our move."

His proximity sent a flutter through her that she immediately suppressed. This close, she could smell the woodsmoke and sandalwood scent of him, could feel the unnatural heat radiating from his skin. He'd fed recently. Preparing.

"And what will you be doing while I'm risking my skin?"

Taking a step to the side, she wanted to put some distance between them.

"Planning." He tapped the blueprints. "And acquiring resources we'll need for the operation."

"Resources?"

"The less you know about that for now, the better." His smile was wolfish. "Trust me."

Trust. Such a dangerous word.

"Fine," she conceded. "When do I start?"

"Tonight. Remember. Observe, don't engage. We need to understand what Braen is hiding. We need *dirt*. Not action. Just enough to get him to meet with me in private."

"Unlike some of us, I know how to follow orders." She smirked up at him. "But why can't I just go in and kill him? I *am* an assassin, after all."

"Very funny." He sighed. "And as for why? Braen's death will raise a great deal of questions over who did the deed and why. Doing this outside of his club will help us control the variables. Fewer possibilities of things going wrong. And if we have dirt on him at that point, something or someone else that his death can be pinned on, all the better."

She sighed. It made sense. Find something horrible about Braen so that when he died, the blame could be shifted to *that* and away from the Nostroms. "This is why I always stayed away from politics."

"Believe me, I side with you on this." He smirked at her.

And with that, she was off. For three nights, Nadi transformed into different employees of The Poisoned Serpent.

It almost felt good, having a "normal" job to do. Something that wasn't caught up in the complexity of whatever was happening between her and Raziel. Something that just involved her, her skills, and the work she had trained herself to do for eighty years.

The first night, she took the form of a young human male—

one she'd observed rushing between the club and a nearby bakery earlier that day. Thin, unremarkable, with the kind of forgettable face that made him invisible to the wealthy patrons. It was his night off.

Well, for *him*. Not for Nadi. He might be confused in two days' time when people referenced him working the night before, but he'd have a bigger check to show for it, so she figured he wouldn't give a damn at the end of the day. Just one of those funny mysteries that people brushed off because there was no logical explanation for it.

The Poisoned Serpent after dark was a different creature entirely from the respectable establishment it appeared to be during daylight hours. Gas lamps cast flickering shadows across richly appointed rooms while well-dressed vampires and their human companions indulged in pleasures that would have shocked the more conservative members of the metropolis.

Nadi kept her head down and her movements efficient as she cleared tables and replaced ashtrays, her enhanced hearing picking up fragments of conversation that painted a picture of Braen's operations. Drug deals disguised as business investments. Sexual favors of the most depraved kind discussed over bottles of wine that cost more than most automobiles.

But it was the casual mention of "special merchandise" that made her skin crawl and immediately grabbed her interest. Unfortunately, it was only the first night, and there was little that she could do immediately.

Patience was key.

She caught her first glimpse of Braen himself near midnight, when he emerged from a private gambling room accompanied by three vampires she didn't recognize. She hadn't tangled much with the Rosovs before. They owned nightclubs and restaurants on the fringes of the metropolis.

But there was no question in her mind that this was him.

Braen was a handsome man with mid-length dark brown

hair gelled back in the modern style. His suit was custom-made and from the height of fashion. And his sweet, almost youthful, beautiful features did nothing to hide the hint of malice in his eyes.

The Rosov family was also an older group of vampires—but one that she didn't know much about. They had always rather kept to themselves. Powerful, but *quiet*. Her attention—and her wrath—had been pointed squarely at the Nostroms.

"The shipment from the eastern territories should arrive next week," one of his companions was saying as they passed near her table. "The quality has been exceptional lately."

"Good," Braen replied, his voice carrying the faint accent of old vampire nobility. "Our clients are becoming increasingly discerning. We can't afford to disappoint them."

As they moved away, Nadi noted the way other patrons deferred to Braen—stepping aside, lowering their voices, watching him with a mixture of respect and fear. This was his domain, and everyone in it knew exactly who held the power.

She spent the rest of the night mapping the club's layout, noting guard positions and shift changes. The basement level was off-limits to staff members like the one she was playing as, but she observed several well-dressed guests being escorted downstairs by club security. Whatever Braen was hiding, it was down there.

It was during that infiltration that she noticed something else odd and out of place. Well, not some*thing*, but some*one*. It was just something about the young woman who was wiping down tables and sweeping the floors that struck Nadi as strange.

Nothing about the otherwise nondescript young woman should have stood out to her. She had shoulder-length dark hair. Medium build. Attractive, but nothing memorable. In fact, it was almost as though she had been purpose-chosen to *blend in*.

As someone who often designed themselves to do exactly that, it was the first thing that Nadi noticed. The second was how the young woman moved. There was just an odd kind of grace in the way she carried herself—subtle, just around the edges, like the hint of an accent that only someone who was from that area could recognize.

The woman was *fae*. Or at least from the Wild. There was no question in Nadi's mind. But was she just a transplant who had come up to the surface to make her way in life, not wholly unlike Nadi herself? Or was there something else going on?

She filed the information into the back of her mind and went about her night. She had work to do. And a single stray child from below was not worth threatening her mission over.

For her second infiltration, Nadi took the form of a vampiric woman she'd seen serving tables—someone with enough authority to move freely through the club but not important enough to attract attention from the management.

This time, she was able to access more of the club's restricted areas, carrying trays of bloodwine to private rooms where the real business was conducted. In one room, she overheard a conversation about shipping schedules. In another, a heated discussion about "product quality." But no other leads and no ways to get down into the basement.

It was in the third-floor private dining room that she saw Zabriel Rosov.

Braen's younger brother was everything the elder wasn't— where Braen seemed to radiate barely contained aggression and unpredictable energy beneath a veneer of polish and expensive clothes, Zabriel possessed an almost supernatural calm.

He was handsome, with long chestnut-brown hair pulled back into a simple, practical ponytail. A pair of thin-framed glasses sat perched on his nose, which was rare for vampires. His eyes were an amber shade of orange and seemed to gaze *through* everything around him.

Zabriel was attractive, no doubt. But in the way that an oil painting was attractive. Distantly so.

He sat perfectly still at the head of a polished table while a group of well-dressed vampires reported on territorial disputes, his pale amber eyes tracking every speaker with the attention of a predator calculating the precise moment to strike.

"The Nostroms think they can dictate terms from their ivory tower," one vampire was saying, his voice carrying nervous energy in the face of Zabriel's silent scrutiny. "But perhaps it's time we reminded them that old blood doesn't guarantee continued power."

Nadi lingered near the door, arranging glasses on her tray while listening to the exchange. Zabriel was younger than Braen by perhaps fifty years in appearance, but there was something unsettling about his stillness—the way he could remain motionless for minutes at a time while others fidgeted under his gaze.

Even older vampires moved instinctively. Even just a little. But not Zabriel.

"What about their new asset?" another vampire asked. "The wife. If the rumors are true, she has some kind of uncommon power. There's no other reason for the Nostroms to leave her alive—"

"Rumors. And nothing more." Zabriel's quiet voice carried easily despite its soft tone. "The Nostroms have always relied on fear and mystique to maintain their position. Half their supposed power is theatrical nonsense designed to keep the other families in line." He paused, his fingers drumming once against the table. "But even theater can be dangerous if enough people believe in the performance."

Interesting. Where others might dismiss her entirely, Zabriel seemed to understand that perception could be as powerful as reality. He was more dangerous than she'd initially assumed.

As the evening wore on, she observed the dynamic between the brothers when they finally occupied the same space. Braen's subtly aggressive energy filled whatever room he entered, demanding attention through sheer force of personality. But when Zabriel spoke, even Braen listened—not with deference, but with the careful attention of someone who understood that still waters often ran deepest.

And once again, she noticed that young woman from the night before—the one from the Wild. It was hard not to keep an eye on her. But for all that Nadi could see, she was just going about her business and doing her job.

Near the end of her shift, she managed to get close enough to their private table to overhear a more personal exchange.

Braen's voice was pitched low but carrying the edge of barely controlled hatred. "It's time we stopped pretending this is about business and reminded them what real power looks like."

Zabriel leaned back in his chair, his expression thoughtful rather than eager. "Violence for its own sake is wasteful, brother. If you are insistent that we must move against them, a matter I disagree with, it should be decisive. Complete." His pale eyes found Braen's. "Are you prepared for what complete means?"

"I've been ready for years." Braen's hands clenched into fists on the table briefly. "And I am the eldest. This is my decision to make. The question is whether you've finally realized that patience without action is just another word for cowardice."

Zabriel's smile was barely visible, but somehow more threatening than any of Braen's obvious displays of aggression. "I've never been accused of cowardice, brother. Only of being thorough."

The look that passed between them was loaded with a kind of weight that Nadi couldn't quite decode. But whatever the Rosov brothers were planning, it likely involved Lana's upcoming wedding—and Nadi didn't know how she felt about that.

Part of her wanted them all to kill each other in a rain of

bullets and bloodshed. The other half of her felt... as though she should *warn* someone. But she still had nothing concrete. No dirt. Nothing she could go back to Raziel with to call the mission a success.

On the next night of reconnaissance, Nadi took the boldest approach yet—replacing the club's bartender, a position that would give her access to conversations with the elite clientele while they were at their most unguarded.

She'd spent the afternoon watching the real bartender, a new employee who hadn't been on the job more than a few days, studying his mannerisms and speech patterns. When she approached him after his shift ended, wearing some stranger's face, offering him enough money to disappear from the job, he'd accepted without asking questions. The metropolis had taught everyone the value of not looking too closely at unexpected opportunities.

The bar at The Poisoned Serpent was positioned at the heart of the main floor, giving her a clear view of nearly every transaction that occurred in the public areas. More importantly, it was where Braen himself came to conduct business when he wanted to be seen doing it.

She'd been working for barely an hour when he appeared, sliding onto a barstool with the fluid grace of a predator claiming territory.

"Bourbon," he said simply, his eyes scanning the room with the attention of someone constantly assessing threats. "The good stuff."

Nadi poured him a glass of the club's finest bourbon, noting the way he held himself—relaxed but ready, like a coiled spring waiting for the right moment to release. This close, she could see the small scars on his hands, evidence of violence that his expensive clothes couldn't quite hide.

"Busy night," she offered, the kind of small talk that bartenders were expected to make.

Braen's attention focused on her for the first time, and she felt the weight of his scrutiny like a physical thing. "New," he observed. It wasn't a question.

"Started this week," she replied, keeping her voice steady. "Still learning everyone's preferences." It was an apology for the small talk, without bending over and eating shit for it.

He studied her for a moment longer, then nodded slightly. "You'll do fine. The key to working here is understanding that what you see and hear doesn't leave this building. Ever."

"Understood, sir."

"Good." He took a sip of his whiskey, and his attention returned to the room. "Trust is a valuable commodity in this business. Those who prove they can be trusted find themselves well-rewarded. Those who can't..." He left the threat unfinished. It didn't need to be.

Throughout the evening, Nadi watched as a steady stream of visitors approached Braen's position at the bar. Some came to pay respects, others to report on various business ventures. But it was near closing time that the most interesting visitor appeared.

A woman Nadi didn't recognize—vampire, by the pale perfection of her skin, but young-looking even by their standards. She carried herself with the certainty of someone three times her size. She had close-cropped hair and wore a man's suit tailored into sharp angles. Her fierce gaze immediately snapped from Braen to Nadi as the bartender, then dismissed her as anything interesting—then went right back to Braen.

"Braen," the woman said, her voice tight with nervousness. "We need to talk."

"Nabrisi, sister dear," Braen replied. Another Rosov sibling. "How lovely to see you. What brings you to my establishment? You rarely *slum it* here with me."

The family resemblance was clear once Nadi knew what to look for—the same dark hair, the same calculating eyes. But where Braen radiated barely controlled violence and Zabriel maintained his unsettling calm, Nabrisi seemed to carry herself with the careful precision of someone who understood she was surrounded by predators. Namely, because she was one too.

Something about her reminded Nadi of the fae berserkers. Battle warriors who would fight to the death to defend their people.

"It's about the Nostrom situation." Nabrisi glanced around the room before continuing. "The family wants to know if you're serious about this... movement of yours."

Braen's expression darkened, his hands clenching slightly. "The family knows exactly how serious I am. The question is whether they're finally ready to stop treating us like children who can't be trusted with real power."

"They're not treating us like children. They're treating us like potential casualties." Nabrisi's voice dropped even lower. "Do you have any idea what Raziel Nostrom is capable of? What he's done to families that crossed them? You of all people should know why we—"

"I know exactly what the Serpent has done." Braen cut off his sister, his tone like ice. "And I know *quite* well what he is capable of. But he is not immortal. None of his family is."

The conversation continued in whispers too low even for Nadi's enhanced hearing to catch, but the body language told its own story. Nabrisi was standoffish and wary—not of the Nostroms, but of whatever her brothers were planning. When she finally left, her movements held the careful control of someone trying not to look like they were ready to smash something expensive.

As the night wound down and the last patrons filtered out, Nadi found herself alone with Braen for a few minutes while the security team conducted their closing procedures. He remained at the bar, nursing his bourbon and staring into the deep amber liquid as if it held answers to questions he wasn't ready to voice.

"Tell me," he said suddenly, still not looking at her, "what do you know about loyalty?"

The question seemed to come from nowhere, but Nadi sensed it was important. "I know it's earned, not given."

"Wise answer." He finally looked up, and she saw something almost vulnerable in his expression—gone so quickly she might have imagined it. "Loyalty is the only currency that matters in this business. Money can be stolen, power can be lost, but loyalty..." He paused. "Loyalty is what determines whether you live or die when everything else falls apart."

Before she could respond, Zabriel appeared from one of the back rooms. "Brother. We're ready."

"Good." Braen finished his whiskey and stood. "Close up for me," he told Nadi. "And remember what I said about trust."

As the brothers disappeared into the back of the club, Nadi began the process of shutting down the bar while her mind raced with everything she'd learned. The Rosovs were planning something that involved the Nostroms. Braen was positioning himself for some kind of power play that his own sister feared. And there was definitely something hidden in the basement level that she hadn't been able to access.

But perhaps most importantly, she'd observed the dynamics between the siblings—the way Braen commanded respect while Zabriel provided council, the way Nabrisi seemed to play *the muscle* of the organization but was reticent to jump into a fight she deemed unwise. And yet the fourth sibling, the other sister, Asha, had not made an appearance yet.

When she finally left the club in the early hours of the morning, Nadi felt the satisfaction of a job well done. She had the intelligence Raziel needed, and more importantly, she had a sense of the Rosovs as people rather than just targets.

Now came the harder part—figuring out how to use what

she'd learned to bring them down. She'd gathered valuable intelligence about the family dynamics and their plans for the Nostrom wedding, but there was still that basement level she hadn't been able to access. Whatever Braen was hiding down there, it was important enough to warrant the club's heaviest security.

She was going in again. This time, she wouldn't be content with observing from the periphery. This time, she was going to find out exactly what the Rosovs were hiding in the depths of The Poisoned Serpent.

Even if it killed her.

EIGHT

On night four, everything changed.

Crystal chandeliers cast rainbows across the polished marble floor, while a jazz quartet played on a raised stage, their melancholy notes winding through the cigarette smoke that hung in the air like fog.

But tonight, Nadi's evening was far away from the luxury of the club. No, her night was consumed by clanging pans and the barking of food orders. She was playing the part of the head chef. The good news was it wasn't the first time she'd had to do the role before in her life. The woman had called in sick, and she'd been the one to intercept the phone call earlier that day, so it had been easy enough to swap into her form and take the position on the line.

It was when she had her head down, prepping scallops for the dinner service, that Braen walked in. "You're late for our downstairs guests."

He gestured at a row of plates on the prep shelf next to him. "These will do. Get a tray. Let's go. My guests are getting impatient, and if they haven't eaten, they're liable to faint before the evening kicks off."

"Yessir. I'm sorry." Grabbing a large black tray from a stack, she filled it up with the plates he had gestured at and followed behind him obediently.

Braen was in a hurry, and she made sure she was appropriately cowed, embarrassed, and afraid of him. When he took her down to the basement, and to a door that shouldn't have been there—as it wasn't on any of the floor plans that Raziel had shown her—she felt the hair on the back of her neck start to stand up.

The vampire reached into the pocket of his coat, pulled out a set of keys, and clicked open a hidden lock tucked away behind a false steam pipe along the wall. Pushing open the bricks, it revealed a corridor that was just as lavish as everything else, if far more dimly lit.

This was still a public-facing space—just far more salacious. *What was going on here?*

Braen's expensive shoes clicked loudly on the wooden floor as he led her deeper into the basement, before turning the corner into a room.

Nadi's heart lurched in her chest. She almost staggered and dropped the plate of food all over the floor.

She almost shifted into Ivan and bludgeoned Braen to death where he stood.

It took every ounce of her will—every shred of self-preservation—every voice in her head screaming *Don't do it, you fool, you'll die*—to keep herself from flying into a rage.

In front of her were men and women. Chained. In various stages of barely clothed or fully nude. All young, all beautiful, all on their knees, all clearly prisoners...

And all of them fae.

"Well?" Braen snapped. "Are you an idiot today? What are you waiting for?" He gestured toward the prisoners. No... The *slaves*.

"S-sorry. Not feeling my best today. Almost called out sick."

She stepped forward with the tray of food, before placing it down on the ground, passing out the plates. The fae in front of her didn't even look up at her. Her hands were shaking as she returned back to the door, clutching the tray hard enough that her knuckles were turning white.

Braen frowned. "Oh, I'm so sorry, Wilma. I shouldn't have been so cross with you, then. Well, then go home, take the rest of the night off. Your work ethic really will be the death of you, you know." He reached out and put his hand gently on her arm, smiling at her with an honestly *sympathetic* and kind smile. "You know how wound up I get on big nights. I shouldn't be taking it out on you. Go on home, I mean it. It's about time one of those lousy line cooks of yours learned how to step up."

The jarring change in his mood was like putting a hot glass plate into a bucket of cold water. It shattered something in her. She just kind of went numb from it all. Nodding, she smiled weakly. "Thanks. I-I'll do that."

The kitchen door swung shut behind her with a soft whoosh, cutting off the distant sounds of clinking glasses and muffled jazz from the dining room. The back alley behind the club was mercifully empty, lit only by a single bulb hanging over the service entrance. Nadi pulled her false cardigan tighter around her shoulders and started walking, her glamor-summoned sensible shoes clicking against the wet pavement.

The cool night air bit at her cheeks, but she welcomed it. Anything was better than the suffocating atmosphere she'd just escaped. Her mind churned as she replayed the conversation, trying to make sense of Braen's sudden shift from anger to sympathy. It felt wrong, like a mask hastily slapped over his true face. The way his fingers had lingered on her arm, the too-practiced concern in his voice—it all left her feeling somehow dirty.

Because it had been *real*. His concern for his employee had been sincere. He cared for "Wilma" as someone he looked after in his company. When he had *Nadi's people* chained up like animals in the basement. The jarring whiplash of it made her want to retch.

But that was simply how the world worked, wasn't it? Some people were always *less than*. Always able to be looked down on. Spat on. Or in this case? Traded. Sold. A commodity like food at a restaurant, and nothing more.

She turned onto the main street, where the glow of illuminated signs framed in bulbs painted everything in gradient tones of yellow and amber. A couple stumbled out of a bar, laughing too loudly, and she stepped aside to let them pass. The normalcy of it—people going about their evening, oblivious to everything going on in the shadows—felt surreal after everything that had happened.

Twenty blocks stretched ahead of her, but she didn't mind. The walking helped, each step putting more distance between her and Braen's sincere kindness and abject cruelty.

Her breath came out in small puffs as she passed under streetlights, each one creating a brief circle of warmth before abandoning her to the shadows again. A taxi honked somewhere in the distance, and she could hear the distant rumble of the elevated train. The city moved around her like a living thing, but she felt separate from it all, wrapped in her own bubble of shock and disgust.

By the time she reached the tenth block, her initial numbness had begun to thaw, replaced by something much more dangerous. Rage, pure and simple, burned through her veins like liquid fire. Raziel had let her walk into that situation blind. He'd sent her to work for someone likely knowing *exactly* what he was up to. There was no way in the pits that he didn't know who Braen was trafficking, who he could have exposed her to— or what could have happened if she got caught. And he'd said nothing.

She was so lost in her fury that she almost didn't notice the sleek black car pulling up to the curb beside her. It was Ivan.

He said nothing as she opened the door and climbed into the back seat and shut it behind her.

All through the silent ride back to Raziel's house, her rage built in silence. Now, it wasn't just pointed at Braen. Now, it was pointed at Raziel. And she could punch *him* in the fucking *face.*

When she got back to the house, she made a line straight for Raziel's office. She didn't bother to say a damn thing to him before walking in and slamming the door behind her hard enough that the paintings on the walls went crooked. *"You motherfucker! Why didn't you tell me?"*

He looked up from his desk, his expression neutral. "You'll need to be more specific."

"Trafficking!" She spat the words like venom. "Not just drugs or weapons. Braen is selling—" Swallowing her words, she was shaking. She forced herself to speak quieter. She knew the house could hear if she shouted. "He is selling *fae.*"

Something flickered across Raziel's face—discomfort, perhaps even shame. "What did you see?"

"There's a basement. A set of rooms that's not on the blueprints." Nadi's jaw clenched as she paced before his desk. "He keeps them collared with iron. I saw at least twelve." Her voice broke slightly. "They're being sold as sex slaves, Raziel. I'm certain. And you *knew.*"

The coin in Raziel's hand stilled. He set it down carefully on the desk. "I was aware he had... tastes. I had seen him with them. I didn't know he was collecting and selling. But I won't lie." He wouldn't meet her eyes. "It's been a rumor for years."

"A rumor?" She laughed bitterly. "That my people are being kidnapped, used, and sold? That was just a *rumor* to you?"

"In the old days, it was hardly an uncommon practice." His voice turned hard, cold. "The fae used to be gathered and then released and hunted for sport. Or kept as pets. Commodities."

"By monsters like you."

For once, he didn't smile at the accusation. Instead, he stood and walked to the window, looking out at the night. "Yes. By monsters like me."

The admission caught her off guard. She'd expected denial, deflection, his usual arrogant dismissal.

"Does it bother you now?" she pressed. "Now that you're working with one of those *commodities?*"

"It bothered me before," he said quietly, surprising her again. "Why do you think Braen and I had our... falling-out? I thought what he was doing was disgusting. Sleeping with fae." He laughed once, as if he actually found it funny.

Nadi studied him, trying to read the truth in his posture, the set of his shoulders. "You expect me to believe you objected on moral grounds?"

"Yes. I did." Raziel turning to face her. "The fae are unpredictable. Savage. Their magic even more so. And at the time, I believed their blood to be poison. Only the most debased of our kind would risk keeping them around. Wild animals can only be broken so far. They are always liable to tear you to pieces when you turn your back."

His words were logical, cold, but something in his eyes told a different story. Discomfort? Regret? She couldn't be sure.

"Why didn't you stop him?"

Raziel moved closer, his gaze locked on hers. "I am hardly one to judge another for their *sexual perversions*, am I? Especially now." He huffed another laugh.

A silence stretched between them, tense with all the things neither was willing to say.

He shook his head. "It doesn't matter anymore. We can use this. Evidence of his trafficking operation would destroy the Rosovs' standing among the vampire clans. Even the most corrupt families have standards, appearances to maintain."

"So that's our new target?" Heading back to his desk, she

looked down at the map thoughtfully. "The records of his trafficking operation?" It could serve her needs nicely. She wanted to destroy this at the roots.

"Precisely." Raziel's expression shifted to one of cold calculation. "With those records, we can force Braen to meet us on our terms, away from his guards and security. Somewhere we can finish this cleanly."

Nadi crossed her arms. "And what about the fae he's holding captive?"

Something flickered across Raziel's face again—that strange, unfamiliar expression she couldn't quite name. "We'll deal with that once we have what we need."

It wasn't enough, not nearly, but it was more than she'd expected. "Fine. When do we move?"

Raziel smiled, and for once, it reached his eyes. Which filled her with far more dread than it should have. "We're going to a party."

Nadi was truly, honestly, starting to *loathe* parties.

NINE

This time, Nadi entered The Poisoned Serpent as a guest, not the staff. She really had a chance to appreciate how lavish it was now that she could look around at it as someone who *hadn't* seen it a thousand times.

Nadi moved through the crowd in the form of a tall, willowy blonde vampire she'd observed at Lana's gatherings—someone important enough to gain entry, but not so significant that her presence would draw attention. Her crimson gown caught the light with each step, with a slit that ran up to her thigh and allowed easy access to the blade strapped just out of sight.

She paused at the bar, glancing at the ornate clock above it. Nine fifteen precisely. According to their carefully choreographed plan, Raziel would be watching the staff entrance now, timing the guard rotations. By nine twenty, she needed to be positioned at the staircase for the shift change.

Raziel was outside, maintaining surveillance from across the street through binoculars, ready to create a diversion if needed. They had decided it was too risky for both of them to enter—

Braen had a great deal of spies, and Raziel's face was too well-known.

She accepted a glass of champagne from a passing waiter, using the moment to scan the room. The plan was precise, relying on her observations from previous visits. If the guards maintained their usual pattern, she had exactly fifteen minutes to reach Braen's office.

And only a few minutes more to search for proof of the trafficking.

Making her way toward the grand staircase, she paused to exchange pleasantries with another vampire she recognized from Volencia's council. The woman didn't give her a second glance—just another beautiful face in a sea of near-immortals.

The second floor was more exclusive, with private gambling rooms and intimate lounges where the true business of the metropolis was conducted. Nadi slipped past them, every one of her senses alert for any sign of trouble.

As she reached the corridor leading to the next set of stairs, she spotted two burly vampires in Rosov uniforms approaching from the east wing. Quickly ducking into a shadowy alcove, she pressed herself against the wall as they strode past, their hands resting on holstered weapons.

She counted to ten slowly after they passed, then continued on her way. The third floor was restricted to Rosov family members and their most trusted associates. As Nadi reached the top of the stairs, a guard stepped forward to block her path.

"This area is private," he said, his tone leaving no room for argument.

Nadi smiled, channeling the haughty arrogance of the vampire whose form she wore. "I'm expected," she said, reaching into her clutch to produce the invitation Raziel had somehow procured—an elegant card bearing the Rosov family crest. It was probably old, she realized now. And it had probably been sent to *him*.

One of the "resources" he had mentioned earlier in the week.

The guard examined it, his expression unchanging. "Wait here."

He stepped away to confer with another security officer, and Nadi braced herself. If they verified the invitation with anyone who knew the real owner...

She glanced at the ornate wall clock, noting with growing concern that she'd spent nearly three minutes at this checkpoint. According to their plan, she should already be approaching Braen's office by now.

The guard returned, nodding curtly. "Follow me."

Relief washed over her, quickly replaced by focus as she was led through a corridor of closed doors. According to her reconnaissance, Braen's office was at the far end, a corner room with windows overlooking the street.

"In here," the guard said, gesturing to a door on the left. "Mr. Rosov will join you shortly."

Shit. That wasn't part of the plan. *Shit, shit, shit!*

Nadi smiled at the guard, stepping into what appeared to be a private lounge. "Thank you. I'll wait here."

The moment the door closed, she moved to examine her surroundings. The room was luxuriously appointed, with velvet sofas and a fully stocked bar along one wall. More importantly, there was another door at the far end—possibly a connection to adjacent rooms.

She glanced at the clock on the mantelpiece. She had perhaps ten minutes before Raziel would expect her at their rendezvous point. If she didn't appear, he would implement their contingency plan—a staged altercation outside to draw attention away from the building's upper floors.

If Braen showed up, the whole operation was blown. Damn it. *Damn it.*

Heading to the door to the connecting room, she tried the

handle. Locked, of course. Time for a change of tactics. Cracking her neck, she changed forms, taking the appearance of one of the guards she'd observed during her reconnaissance—a broad-shouldered man with a scar running down his left cheek.

The lock was simple enough to pick with the hairpins she kept for just such occasions. Within moments, she was through the door and into a narrow service corridor.

According to her previous reconnaissance, the third door on the right should connect to a maintenance closet that backed up to Braen's office. She found it exactly where expected, and sure enough, a large ventilation grille was set into the wall at floor level. Removing it as quietly as possible, she shifted once more—this time into a more familiar, lithe figure of a young woman that could navigate the cramped space. She didn't even remember who it belonged to. Some teenager she saw on the street once, ages ago. She used it occasionally when she had needs like this.

The metal duct was cold against her skin as she crawled through. After what felt like an eternity of claustrophobic darkness, she reached another grille—this one looking down into Braen's office.

The room was empty, but she could hear voices approaching from the corridor outside. Quickly, she removed the grille and dropped silently to the floor, immediately taking the form of one of Braen's personal assistants—a petite vampire with auburn hair.

She glanced at the grandfather clock in the corner. Five minutes until Raziel would expect her at their meeting point. She needed to move fast.

Nadi went directly to the desk. The first drawer slid open with a soft click, revealing a leather-bound ledger and a small lockbox. Picking up the ledger, she quickly opened it and scanned through it. Her heart soared and sank in the same moment. Because inside it was everything they needed.

Names. Dates. Prices. Buyers. *Everything.* Shipments of people coming in. And the names of the vampire lords and ladies who were procuring the fae from the bastard going out.

"Got you, you *idiot*," she whispered as she slipped the ledger into her clutch. Moving toward the ventilation duct, she went as fast as she could, trying to balance speed and silence. But before she could reach it, she heard the click of the door lock.

Fuck.

Too late.

Thinking quickly, she positioned herself by a filing cabinet as if searching for something, and composed her features into a mask of efficient professionalism.

The door opened, and Braen Rosov entered.

He looked at her with a blink, voice tinged with surprise. "Elise. I wasn't expecting you."

Nadi adopted the slightly nervous demeanor she'd observed in the real assistant. "My apologies, sir. Mr. Zabriel requested the Falkirk files, and I knew you kept them in here." Raziel had given her a bunch of names as backup noise, in case something happened. One always went in with backup noise for this reason. Falkirk was another vampire that Braen had double-crossed recently.

Braen studied her for a long moment, his expression unreadable. "Did he? Interesting."

He moved to his desk, and Nadi's heart leaped into her throat as his gaze fell upon the drawer—still slightly ajar.

"Sir," she said quickly, hoping to distract him, "there's also the matter of the guest in the Azure Lounge. The blonde vampire? She presented an invitation, but I don't recognize her from the list."

Braen's attention shifted away from the drawer. "What invitation?"

"A Rosov seal, sir. Third-tier authorization."

His eyes narrowed. "Show me." Turning, he led the way.

"Sir, before we go—" she began, but was cut off as Braen suddenly whirled around, his hand closing around her throat with inhuman speed. Before she could react, she was slammed up against the wall with a merciless brutality. Spots appeared in her vision.

He was pressed up against her, his body warm against hers. "You're not Elise," he said, his voice deadly quiet. "Who are you?" His lips were close to hers, his breath washing against her skin.

Panic rose in her chest. His grip was like iron, cutting off her air.

"Your smell is wrong," Braen continued, his brown-and-red-flecked eyes boring into hers. "Elise uses jasmine perfume. You smell of the sea."

She didn't know what to say. Didn't know what to do. When he leaned in and kissed her, slowly, savoringly, his tongue slipping into her mouth, running along hers, she instinctually bit down.

She expected him to snarl or strike her. She didn't expect him to laugh. Didn't expect him to press his hips against her body. Didn't expect to feel the length of his desire grinding against her.

He pulled his head back, eyes almost black with lust. "*Oh, you are a fae...* how delicious! Come to save your friends, have you? You must have been the one masquerading as Wilma the other day... and James the day before that... and Alex before that... I'm so glad you came back. I was wondering who you might be... my little ghost." He relented from the pressure against her only to press closer again, groaning in bliss. His teeth were stained red with his own blood. She could taste it on her lips, coppery and bitter. "I like the smell of you, little fae. I like the taste of you even more. Promise me you'll stay forever and ever."

His smile was one of madness.

Pure and *total insanity*.

Fear gripped her—far harder than the hand at her throat.

"I'm going to keep you all for myself." He rutted against her again. "Show me your real face, won't you? If you don't, I might have to peel that one off..." Squeezing her throat harder, he didn't seem to care she was about to black out.

With her last ounce of strength, Nadi reached into her bag and pulled out a device that Raziel had given her in case of emergencies. And this was an emergency. A small smoke bomb. She dropped it at their feet. Dense gray smoke billowed upward, and Braen's grip loosened just enough for her to break free.

Gasping for air, she shifted forms again—this time into a nondescript club patron—and stumbled toward the door.

"Come back! Come back, my love! Don't go!" Braen shouted after her, hidden now by smoke. "Guards! *Guards!*"

The corridor outside was chaos, with guards rushing toward Braen's office and guests streaming toward the stairs. But for a split second, she caught sight of someone unexpected. That young woman—the one from the Wild she had seen before. She was running in the *wrong direction.*

She was running toward the basement with a gun in her hand.

Nadi's heart soared. There was hope. But she couldn't help her—no matter how hard she wanted to. She allowed herself to be swept along with the crowd, clutching her purse with its precious cargo.

She had to reach the rendezvous point. If Raziel saw the commotion, he would know something had gone wrong, but he'd wait for her at their predetermined location before implementing the backup plan.

Heart racing, Nadi pushed her way through the panicking

crowd, taking the stairs two at a time. The smoke had spread to the second floor, adding to the confusion.

She reached the ground floor and cut through the main dining room, now empty as guests fled. The kitchen was ahead, its doors swinging as staff abandoned their posts.

As she pushed through the kitchen doors, a hard body slammed into her, driving her against the wall. A guard—one she recognized from her reconnaissance—held a gun to her head.

"Don't move," he growled. "I just saw the exact same *you* come through here ten seconds ago. What the fuck *are* you?"

Her hand inched toward the blade strapped to her thigh, but before she could reach it, another figure appeared behind the guard—Raziel, his movements a blur as he gripped the man's head and twisted. The sickening crack of breaking bone was followed by the guard's body crumpling to the floor.

"We need to go. Now." Raziel took her arm, pulling her toward the service entrance. "Braen's men are locking down the streets outside."

"How did you know?" she asked as they ran.

"I saw the smoke. Figured you'd gone to our contingency." His lips twitched in what might have been a smile. "Besides, you're remarkably punctual. When you didn't appear at our meeting point, I knew something had gone wrong."

They burst through the door into a narrow alley behind the club. The night air was cool against Nadi's flushed skin as they ran, the sounds of pursuit growing louder behind them.

"This way," Raziel urged, pulling her into a recessed doorway. "There's a warehouse we can cut through. We can lose them on the other side."

"You can turn into bats. Go. I'll be fine." She was suddenly jealous of the Nostrom family ability to shift their forms into the flying rodents. It would come in handy right about now.

"And leave you to be captured and tortured for information?" He huffed. "Hardly." He put his shoulder into the metal door, breaking the lock with a loud *wham*. It would alert the guards to where they were, but it was a calculated risk. It also gave them the means to escape. The warehouse on the other side was deserted, and it was fast enough to cross. When they got through to the alley on the other side, it was empty.

"Did you get the proof?" Raziel asked as they paused to catch their breath. It had been raining recently, and the damp cool air was a blessing.

Nadi nodded, patting her purse. "He kept a ledger. I assume as dirt. Transaction records. Buyers. I hope it's enough. But Braen—he knew I wasn't his assistant. He knows I was fae." She kept out the knowledge of the other one she saw there. That wasn't important to Raziel.

"He's more perceptive than most," Raziel admitted. "But it doesn't matter. We have what we need. He doesn't know we're working together, and he won't connect the dots."

A distant shout echoed through the warehouse—the Rosovs had found their escape route.

"Time to go," Nadi warned.

Raziel's expression hardened. "We keep to the alleys. Ivan is waiting six streets up, but we have to keep to the shadows. This is Rosov territory."

They ran through the darkness, using the twisting network of overhead roads in the metropolis to shadow them. Here, on the outskirts, it was almost as good as being underground in the Wild, for as little light reached them.

Raziel moved fast, and had no pity for her shorter legs. Nadi's lungs burned as she pushed herself harder, her fae blood singing with the familiar thrill of the hunt—even when she was the prey. Behind them, the heavy boots of Braen's men echoed off the brick walls, growing closer despite their best efforts to lose them in the labyrinthine streets.

"This way," Raziel hissed, pulling her sharply to the left

into an even narrower passage between two crumbling tenements. The space was barely wide enough for them both, forcing them to run single file. Poorly maintained mortar crumbled from between the bricks as they scraped against the walls, leaving chalky streaks on their clothes.

Water dripped from the overpasses, forming puddles that splashed beneath their feet in the low areas of the cobblestones of the alleys and dripped from the rusted fire escapes of the closely crowded buildings.

The shouts grew louder. "There they are! Stop!"

Gunfire erupted, bullets ricocheting off the concrete walls around them. Raziel pulled Nadi behind a support column, shielding her with his body. "The exit is just ahead," he said, his voice tight. "But we'll never make it with them right behind us."

Nadi peered around the column, counting at least six pursuers. "We're outnumbered."

Raziel's eyes gleamed in the darkness, his fangs extending. "Not for long."

Before she could stop him, he stepped out from their cover, facing the oncoming guards. His voice, when he spoke, carried a power she had felt before.

"Kill each other." The phrase was simple. Elegant. Unavoidable.

The effect was immediate and horrifying.

The guards turned on one another, their expressions blank as they obeyed without question. Gunfire erupted once more, but this time directed at their own ranks. In seconds, the tunnel was quiet again, save for the moans of the dying.

Nadi stared at the carnage, stunned despite knowing what Raziel was capable of.

She had seen it herself. She *knew* what he could do. But to just... see it done like that. So effortlessly? The ease with which he had condemned those men to death?

"Don't look so shocked." He shook his head. "They would have done the same to us."

Before she could respond, another figure emerged from the shadows ahead—a guard who must have circled around to cut off their escape. He raised his weapon, aiming directly at Raziel's back.

"Raziel!" Nadi lunged forward to push him aside.

The gun fired, the bullet grazing her arm as they both tumbled to the ground. Raziel rolled, coming up in a crouch, then launching himself at the guard with inhuman speed.

The fight was brief and brutal. The guard, though skilled, was no match for a vampire of Raziel's power. Within moments, he lay broken on the tunnel floor, his neck twisted at an impossible angle.

Raziel turned to Nadi, his eyes wild, fangs extended in rage. "Are you hurt?"

She shook her head, clutching her arm where the bullet had grazed her. Checking it, there was blood, but not much. "It's nothing. Just a scratch."

He was beside her in an instant, examining the wound with gentle fingers that belied his ferocious appearance. The contrast was jarring—this creature who could command men to slaughter each other, now tending to her injury with caution.

"It's already healing." Clearly fascinated, he watched as her fae physiology closed the wound before his eyes. "It must have been a struggle to pretend to be wounded after the wedding."

"It was a serious pain in the ass, actually." She chuckled weakly.

"You continue to surprise me, little assassin."

His proximity was intoxicating, the adrenaline of their escape still coursing through both of them. Nadi could feel his breath on her skin, could see the hunger in his eyes—not just for blood, but for *her*.

"We should go," she said, her voice unsteady. "Before more guards arrive."

Raziel didn't move away. Instead, his hand slid to the back of her neck, fingers tangling in her hair. "Tell me what happened between you and Braen. Every detail."

"Now's not the t—"

"Would I see bruises at your throat, if it weren't for this magic of yours?" He backed her slowly into the wall. "Bruises from *his* hands on your body?"

"Yes..."

"Did you like it?"

"No."

He slid his hand to her throat, his fingers taking the place where Braen's had been only so many short minutes before. "Why not?" He pressed her gently to the wall. It was such a familiar situation—and yet so different than it had been with the other vampire.

She felt like she couldn't breathe. "Raziel, we need to g—"

"Answer me. Why didn't you like it?"

"He was going to hurt me..."

"And you don't think I will?" His hand tightened just a little. "Do you *trust* me, Nadi?" His question was almost breathless—filled with disbelief.

She swallowed the rock in her throat. Did she? Her whole body was trembling. This was all too much.

The tension between them was electric, charged with danger and desire in equal measure. Nadi knew she should push him away, maintain the emotional distance that was her only protection against him.

But when his lips claimed hers, fierce and demanding, she couldn't resist responding with equal hunger. The kiss was raw, honest, born from the heady rush of survival.

His hand tightened at her throat—just enough—proving to her the difference between the two men. Pulling her from the wall, he tilted her head back to deepen the kiss. Nadi clutched at his shoulders, her resolve crumbling as her body betrayed her once again. She wanted him—here, now, surrounded by death and darkness. The realization was as terrifying as it was exhilarating.

When they finally broke apart, both breathing hard, Nadi felt a surge of frustration—at herself, at him, at this impossible situation. She pushed him away, creating physical distance to match the emotional barriers she was struggling to maintain.

"Don't," she warned, her voice low. "This doesn't change anything between us."

Raziel's smile was knowing, infuriating in its confidence. "Doesn't it?"

Before she could respond, the distant sound of voices echoed through the warehouse—more guards.

Sighing, Raziel's posture changed. He was suddenly all business again. "Let's go."

As they ran through the darkness, the ledger secure in her purse and the taste of him still on her lips, Nadi fought against the confusion in her heart. She had come to destroy the Nostroms, to avenge her family and her clan. Getting closer to Raziel was supposed to be a means to that end, nothing more.

So, why did it feel increasingly like she was losing herself in the process? And why, despite everything she knew about him— the monster he was, the blood on his hands—could she not resist him?

These questions haunted her as they emerged from the alleys onto the main street, glistening like a river after the rainstorm. Ivan was waiting for them in the car.

She shouldn't have felt relief when she saw it. Because it shouldn't have felt like freedom to her. Freedom—or another kind of prison. She wasn't sure which anymore.

Climbing into the car, she slid onto the bench to make room for Raziel.

"Go." The command to Ivan was urgent. No hypnotism needed to get his friend and bodyguard to stomp the gas.

But it seemed she wasn't going to be given any time to relax. Raziel pulled her into his lap, rolling up her sleeve to inspect the wound on her arm. It was closed, but the blood remained.

Lowering his head, he lapped up the red stain slowly, his eyes boring into hers. "We have a discussion to finish when we get home, Monica."

A knot twisted in her stomach even as her face went warm in anticipation.

Everything was becoming too complicated.

And complicated was going to get her killed.

But for now, all she could think about was the taste of his lips.

And the sensation of his body against hers.

I am losing my mind.

This has to stop.

One way or another.

TEN

"Show me."

The door had barely shut behind Raziel before he pushed Nadi onto the bed, climbing atop her and straddling her legs to pin her down. Her instinct had been immediately to fight him tooth and nail—she wasn't used to her enemy manhandling her like it was nothing out of the ordinary.

But when she saw the look on his face, she froze.

The desire in his expression was gone. At least for the moment. Instead, it was a strained, almost panicked look of desperation.

Fear.

His eyes were wild, his movements frantic as he loomed over her. Instead of the predatory lust she'd come to expect, his expression was raw and unsettled.

"Let me see," he demanded, his voice rough.

"See what?" She pushed herself up onto her elbows, confusion momentarily outweighing all else.

"Your throat." His hands were already reaching for her, fingers hovering just above the place where Braen's had wrapped around her neck. "The bruises. Let me see them. Drop this hideous illusion of yours and let me *see*."

"They're gone." She tried to worm out from underneath him. "I heal quickly, the bullet proved that."

His hand pressed down on her shoulder, once more flattening her to the bed. "Show me anyway."

There was something in his tone—something that went beyond just his usual obnoxious commands—that made her pause. She tilted her head back, baring her throat to him in a gesture that felt far more vulnerable than it should have.

And dropped her glamor. At least far enough that she still had her legs.

His fingers traced where the bruises should have been, featherlight and searching. When he found nothing, some of the tension seemed to bleed from his shoulders, though his expression remained tight.

"What is this about?" She almost didn't dare ask. "You're acting like—"

"Like what?" he snapped, drawing back.

"Like you care," she finished, holding his gaze.

A muscle in his jaw ticked. "You're not his to touch."

The words should have enraged her. To a certain extent, they did—a flare of indignation burned inside her chest. But there was more to it than simple possession.

"Is that what this is? Your property was touched by someone else, and now you need to make sure it's unmarked?"

"No." The denial was quick, forceful. Almost desperate in its vehemence.

"Then what?"

"I know what he does—" Raziel turned away, running a hand through his hair. The usually composed vampire looked utterly undone. "When you told me—"

"You've seen me nearly die before," she reminded him. "You've watched me get shot."

"That was different."

"How?"

"Because it wasn't personal then." He met her gaze again, his eyes blazing crimson. "Because it wasn't someone putting their hands on you with the intention of taking you for themselves."

There it was again—that possessiveness. But beneath it, something else lurked. Something that made her breath catch.

"I am not yours to own." The words came out far weaker than she'd intended.

"No." He leaned in closer, reaching out to brush her hair back from her face. "You're not. You're something much more dangerous to me."

The confession hung between them, neither quite willing to define exactly what she had become to him. What they had become to each other.

"This wasn't supposed to happen," she whispered, her throat tight. "I came here to fucking *kill* you."

"And you were meant to be a foolish little human girl that I was going to break and discard in the span of two weeks." His thumb traced her cheekbone. "Yet here we are."

"Where exactly is that?" she asked, hating how she leaned into his touch despite herself. "What are we doing, Raziel?"

His answer came in the form of a kiss. It wasn't the calculated seduction she'd come to expect from him, nor was it the rough claiming of previous encounters.

This was raw, searching, seeking—an embrace from a man deep beneath the waves, clawing for the surface, trying to find a lungful of air.

When he pulled back, his eyes seemed to search her face for something. "Tell me you hate me," he demanded.

"What?"

"Tell me you still hate me." His fingers tangled in her hair, pulling her head from the mattress. "Tell me you still want me dead."

"First you want me to admit there's more to this than just lust, now you want me to admit that I hate you?"

"Just *say it*, Nadi," he snarled, his fangs extended.

She opened her mouth to reassure them both that nothing had changed. That despite everything, she was still the vengeful fae who had infiltrated his life to destroy him. That her mission remained intact.

But the lie wouldn't form.

It just *wouldn't*.

In the silence, something between agony and relief crossed his face before he kissed her again, harder this time. She responded in kind, pouring all her confusion and frustration and unwanted desire into the contact.

Their kiss turned hungry, desperate, his hands roaming over her body as if trying to confirm she was whole, unharmed, and still there with him. She found herself returning the gesture, fingers tracing paths over his chest, his shoulders, as if reassuring herself of the same.

It was then that she realized she had never actually touched him. Not meaningfully. Not in any way that *mattered*.

When he tried to catch her wrists to press her back onto the bed, however, she resisted. "No."

He pulled back, confused.

It was reckless. Dangerous. She was playing with fire. She licked her bottom lip. "Not this time."

Understanding dawned in his eyes, followed by a flicker of hesitation. Then, startlingly, a smile. It was sharp and dangerous, but with a hint of something that might have been anticipation.

He laughed, low and sinister. For a moment, she was worried he would snap and lash out. The Serpent was notorious, and she'd experienced his proclivities firsthand. His control was just as much a part of him as his fangs. The idea that he'd surrender it? To *her*? It lit a fire in her.

Slowly, carefully, like a stalking predator, he rose from the bed. "Very well, Nadi..."

The words sent a jolt through her. She almost didn't know what to do at first. Was this *real*? Or was he toying with her? Waiting for her to let her guard down, only to turn the tables.

But he only stood there. And waited.

She climbed from the bed to circle him, like he'd so often circled her—feeling for once like she was the predator, if only for the moment. Never once had she been able to explore his body. He'd always been in control. Always calling the shots.

Running her hand along his back, she felt his muscles tighten. Delicious. She pulled his shirt out from under his pants. It'd be easier to tell him to undress, but where was the fun in that? She wanted to take her time. She wanted to feel every inch of his body. She wanted to savor it.

Besides. The last time someone had told him to strip... The memory of Volencia's cruelty lingered in Nadi's mind.

No, this was going to be *her* hands doing the deed. She undid his tie and tossed it aside. His coat went next. Then his vest. Raziel helped with what she couldn't get undone on her own.

Crimson eyes watched her every move, expression unreadable. There was no shame in him, no hint of the vulnerable discomfort most would feel. There was a tension to his frame that spoke of restraint—of power deliberately held in check.

Soon, he was fully naked in front of her. Letting her hands roam, she bit back a groan at how much she *loved* how it felt. Stepping closer, she trailed her fingers down to his hips. His muscles twitched and tensed beneath her touch.

Now came the real risk. "Kneel."

This command met with the briefest pause—the barest

flicker of resistance in his eyes—before he lowered himself to his knees before her.

The Serpent, kneeling at her feet.

Her enemy.

The man who murdered her family.

Who she had sworn to kill.

The thought sent a thrill of power through her that was *intoxicating.*

She tangled her fingers in his hair, tilting his head back to look at her. "How does it feel?" she asked, genuinely curious. There was no haughty ego in her voice, just a kind of breathless awe. "Not to be the one giving orders?"

"Strange," he admitted, voice rougher than usual. "But not... unpleasant."

Oh, she could very much get used to that. Smiling, she traced her thumb along his lower lip. Slowly, deliberately, she began to undress herself. It wasn't a seductive performance, not in the way she might have expected herself to play the role as she had so many times for her targets.

Instead, it was methodical, almost clinical—a display of control that she knew would torment him more than any teasing ever could. When she was as bare as he was, she stepped behind him.

"You're not allowed to move. Not until I say so." Running her hands along his back, she hummed thoughtfully. "You do, and I sleep in another room for the rest of the night."

After a pause, he nodded once, though his shoulders were tense.

She circled him again, trailing her fingers over his shoulders, his back, his chest. Taking her time to explore what had always been out of reach. She felt him shudder under her touch, saw the way his hands clenched at his sides as he fought to obey.

Glancing down, she was impressed. And honestly, a little

surprised. "You're enjoying this," she observed, a hint of wonder in her voice. "You actually like not being in control?"

"I like it with *you*." He grimaced.

The distinction was the same thing he had demanded of her in the alley. Why did she enjoy *his* hand at her throat but not Braen's? The admission was one she didn't want to examine. Couldn't examine. It was too much. Too tangled. She pushed it into a box and put it in the corner with everything else. "Get on the bed."

He did so without question, lying on the bed flat on his back. She followed after him, straddling his lap. It was so similar to how they had been in the church, only the circumstances were so very, very different.

Shifting, she settled herself down on his upper thighs. Taking his length into her hand, she stroked him slowly, feeling him twitch and throb.

Groaning, he shut his eyes before pressing his head back into the pillow.

He was *beautiful*. A true work of art. She could admit that freely now. Lowering herself down to him, she ran her tongue up his length, just as meanderingly as she had done with the rest of her teasing, before swirling around the tip and taking him into her mouth.

"Nadi—*fuck*—" His hands clutched the air uselessly beside her head before fisting in the sheets in a desperate attempt to keep from losing control.

Chuckling, muffled against him, she focused on the task at hand. And it was quite the task. One now she could fully appreciate without the distraction of his bindings and overwhelming presence. She could just enjoy *him*.

"Yes, ah—my little, beautiful killer, yes—" Words spilled from him, quiet and moaned, dusky with lust and need. "My fae, my perfect, deadly fae—yes, deeper—*please*—"

He was begging her.

Raziel Nostrom.

Was begging her.

Her head spun at the bliss of it all.

And she could only oblige him. She drove him into her throat, taking him all the way again, and again, but careful and slow—never enough to bring him to a peak. Just enough to get him brutally close.

When she lifted her head from him finally, he was a sight—lips parted, fangs extended, his eyes blown out and nearly black from pure lust. His nails were dug deep into the sheets as he watched her, a sweat forming on his brow.

Licking her lips, she slid up his body. His pale, white-gray vampiric skin to her pale, green-blue fae skin. What a pair they made. And in this moment, that was what they were.

A pair.

This wasn't about revenge anymore. It wasn't even about the complex web they'd entangled themselves in. This was simply *them. Only* them.

Leaning down, she kissed him. It was a tender kiss, as much as she could manage with how much she needed him in the moment. But she couldn't put into words what was lurking in her heart. She just wasn't ready for it.

So that would have to do.

Running her thumb along the line of his lower lip, she studied him. He was a caged tiger. Begging, *starving.* And she was a rare steak on the other side of the cage bars.

"Now," she whispered.

She was on her back before she could blink. His lips crashed against hers, devouring, hungry—but pouring into her such emotion that she could barely stand it.

He hooked her leg into the crook of his arm, and with one swift movement, buried himself to the hilt in her body. The cry that left her was met by his moan, both muffled in the kiss they both still shared.

The dance was unlike any they'd shared before. There was no control. There was no *purpose*. There was no one at the wheel of the car. It simply *was*. She drove her hips up to meet his, matching the rhythm, wanting, needing more. Desperately seeking every perfect, aching bit of him that filled her.

His strength. His power. *Raziel*.

It felt like something was changing. And if she was smart, she would have dug out the gun in the bedside table and blown his brains out. But she couldn't. Wouldn't. *Didn't want to*.

"Raziel—" she clung to him, dug her nails into his back. "I —" All thoughts became white noise briefly as her pleasure crested, her muscles spasming as everything turned to bliss.

"Let go, I have you—" He buried his head into the crook of her neck. He clutched her close, his thrusts growing erratic as her release triggered his.

This time, without his even needing to purr, she turned her head away, baring her throat to him. She wanted to feel it. Wanted him to *take* it. Wanted him to erase the feeling of that bastard's hands around her throat. Wanted Raziel to remind her of whose bed she belonged in.

A brief sting at her throat.

Nadi was flooded with euphoria. She held him, weakly, as he drank her blood. He shuddered, moaning against her skin. The purring had begun, reverberating through her.

After a few moments, he pulled his fangs from her throat and settled down on top of her, gently kissing at the bite wounds. He rolled onto his side next to her, pulling her into his arms.

It was then that a realization settled over her. This should have been an ending. All of it. This whole nonsense. It was meant to be an *end*. Not a beginning.

She'd come here with a single purpose—vengeance. Revenge against the monster who had slaughtered her family, who had laughed as he did so.

Yet here she was, curled against that same monster's chest, listening to the slow beat of his heart, briefly having lurched to life from her blood in his system, feeling something dangerously close to... to *happiness*.

"If you have to kill me, kill me like that," she murmured to him.

"Should it come to that, gladly." He kissed the top of her head.

A long stretch of silence passed between them before she had to voice the question echoing in her mind. "What are we doing?"

He was silent for so long she thought he might not answer. Then, his voice equally soft, he replied, "I don't know."

The honesty in his tone was more unsettling than any lie might have been.

"This changes nothing," she said, trying to convince herself as much as him. "Your entire family still needs to fall. And then the two of us still have a score to settle."

"Yes." His fingers traced patterns on her back, gentle in a way that made her heart ache. "I know."

Closing her eyes, she fought exhaustion. "When this is over, if you win and your family is destroyed and you have what you want—what are your plans for me, assuming I don't kill you first?"

His hand stilled on her back. "I haven't decided." He paused. "What do you want to happen? Well... besides your previous request about the method."

The question caught her off guard. What did she want? She'd never allowed herself to think beyond revenge. Beyond destroying the Nostroms and avenging her family. The future had always been a blank, unexamined thing.

But now?

"I want to be free," she said finally, the answer surprising even her with its simplicity. "Not owned. Not controlled. Just... free to choose."

He was silent for a long moment, his fingers resuming their gentle tracing on her skin. When he spoke, his voice was soft, almost vulnerable.

"Perhaps," he said, "we could be free to choose together."

The words hung in the air between them, heavy.

She didn't answer. Couldn't. She still couldn't reconcile the monster who had destroyed her life with the man who now held her with such careful tenderness.

Instead, she closed her eyes and listened to his already-fading heartbeat, steady and strong beneath her ear. Tomorrow would bring new challenges, new complications. Tomorrow they would have to face the web they'd woven, the enemies they'd made, the family they planned to destroy.

Yet there, in the back of her mind, clawing away at her consciousness like the dripping of water from a faucet she just couldn't tune out, was the offer from Mael. The open door to another partnership that stood a much higher likelihood of success. Because the odds were high that she was on the losing side.

And she had to weigh that on the scales. She had come here with a job to do, long before she let herself get tangled up in sheets and emotions with her enemy.

But tonight—just for tonight—she would allow herself this moment of peace in the arms of the man she should hate.

The man she increasingly feared she might have feelings for instead.

ELEVEN

Sunlight filtered through the curtains, casting golden patterns across the rumpled sheets. Nadi stared at the ceiling, her mind racing despite her body's exhaustion. Last night had changed something between her and Raziel—shifted the boundaries that had once seemed so immutable.

And in the light of the dawn, it twisted something in her stomach that was closer to disgust than anything else.

Disgust at *herself*. This had to stop. It *had* to.

And she had a way out. Mael. She just had to be brave enough to take it. How many people had she seen in her life die by drug addiction? It didn't matter how good Raziel made her *feel*, it was going to destroy her in the end. And she had to cut that part of her life out before it was too late.

The bed beside her was empty. Through the vague memory of sleep, she remembered Raziel leaving at dawn, murmuring something about meeting with Ivan to discuss their next moves against Braen. But his absence gave her the space she desperately needed to think.

She'd come to the Nostroms for one reason—revenge. To destroy the family that had destroyed hers, starting with the

Serpent himself. But now, lying in his bed with his scent still clinging to her skin, she had to face an uncomfortable truth.

She was getting too close. Developing real feelings for a monster.

Sitting up, she ran her hands through her hair and took a steadying breath. "Enough is enough," she whispered to the empty room. "You're losing yourself." He was killing her slowly. Piece by piece.

Mael's offer echoed in her mind. It was a way out of Raziel's control that would still allow her to complete her mission. It had seemed too good to be true when he'd first proposed it, but now it looked increasingly like her only viable option.

The more entangled she became with Raziel, the more she risked compromising everything she'd worked for. Everything she had ever killed for.

Rising from the bed, she headed for the shower, letting the hot water wash away the evidence of the night before. As the steam filled the bathroom, she tried to clear her mind, to reclaim some of the clarity she'd had when she first arrived.

Focus on the mission. Not on him.

By the time she stepped out of the shower, she'd made up her mind.

She would take Mael's offer. It was the only sane choice.

She would find a way to extricate herself from Raziel's orbit while maintaining her cover and her purpose. It was the only way. No matter how much it made something in her hurt, she had no choice. It was a weed, winding itself around her heart, and she had to rip it out before it grew too deep.

She was wrapping herself in a robe when the phone in the bedroom rang. Frowning—few people called the private line— she moved to answer it.

"Hello?"

"Monica, darling!" Lana's voice, saccharine sweet and

buzzing with energy, came through the line. "I hope I haven't caught you at a bad time."

Nadi straightened, instantly on alert. If Lana was calling her directly, that meant she knew Raziel was out of the house. That meant the Sweetheart Mistress was *up* to something. "Not at all. What can I do for you?"

"I've been thinking about the wedding," Lana continued, "and there are some details we really must discuss. Would you be a dear and come by my estate this morning? Say, in an hour or two?"

"The wedding?" Nadi repeated, momentarily confused. Then, she remembered—Lana's upcoming marriage to Zabriel Rosov. "Right. Yes. Sorry. Everything's been such a blur."

"Of course! You poor thing. But I was hoping to get your help with some of the preparations." She paused. "It's important, Monica. I wouldn't ask if it weren't."

It made her uneasy. Lana was definitely up to something. But Nadi couldn't refuse without raising suspicion. And, moreover, she wanted to know what was going on. "Of course. I'll be there."

"Wonderful! Just come alone, would you? Girl talk and all that."

The line went dead before Nadi could respond, leaving her with a growing sense of unease.

Lana was playing some kind of game—she always was—but what exactly did she want?

There was only one way to find out.

Lana's estate was a sprawling, modernist monstrosity at the edge of the metropolis, all sharp angles and gleaming surfaces. It couldn't have been more different from Raziel's home with its modern lines and sleek, polished luxury.

A human servant met Nadi at the door, ushering her

through a series of stark white corridors to a sunroom at the back of the house.

Azazel was sprawled out on a chaise longue, reading a book, eating grapes in a manner that she was certain was meant to be annoying.

And there, surrounded by exotic plants in glass terrariums—each carefully sealed to prevent any infection from the Wild—sat Lana, resplendent in a pale pink dress that made her look almost innocent.

An illusion that couldn't be further from the truth.

"Monica! Right on time." Lana gestured to the seat across from her. "Come, sit. Would you like some tea? Or blood, perhaps?"

"Tea would be fine," Nadi replied, taking the offered seat cautiously. Every instinct she had was screaming danger. "My stomach is still getting adjusted to blood." She glanced over at Azazel. "I thought you said this was girl talk."

"Who, Azazel? He doesn't count." Lana waved dismissively at the servant, who bowed and retreated, closing the doors behind him. The moment they were alone, save for Lana's favorite boy toy, something shifted in the vampire's demeanor. The playful facade fell away, replaced by a sharp, calculating assessment.

"You know," Lana began, pouring tea with practiced elegance, "I've been watching you quite closely since my dear brother brought you home."

Nadi accepted the cup, careful to keep her expression neutral. "Have you?"

"Mm." Lana's smile was all teeth now. "And I must say, I'm impressed. Most humans barely last a week in Raziel's company before they're begging for death. Yet here you are, not only surviving but..." She leaned forward, magenta eyes gleaming. "Thriving."

Nadi sipped her tea, using the moment to compose her response. "I'm stronger than I look. The outer cities are rough."

"Clearly." Lana set her own cup down with a soft clink. "But that's just it, isn't it? They're rough. But they aren't *that* rough. No rancher's daughter from the outer cities handles herself the way you did at The Poisoned Serpent."

Ice slid down Nadi's spine. So that was it. Lana had been watching her, monitoring her movements.

"You had people there." She kept her words calm. All the while, she was debating how quickly she could grab the small pistol from her purse and put a bullet between Lana's eyes.

She could kill Lana fast enough. Azazel was the unknown variable. Would he kill her? Or would he just sit there? Maybe he would even applaud or help her escape. There was no telling.

Lana laughed, the sound like breaking glass. "Oh, Monica—or whatever your name *really* is—I have eyes everywhere. Did you think I wouldn't station my own people at Braen's club when I knew my brother would be sending his new pet there?"

"I don't know what you're talking about." Nadi kept her voice level, though her heart was racing. "My name is Monica Valan—"

"Please." Lana cut her off with a dismissive wave. "Let's not insult each other's intelligence. Mael may be too soft-hearted—and frankly, too *horny*—to put two and two together, but I know what you are."

"And what is that?" *Fuck, fuck, fuck!*

"A spy." Lana's eyes glittered with triumph. "Though I can't quite tell who you're working for. Not yet. Either Raziel replaced Monica with you, some secret vampire operative he's been keeping hidden, deciding he wanted nothing to do with whatever little cow they sent along as a sacrifice, or you're a plant from a rival family, or you're some new, unknown entity entirely. Either way..."

Nadi said nothing, waiting for the other shoe to drop, and just waited.

Lana leaned back in her chair. "I think it's absolutely *fantastic*."

That, Nadi hadn't expected. She blinked. "Excuse me?"

"Whoever sent you—whatever your purpose—I assume it involves tearing my family apart in some fashion. Either because Raziel wants you to, or because you're doing it on your own." Lana's smile was almost genuine now. "Which aligns perfectly with my own interests."

Nadi glanced over at Azazel.

"Don't worry about him." She waved her hand. "He's furniture."

Nadi felt a pang of sympathy for Azazel once more. But she had to focus on her own situation at the moment. Turning her attention back to Lana, she considered the woman's words. "You want me to tear apart your family?"

"Not my entire family. Just a few... specific members." Lana traced the rim of her teacup with one perfectly manicured finger. "I have a proposition for you."

The game board just kept growing more and more complex. "I'm listening."

"You and Raziel are set to assassinate Braen. A deed that my mother has designed to punish my dear brother for his lack of loyalty. Killing the only one who has ever truly loved him... how wonderful." Her smile turned sharp. "But what if, during this confrontation, *both* men were to tragically perish?"

Nadi kept her expression carefully blank. That was new subtext to process, but she couldn't do it now. "And how would that benefit me?"

"Mm. I knew I liked you." Lana chuckled. "With Raziel gone, his seat at the family table would be empty, wouldn't it?" Her eyes gleamed with cold calculation. "A seat I could ensure goes to his poor, grieving widow. Coupled with Mael's overtures to you, you would be sitting quite nicely with Raziel dead and gone, wouldn't you?"

What the *fuck* was wrong with this family? But with all the pieces seemingly shifting their positions on the board, Nadi now had all three siblings with doors open to her. And *her* specifically. Mael's offer was tempting enough on its own. But now? She would be positioned exactly where she needed to be to continue dismantling the Nostroms from within—with Lana's blessing and Mael's protection.

Raziel was now clearly the poorest choice. The *wrong* choice. The one holding none of the cards in his hand and yet believing he was bluffing them all.

Fuck.

"Why would you do this if you suspect I'm not who I claim to be?" Nadi asked, setting her tea aside. "If you know I likely came here for revenge of some kind? How can you be so sure it stops with him?"

Lana sighed, a theatrical sound that did nothing to mask the very real cynicism beneath it. "Because I'm sick of playing my family's games. Sick of being the pretty face, the bargaining chip, the *Sweetheart Mistress*." She practically spat the title. "I want to play my own games. Wield my own power. And I'm willing to buy my supporters by any means necessary."

"And I would be one of those supporters."

"Yes. But you would be beside me as my partner, not some subordinate. Whoever you are, you've impressed me." Lana's smile returned. "With your talents, and my resources, we could reshape the whole metropolis. Whatever you're after, whatever my family did to hurt you—I can guarantee I wasn't a direct part in it."

No. She hadn't been. Lana's only sin against the Iltanis was one of blood relation. Lana had plenty of crimes of her own— flesh trading most notoriously—but nothing against her own family.

It was tempting. Moons, it was tempting. A clear path to completing her mission, without the complication of her growing feelings for Raziel. A way to justify everything she'd done, everything she'd sacrificed.

"And what would you gain from this arrangement?" It was a struggle to keep her tone curious rather than suspicious. "Volencia seems well on her way to removing Raziel without any help."

"For all her cruelty, Mother is too sentimental." She sighed. "Fine. All good business relationships are built on a little bit of trust. I'm searching for *freedom*, 'Monica,' like I suspect we all are in the end." Lana's face briefly showed something that looked almost like genuine emotion. "A chance to step out from *dear mother* Volencia's shadow. To be more than just the pretty daughter who sells flesh and spreads her legs for political advantage."

The raw honesty in her voice was startling. For a moment, Nadi could almost believe her. And maybe she did.

Then, Lana's mask slipped back into place, the vulnerability gone as quickly as it had appeared. "So, do we have a deal?"

"I'll need to think about it," Nadi replied cautiously. "This is... a lot to consider."

"Of course." Lana's smile was understanding, though her eyes remained calculating. "But don't think too long. Our window of opportunity is narrow." She stood, signaling the end of their meeting. "Oh, and Monica? If I were you, I wouldn't mention to Raziel that we spoke. He can be so possessive of his toys."

Nadi rose as well, forcing herself to smile through gritted teeth. "Thank you for the tea, Lana. If he knows where I was, I'll tell him I was giving wedding advice."

"Naturally. Hopefully, mine ends better than yours." Lana gestured toward the door. "I'm sure you can find your way out."

The drive back to Raziel's home gave Nadi time to process what had just happened. Lana knew that she wasn't the real Monica Valan. That she had infiltrated the Nostrom family for some purpose of her own. Who and what she really was, still remained a mystery, at least.

And instead of exposing her, Lana wanted to use her.

It aligned perfectly with Nadi's original plan—kill Raziel, work her way through the rest of the family, avenge the massacre of her clan. She should have been elated at this unexpected opportunity. It was perfect. *Flawless.* Let Raziel kill Braen. Then, kill Raziel.

She couldn't have asked for a better setup.

Instead, she felt hollow.

The car pulled up to Raziel's manor, and she stepped out, nodding absently to the driver. As she walked toward the entrance, her thoughts continued to tumble over one another.

Could she do it? Could she kill Raziel now, after everything?

He murdered your family, she reminded herself harshly. *He laughed as your mother died.*

But the Raziel who had held her last night, who had surrendered control to her, who had looked at her with something so close to vulnerability... he seemed like a different man entirely from the monster of her memories.

Shaking her head, she pushed through the door, determined to find some quiet corner where she could sort through her thoughts.

Instead, she found Raziel waiting for her in the foyer, his expression unreadable. He took her to his office, shutting the door behind them so that they could speak in private.

"Where have you been?" he asked, voice deceptively casual.

"Lana invited me over," she replied, seeing no reason to lie about that much. Even if Lana had warned her otherwise, Raziel's driver would already have told him where she had been. "Wedding preparations." She knew she had to give him more than that. "Supposedly."

His eyes narrowed slightly. "And was it?"

"No." She sighed, suddenly exhausted by all the deception. "But I didn't learn anything useful, if that's what you're asking."

He studied her for a long moment, as if trying to decide whether to believe her. Then, apparently satisfied, he nodded once.

"I have news," he said, changing the subject. "We've confirmed Braen's location for the next three days. He'll be staying at his house on the west end of the metropolis since we... disrupted his apartments above The Poisoned Serpent."

"The perfect opportunity for our assassination," she observed. She tried to recall what she knew about Braen's home. "It's a pretty big property, if I remember correctly."

Raziel nodded grimly. "Trafficking fae is banned by all vampiric councils. The ledger you stole from him is proof positive of his activities. I would have had *more* proof, but when I had one of my men go into the basement to take a few of his captives as insurance, he found they were already missing." He shot her a cold look. "You wouldn't happen to know anything about that, would you?"

The woman from the Wild Nadi had seen running through the chaos. So, she had been successful. Or at least, up and to a point. That was, if Braen's men hadn't been under orders to *dispose of evidence* if there was an issue. Therefore, her answer wasn't a lie. She had no conclusive knowledge. "I don't."

He let out a hum. It seemed he believed her, at least well enough. "I will send a letter to Braen informing him that I have evidence of his lucrative *side-hobby* and threaten to expose him to the council of all the vampire elders if he does not meet with me. It would destroy the Rosovs if news came out. He will come."

"That, and your previous history together, and I think

you're right." Nadi left the door open for him to explain more of his complex past with Braen.

It seemed he was uninterested in taking the bait. He took his hair out of the tie at the back of his neck, running his fingers through the gleaming black strands. "I've been working with Ivan to finalize our approach. With any luck, we'll have him isolated. It's on his turf, which I don't like. But the odds we get him off his family grounds without guards are much lower. I would rather have him unguarded."

She couldn't help but be distracted by the confident set of his shoulders, the fluid grace of his movements. He was beautiful, in the way that predators often were. Deadly and magnetic all at once.

This is a man who killed your family, she reminded herself again.

But he was also a man who had suffered. Who had been shaped by cruelty into a weapon. A man who, despite everything, had shown her glimpses of something almost like tenderness.

"What's troubling you?" Raziel asked suddenly, turning to face her. "You're unusually quiet."

"Just thinking about what's ahead." It wasn't a lie.

He moved closer, studying her face with an intensity that made her want to look away. "There's something you're not telling me."

It wasn't a question. She forced herself to meet his gaze steadily.

"We both still have our secrets, Raziel."

Something flashed in his eyes. Anger? Hurt? It was gone before she could identify it.

"True enough." He took a step back. "But secrets between allies can be dangerous."

"Is that what we are now? Allies?" She couldn't keep the bitter edge from her voice.

He tilted his head, regarding her curiously. "What would you call us?"

Impossible. Wrong. A travesty. A nightmare. "Messy," she said instead.

A smile ghosted across his lips. "An understatement if ever I heard one."

He moved to his desk, spreading out several papers—more maps and floor plans, she realized. "Come. Help me plan our approach to Braen. The sooner we deal with him, the sooner we can move against our true enemies."

True enemies. True enemies she was debating siding with.

She crossed to stand beside him, glancing over the documents. Despite everything, despite the turmoil in her heart and the offers weighing on her mind, she found herself drawn into the tactical discussion.

This, at least, was familiar territory. Planning. Strategy. The clinical approach to ending a life.

Far easier than confronting what she truly felt for the man standing beside her.

And the real question was... would one life be ending tonight?

Or two?

TWELVE

Dawn came too quickly. Nadi was getting really sick of the late nights and early mornings.

But with the sunlight, came another phone call. For *her*.

Raziel was out with Ivan, getting things ready for the hit that night on Braen. She knew that was precisely why the caller felt safe to ring the private line in the bedroom.

This time it wasn't Lana. It was Mael.

"Good morning, Monica. I hope I didn't wake you." His voice was warm—she could hear the smile in it.

"You're taking a risk. The line could be bugged. Or recorded." She rubbed her hand over her face.

"It's neither." Mael paused, clearly trying to decide how much to tell her. How much to trust her. "I have people within his people."

And she was certain that Raziel had people working among Mael's staff, as well.

This was precisely why Nadi always worked alone. Sitting down on the edge of the bed, she leaned her shoulder against the headboard and pined desperately for a cup of coffee. "Well, to what do I owe the pleasure this morning?"

"I want to know if you've considered my offer."

She paused. "I have."

"And?"

She kept her voice natural, nonchalant. "I'm considering offers from multiple brokers."

Mael laughed. *Hard.* "Oh, you truly are a natural at this. Lana told me you two spoke."

Ah. Well, that answered that question. The brother and the sister were working together, at least to some degree. *Damn.* She was hoping she could play them against each other. "And what did she tell you?"

"About tonight. About what she offered you, should... things go slightly awry." Silence stretched between them for what could have been thirty seconds. Nadi wasn't going to give up anything. This was Mael's call, it was up to him to provide more. This was *his* move. Finally, he relented. "I... would obviously support you, if this... tragic incident were to take place."

"That's lovely to know."

More silence. "But I feel like I must warn you."

"Oh?"

"I've noticed a change in Raziel." His tone grew softer, more thoughtful. "You're different from his other companions. You've survived longer, for one thing." He chuckled. "But there's something else."

Once more, she said nothing.

"He's more focused. More disciplined. Almost as if there's a goal he's fighting for beyond his twisted pleasures. He's working toward something—and it's been ever since you arrived. But I don't know *what*. Either the bastard is truly in love with you—"

They both paused to laugh at that.

"—or he's scheming. Something big. Something that could tear us all apart."

Oh. *Oh.* Lana hadn't told Mael that "Monica" wasn't really "Monica." Lana might have told him that she had asked Nadi to take out Raziel during the Braen hit... but everything after that? *Interesting.*

"Why do you think he's choosing to move now? It certainly can't be because of me."

"Potentially, it could. The Nostrom family is at a crossroads. Volencia is losing her grip on reality, becoming more paranoid and vindictive by the day. Lana schemes in her corners. Now, if she has access to the Rosovs and their resources? She's a real threat. If Raziel has dreams of power, he may see this as a now-or-never moment."

"I've never known Raziel to be anything but loyal to the family." The lie left her easily. Sometimes, she really wondered about herself.

"I appreciate the fact that you want to believe in him. I truly do. But..." He paused. "Raziel has always been a loose cannon."

"Killing him won't be easy." That was true. "Braen will be hard enough. I may not get the opportunity." This was just simple logistical facts.

"I know. He is... *damn* hard to kill. Trust me, we've tried. However, there could be another way."

Nadi said nothing, once more waiting for him to continue.

"You give us leverage we've never had before."

"You want me to be a leash on your rabid brother?" The idea was as offensive as it was absurd. She snorted in laughter. "You think that'll *work?*"

"No. Not a leash. A bridge. A way for me to reach him—influence him—without triggering his paranoia and rage. If he can't be killed, then I want to work with him. He's my *brother,* Monica. I love him, no matter what you might believe. In the end, I would much prefer he be alive and at my side. I just can't trust him. But I *can* trust you."

Oh, buddy...

But this wasn't what she'd expected. She heard true sadness in Mael's voice. True remorse. This was a man looking at his rabid family dog, the one he'd loved his entire life, and putting it down with tears in his eyes.

This wasn't Lana's gleeful ladder-climbing. This was a man who honestly wanted what was *best* for him and his people.

"Raziel and I, together, truly aligned? We could create a new kind of order in the metropolis. One free of the old-world cruelty and stagnation that my mother so very much adores."

It almost sounded noble, put that way. Almost kind.

But Nadi had lived too long among liars to take his words at face value.

"And what happens if I refuse?" Now, that was the kicker. How would he respond to that?

Mael's tone hardened. "Then, you remain under Raziel's... protection. Until his interest wanes or his mood darkens. And we both know how that story ends."

The threat was clear. Play my game, or face Raziel's inevitable betrayal alone. "Tonight is the hit on Braen. Depending on how that goes... I'll need time to think."

"Of course. But events will move quickly. You may not have much time. I can protect you from him. Remember that."

It was a fight to keep her voice neutral. "I will. Thank you."

"Oh. One more thing."

She furrowed her brow and waited.

"Whatever Lana has offered you?" His voice was suddenly harsh. Bitter. "Whatever it is, she's lying. Or she plans to betray you. That is what she *does*. Do not let her control you or influence you. There is no room in her world for anyone but Lana."

Swallowing, she hesitated before replying. "Noted."

"My sister plays games within games. And those who trust her tend to end up dead." He let out a heavy sigh. "Good luck tonight, Monica. Please... be careful. I would hate to see you get hurt."

By the moons, that sounded *real*. Either Mael was the best

liar of the Nostrom clan, or he *truly* was giving in to feelings for his brother's arranged wife.

It almost made her want to laugh. Instead, she summoned as much softness into her voice as she could. "I will, Mael. Thank you again."

A click on the line signaled he had hung up. She did the same a second later, and flopped backward onto the bed, staring up at the ceiling. With a groan, she pressed the heels of her hands against her cheekbones. The weight of her situation was starting to bear down on her like a physical force.

Trapped between three siblings, all trying to use her for their own ends.

One knew what she really was and had her.

One suspected what she was and wanted to use her.

And one seemed to just *want* her.

She'd thought she'd been so clever, infiltrating the Nostrom family to destroy them from within. But now she was the one who felt destroyed—torn between vengeance and something *else.*

Between her past and a future she could barely imagine.

As she finally got up and started preparing for the day's chaos, one thought burned through her mind—

I'm running out of time to choose a side.

Including my own.

Nadi crouched in the darkness of the Rosov estate's eastern garden, the smell of night-blooming jasmine heavy in the air. The sweet scent mingled with the metallic tang of her freshly sharpened knives—a combination that reminded her of perfumed death. Something she'd dealt with a great many times.

Also fitting, considering what they were here to do.

She repositioned herself behind an ornamental bush. She

was wearing a form that she used on occasions like this—a muscular, slender human woman with dark hair and unremarkable features—perfect for blending into the background. That, coupled with simple black clothing, and the whole thing almost felt routine. Raziel had given her guff about how *mundane* she looked. But she'd simply rolled her eyes and told him it wasn't her job to look sexy for him this evening. Her job was to kill.

"Braen's not coming," she muttered, barely audible even to herself.

Raziel was stationed behind a decorative column nearby, a shadow among shadows. "Patience, my little murderer. He'll arrive."

The moonlight caught his profile, highlighting the sharp angles of his face. Even after all that had happened, she couldn't deny that he was beautiful—deadly and beautiful, like a perfectly crafted blade.

"We've been here for nearly two hours," she replied, fighting to keep her voice steady despite the competing urges to either flee, stab him to death, or pin him to the ground and have her way with him. All options had their appeal.

"Which means we're closer to success than we were two hours ago." His low voice carried a hint of amusement that set her teeth on edge.

"Easy for you to say. But I can't feel my feet anymore."

He glanced at her, those crimson eyes faintly luminous in the darkness. "It will be worth it."

Nadi fell silent, her thoughts turning to the competing offers from Mael and Lana. One brother and one sister, both offering her a place at the vampire court if she betrayed Raziel. Why did everyone in this family insist on playing games with each other's lives? The Nostroms were a pit of vipers, and she had somehow found herself swimming in their midst.

"I believe it is time for you to finally tell me the truth."

She huffed a half-laugh. "Like you're telling me all your schemes. Be reasonable, Raziel."

His movement was too fast to track. One moment he was several feet away, the next he was directly in front of her, his face inches from hers, one hand wrapped around her throat—not squeezing, but present. A reminder of what he was capable of.

"There's something you should understand about our situation, Nadi." His breath was warm against her face, smelling of rich wine and something metallic. Blood. "I don't share my true plans with anyone. Not even you."

"Especially not me, you mean." She refused to flinch, to look away. "You're still keeping secrets. And you have the balls to challenge me on mine?"

His grip tightened fractionally. "Mine aren't going to get us *killed*. Shall we discuss your meetings with my siblings? Or perhaps how Mael has been contacting you privately? Or maybe we should talk about Lana's offer to you?"

Ice flooded her veins. He knew. Of course he knew.

"You've been watching me."

"I've been watching everyone," he corrected, releasing her throat but not stepping back. "Did you really think I wouldn't notice? I've been playing this game since before you were born."

"This isn't a game to me." Her anger was making her reckless. She had to be careful. "This is my life. My revenge."

"Your *revenge*?" His laugh was soft and cutting. "Oh, my sweet, naive little fae. You think killing me or my family will fill that emptiness inside you? That it might bring you some kind of *peace*?" He placed a hand over her heart, the gesture somehow more intimate than his grip on her throat had been. "Nothing will. Trust me, I know."

She slapped his hand away. "Don't pretend to understand what I feel."

"But I *do* understand." His voice dropped, became almost gentle. "Why do you think I hate them so much? My own family? You think it's just ambition that drives me?"

Nadi said nothing, waiting.

"I told you how my mother chained me in the fountain when I was eighty." Raziel grimaced. "I lied. I was *eight*."

She stared at him, eyes flicking between his in disbelief.

"And it wasn't just once. Every time she held a soiree I was taken back. For a week prior and a week after. *Raziel the mad dog couldn't be trusted to speak. Might do something untoward or gauche.*" He bared his teeth, his fangs extended.

"And... what would Mael and Lana do?"

"Lana would laugh and feed the pet fish my mother kept in the fountain. Mael would frown and claim he disapproved. But he never did anything to stop it." He turned away from her, his shoulders rigid. The moonlight cast his shadow long across the garden path, a darkness stretching toward the deeper shadows beyond.

"You can breathe underwater. You do not know what it's like to drown," he continued, voice so low she had to strain to hear it. "Each time, I'd feel my lungs fill with water. I'd feel the burning, the panic. It would never stop. Eventually, the agony of it would blend with some part of my mind that sought shelter from the pain. I am a madman, Nadi—make no mistake. But I cannot say if I was this way before... or only after. I do not remember."

Nadi found herself stepping closer to him, drawn by something she couldn't name.

"The worst part wasn't the drowning." His voice was hollow now. "It was when they would drag me from the water. It was being pulled from whatever place in my mind I had retreated to. The world I had made that was *safe*. And far away from *them*. But when air filled my lungs, my mother was there. Mael was there. Lana was there. And I knew it wasn't over. That until they were dead, it would *never* be over."

She placed a hand on his back. She didn't even know what she was trying to do. She had no words.

"Why haven't you killed me yet, Nadi?" There was a pain in his voice, an ache that was raw. Exposed. A bleeding wound. "Can you say the words to me?"

"I..." The words caught in her throat. "No. I can't." She felt the words turn into poison. "Tell me something. When you killed my family, were you just following orders? Did you have a choice?"

Raziel lowered his head, his eyes shutting. His expression was unreadable. "I barely remember them, Nadi." He didn't try to soften it. She was grateful for that. "They were nothing special to me. Just another day. Just another assignment."

"My father's name was Talien Iltani. My mother was a human, Essira. My brother, Kaen. My two sisters were Meri and Lissa." She had to say their names. She had to make sure he *knew them*. Because there were good odds that one or both of them didn't survive tonight.

He nodded. "The warehouse beneath the overpass in the seventh district. I remember why, I don't remember their faces. Your father was helping Luciento smuggle more than just drugs —they were smuggling weapons, to a group of humans planning an insurrection against us. Mael ordered a message to be sent. No survivors."

All of that, she knew. All of that, she could understand. But he hadn't answered the most important question. "Did you enjoy it?"

Silence. He lifted his head again to gaze out at the Rosov estate. "Yes."

There was no apology. Nothing but honesty.

He enjoyed it. Because he had been trained to. Raised to.

He was a product of the world that had made him. And... so was she. She should have hated him in that moment. She should have taken the knife in her belt and plunged into his back between his ribs like she'd done to so many of her marks before him.

Instead, she wondered if she had ever found herself enjoying her job. She thought back on every hit she'd ever performed. Every life she'd ever taken. And tried to remember a time she'd ever felt *enjoyment* over it.

She honestly... didn't know.

But *righteous*? Righteousness, certainly. Taking out vampires and their goons, people who furthered the Nostrom family goals—that she had felt *justice* in doing.

And that was a slippery slope. Revenge was clear-cut. *Justice* was a moral high ground that she wasn't sure she'd ever had any right to claim.

Definitely not anymore.

Not since she'd stared into the dead eyes of Luciento Iltani.

Every day that went by, every moment she spent by Raziel's side, she hated how much more like him she felt.

He has to die. I have to kill him. I'm losing myself in him. Little by little, inch by inch, she was being devoured by the Serpent.

"Why are you telling me this?" She needed to find a way out of this damnable conversation.

"Because you need to understand why I want them dead as much as you do." His hands tightened into fists at his sides. "This isn't just about power. It's about breaking a cycle that's lasted centuries."

"And after, if we succeed and your family falls—you take the throne?" It still sounded more like madness than anything else he'd said so far.

"Yes. Precisely." His answer was immediate, absolute. "I

rebuild this city into something better. Something that doesn't thrive on suffering."

She almost laughed. "You? The Serpent? Creating a kinder world?"

"Not kinder." His smile was cold. "More honest. Under my rule, the predators would know they're predators. The prey would understand their place. There would be... balance."

"And what would be my role in this new world order?"

Taking his eyes off the estate, Raziel turned to her. He reached out, brushing a strand of hair from her face with surprising gentleness. "That depends on you, Nadi. On what you choose."

The moment stretched between them, taut as a wire. Something was changing—had already changed—between them. Something that terrified her far more than his rage ever could.

Before she could respond, a faint sound drew their attention. Raziel moved back into the shadows, motioning for her to do the same.

"He's here," he whispered.

The crunch of gravel signaled an approaching figure. Through the garden gate emerged the tall, lean figure of Braen Rosov, accompanied by two bodyguards. He looked much as he had at the club—impeccably dressed in a tailored suit, his dark hair gelled back and shining in the moonlight, his posture that of a man who feared nothing.

"Remember the plan," Raziel murmured, his voice barely audible even to her fae hearing. "Let me confront him first. You stay hidden until I give the signal."

Nadi nodded, though doubt ate at her. After what Raziel had just revealed about the fae captives, after his confession about her family—could she trust him to follow their agreed plan? Or did he have his own agenda, as always?

She glanced at his profile, remembering the vulnerability

she'd glimpsed moments ago. Had it been real, or just another manipulation? With Raziel, she could never be certain.

But one thing was clear—she was running out of time to decide whose side she was truly on. Mael, Lana, Raziel... or perhaps only her own.

She touched the knife at her waist, feeling its reassuring weight. Whatever she decided, she would need it soon.

She watched as Raziel stepped from the shadows, moving into Braen's path with the casual grace of a panther. The older vampire stopped, dismissing his guards with a wave of his hand.

"Raziel." Braen's voice was smooth as aged brandy. "Your letter was a surprise. I didn't take you for a man who made veiled threats. Or have you simply decided your new wife is lacking and you yearn for what you once had?" He chuckled, his smile flashing white. "It was *you* who broke it off between us, remember."

"I regret to say this isn't a veiled threat, Braen." Raziel's stance was relaxed, deceptively so. "We have very real issues to discuss."

Braen raised an eyebrow. "Do we? Since when have you seen fit to meddle in my affairs again?"

"I have had my reasons of late." Raziel's smile was razor-sharp. "Let's discuss this business somewhere more private than here. Somewhere we won't be disturbed."

"Is that so?" Braen's expression remained pleasant, but something dangerous flickered in his eyes. "And what would this... business entail?"

Raziel stroked his chin thoughtfully. "Business that required detailed record keeping, Braen. Until recently." The implication was clear without spelling it out. Just enough to leave the door open that this was merely about two men with a complex past.

Braen's pleasant mask slipped, just for a moment. "You have always had a flair for the dramatic, Raziel. What is this about?"

"As I said, let's go somewhere more private."

Braen hesitated, then nodded. As the two vampires moved deeper into the garden, Nadi slipped silently after them, her hand on the knife at her waist.

Whatever happened next, someone wasn't leaving this place alive.

THIRTEEN

The air was heavy with the scent of night-blooming flowers, their perfume almost suffocating in the enclosed garden space. All of them encased in iron rings, jagged metal barbs facing inward to keep them from outgrowing their carefully arranged spaces.

Lest they grow *wild*, after all.

Moonlight streamed through the gaps in the carefully arranged foliage, casting dappled shadows across the stone path. The home of the Rosov family had gardens that were renowned for their beauty, but tonight they felt like a labyrinth designed to trap unwary visitors.

Nadi kept to the shadows. From her vantage point behind a large decorative urn, she could see both vampires clearly while remaining hidden herself.

Braen walked with the confidence of a predator in his own territory, seemingly unfazed. If he knew this was a blackmail attempt, it didn't seem to bother him. "You know," he said, pausing by a fountain depicting a mermaid-like fae with an eerily familiar face, "I was always waiting for our bad blood to come calling. I had hoped you would be the one to end me." He ran a finger along the mermaid's stone cheek. "I assume you plan to kill me tonight."

"This isn't about our old history." Raziel shrugged, though his voice held an edge that suggested otherwise.

"Isn't it?" Braen turned, brown-and-red-flecked eyes glinting in the moonlight. "Though I suppose nothing is ever simple with the Nostroms. Especially not with you."

Reaching into his pocket, Raziel held up the ledger. "This is simple enough. You've been running a trafficking ring from your club, selling fae to the highest bidders. This would destroy the Rosovs completely, Braen. The elders of every vampire clan would blacklist you and your entire family."

Braen froze. "You were involved..." He grimaced. "I should have known that was a coordinated attack. That delicious little creature was working with you the entire time?" Chuckling, he stroked a hand over his smoothed-back hair. "Forgive me for underestimating you."

"Forgiven." Raziel tucked the ledger back into his pocket. "Zabriel is marrying Lana. And they need you removed from the equation. This shameful business—"

"Which they *all know I conduct*—" Braen snarled, his fangs extended in a sudden burst of fury. "Those hypocrites! Loathsome *slime*! My siblings know full well what I do! What I enjoy! And half those elders you speak of are in that damnable book you're holding!"

"I don't doubt it." Raziel shrugged again. "But I have a job to do. And here we are."

Braen took a deep breath, smoothing out his suit coat. And let out his lungful of air in a long, heavy, weary sigh. "Yes. Here we are. Volencia's attack dog has come to feast."

The words hung in the air between them, heavy as an approaching thunderstorm. For a moment, neither of them moved.

Nadi shifted slightly, trying to get a better view while staying hidden. There was something in Braen's tone—a familiarity, a bitterness. It was clear to her before now that his relationship with Raziel was more than just political, but now it was confirmed.

"This doesn't have to end in blood." Braen's hands fidgeted at his sides. "I can close the operation. Disappear. I'll give you proof of my death for you to take back to Volencia."

"And you think a token will work?" Raziel smirked. He took a step closer to Braen, his movements fluid and precise. "She won't rest until she has reports of your death from people she trusts. People *other than me*. And do you know why?"

Braen's expression remained impassive, but something flickered in his eyes. "Enlighten me."

"Because she doesn't trust me, Braen." Raziel circled Braen slowly, danger in every movement. "And she never has. Certainly not when it comes to us. Not after what she did to us."

Braen grimaced. "And you have the audacity to tell me this is about some *false wedding*. Some political bullshit. This is about what she did to you. What she *really* made you into. The monster that's standing in front of me. The one who would kill me on a whim. The one who forgot all those sweet words he told me as the sun came up over the horizon. I know what really happened."

Raziel hesitated as he stood in front of Braen, uncertainty in his expression.

Nadi tensed, sensing the shift in the atmosphere. This was veering away from their plan—Braen was supposed to be distracted by the blackmail, giving her a clean shot from the shadows. Instead, he seemed to be drawing Raziel into some dangerous verbal dance.

"And what exactly do you think you know?" Raziel's voice had dropped an octave, taking on a dangerous edge.

"I know what she did after she found out about us." Braen's hand slid over Raziel's shoulders, his brown eyes locked on Raziel's crimson ones. "How she turned me against you. Made me believe your affection was nothing but manipulation. Just your hypnotism at work." He laughed, but there was no humor in it. "Imagine my surprise when I learned years later that your gift doesn't work that way at all."

Raziel had gone absolutely still, his face a careful mask. But Nadi could see the tension in his shoulders, the way his hands had curled into fists at his sides. "You're lying."

"Am I?" Braen raised an eyebrow. "She came to me, you know. The night before you and I..." He trailed off, letting the implication hang in the air. "She showed me reports of your 'episodes.' The bodies. What you'd done to your former lovers. Told me how you'd been manipulating my emotions all along. That nothing I felt was real. That was why she told me I had to drive you away. She told me I needed to betray you. To make you feel like it was *your* choice."

Nadi's mind raced. What was Braen talking about? She knew Volencia was cruel to Raziel, but this sounded like something more manipulative. More subtle.

"She lied." Raziel's voice was tight.

"Perhaps." Braen hummed, deceptively lighthearted. "Or perhaps you're the one lying now. Who can say? Volencia certainly made it impossible to tell." He moved closer, until he was mere inches from Raziel. "I think she couldn't stand the thought of you having connections outside the family. Someone who might see beyond the Serpent to the man beneath. So she severed them. All of them. Can you imagine my surprise that you *turned* your new wife? Tell me. Did you do it to spite your cunt of a mother?"

Raziel hesitated, frozen solid, as if he were one of the statues in the garden. "No."

"For power, then?" Braen laughed. "The cowgirl can't have any kind of leverage."

Raziel stayed silent.

Braen's eyes went wide in shock. "You're *kidding me*. Tell me you're fooling me! Oh, Raziel, *Raziel*. My handsome, cruel, wonderful Raziel... you can't mean it." Reaching up, the smaller man took the Serpent's face in his palms. "You can't possibly *love* her."

Silence. It echoed. Nadi's ears rang with it like they had after a grenade was thrown into the middle of her wedding. *Raziel, do something—say something—why aren't you talking?*

Raziel's control was slipping. Whatever had passed between the vampires long ago was too personal, too volatile. Too dangerous.

"Why are you telling me all this now?" Raziel deflected from the topic of Monica, and for the first time, Nadi heard something like uncertainty in his voice.

"A shame. I wanted to hear you say you loved her." Braen's smile was almost gentle, a stark contrast to the hardness in his eyes. "As for why now? Because I want you to understand why I'm going to enjoy killing you." His hand moved in a blur, and suddenly he was holding a gun. "It's nothing personal, old friend. Just survival."

Three shots, muffled against fabric and flesh.

That was all it took.

Fuck. No. No!

Raziel staggered backward, crimson blooming across his white shirt. One shot to the chest, two to the stomach. The shock on his face was genuine as he fell to his knees, blood spilling between the fingers he pressed to his wounds.

That was too fast. Braen had broken the script. Raziel had allowed himself to get suckered in.

Nadi froze, her heart hammering in her chest. This wasn't

how it was supposed to happen. Raziel was supposed to distract Braen while she moved in for the kill—clean, quick, untraceable. Not this. Not Raziel bleeding out on the ground with Braen standing over him, gun still raised.

"Do you know what the worst part was? About being with you?" Braen asked, crouching down to Raziel's level. "The uncertainty. Never knowing if what I felt for you was real or just another one of your mind games." He pressed the barrel of the gun against Raziel's forehead. "In the end, I suppose it doesn't matter. The result is the same. Now... are you truly *you*, I wonder? Or your little fae shifter pet? Time to find out, I suppose."

Nadi was moving before she'd fully processed her decision, her form shifting as she stepped from the shadows. No longer a servant but a predator, sleek and deadly. The knife she'd kept hidden was now in her hand, its blade gleaming in the moonlight.

"I have to admit," Braen chuckled down at Raziel, "if it *is* you, I'm a little disappointed. I expected more of a fight from the Serpent. Any last words before I send you to join all those humans you've commanded to their deaths?"

Raziel was too good to give up her approach. Too good to reveal that Nadi was already in action. He merely smiled up at him, his teeth already stained with his own blood. "I thought I loved you, once. That wasn't a lie. But now I know what love *is*, Braen"—he coughed—"and I love her with an intensity and passion that you have never known in your life."

Braen tensed, beginning to turn, but it was too late. Nadi was already in motion, her blade finding its mark between his ribs with surgical precision. She drove it in between his ribs. Once. Twice. She had six strikes before he even managed to register the first, putting the full force of her body behind each of the thrusts.

Braen made a strangled sound, more surprise than pain.

The gun fell from suddenly nerveless fingers as he crumpled to the ground, eyes wide with shock.

"You..." he gasped, blood bubbling between his lips as he looked up at Nadi. "The shifter...?"

She leaned in close, letting her glamor slip just enough for him to see a hint of her true nature—the opalescent gleam in her eyes, the faintest tint of green to her skin. "I'm the face of every single fae you have tortured and sold," she said softly. "And I am your *fucking* reckoning."

With a final, vicious twist of the blade, she severed the connection between heart and body. She watched the light fade from Braen's eyes, waiting until she was certain he was dead before turning to Raziel.

He had slumped against the base of the fountain, his blood staining the white stone crimson. His face was alarmingly pale, even for a vampire, and his breathing came in shallow, ragged gasps.

"Raziel—" She rushed to his side, pressing her hands over the worst of the wounds to stem the bleeding. "How bad is it? I —" A choked quiet laugh came out of her as she babbled out, "I've never tried to *save* a vampire—"

"It's bad enough," he managed, his voice barely audible. "The bullets... silver."

Silver. Of course. Braen would have come prepared to kill a vampire. Silver slowed their healing and made them vulnerable to blood loss.

"We need to get you out of here." Glancing around frantically, she tried to think. They needed to leave before someone came to investigate—the guards knew where Braen was, and more importantly, *who he was with*. But Raziel was in no condition to walk, let alone run.

This was the moment, she realized with sudden clarity. This was her chance. With Raziel incapacitated and Braen dead, she could complete her original mission.

She could kill the Serpent, avenge her family, side with Lana and Mael, secure her own position within the Nostrom hierarchy, destroy them all.

It would be so easy. He was already dying. All she had to do was leave him here and let nature take its course. Two sadistic, vampiric ex-lovers who killed each other in an argument. It would be perfect. Not a single bit of the story would seem unusual.

Raziel seemed to read her thoughts, a pained smile twisting his lips. "Go ahead," he whispered, voice thick with the blood in his throat. "Finish what you started."

His eyes held hers, those crimson orbs that had once terrified her now clouded with pain but still somehow... understanding. As if he'd always known this moment would come, had accepted it long ago.

And suddenly, Nadi *couldn't do it*.

The thought of leaving him here, of watching the light fade from those eyes, made something in her chest constrict painfully. It wasn't forgiveness—she would never forgive him for what he'd done to her family. It was something else. Something she wasn't ready to name.

But it *was* a choice.

"Shut up," she muttered, tearing strips from his shirt to create makeshift bandages. "I'm not letting you die before I'm finished making you suffer."

A weak laugh escaped him, ending in a cough that brought up more blood. "What... are you going to do?"

A plan was already forming in her mind. "First, I'm going to make sure no one follows us."

Concentrating, she shifted her form, taking on the appearance of Braen Rosov. It was an unsettling sensation, wearing the face of the man she'd just killed, but it wasn't the first or the last time she'd had to do it. With Braen's voice and mannerisms, she ordered the nearby guards to secure the perimeter, claiming there had been an intruder that had already been dealt with.

The guards didn't question it. Why would they?

Once they were gone, she shifted again—this time taking on Ivan's massive form. The added strength would make it easier to carry Raziel. She hated how often the bodyguard came in handy—both literally and figuratively. But he did.

"Hold on," she told him, using Ivan's voice, and carefully lifted his bloodied form. She held him in her now-massive arms, afraid to throw him over her shoulder for fear of what it would do.

"A compelling performance," Raziel managed through gritted teeth. "You made... a decent Braen, back there." His eyes rolled into his head for a moment before they snapped back to her. "For better or worse..."

She decided not to let her thoughts linger on that. The night was complicated enough as it was. "Shut up and focus on not dying," she responded, but there was no real heat in her words.

As she carried him away from the garden, retracing their steps through the estate grounds, she had to keep her focus purely on the task at hand—escape. Survival.

Nadi was acutely aware of his weight in her arms, the warmth of his blood seeping into her borrowed form. The smell of it was overwhelming—coppery and rich, mingled with the unique scent that was distinctly Raziel.

His words echoed in her mind. A confession of love to an enemy. Had it been a distraction tactic? Just something to torture Braen moments before his death? Or... had it been real?

Now wasn't the time to ask.

She thought of Lana's offer, of the position and power she'd promised if Nadi eliminated both Raziel and Braen. She thought of Mael's earnest assurances that he would protect her. She thought of her original mission, the one that had driven her for so many years—to destroy the Nostroms, to avenge her slaughtered family.

And yet, here she was, carrying Raziel to safety, his blood on her hands in a way she'd never anticipated.

What was happening to her? When had the line between hatred and *whatever this was* become so blurred? Had there even been a single moment?

"They're going to come after us," Raziel murmured, his voice fading. "Both of us. For killing Braen. And my family... will allow it."

"I know. Let them come," she replied, surprising herself with the fierceness in her voice. "We'll be ready."

As they reached the car where Ivan—the real Ivan—was waiting, she was finally able to shift out of the bodyguard's form as the real one took over. She let out a breath of exhaustion as she resumed her own shape as soon as she could, knowing how much her assuming Ivan's form unsettled him. And while *she* didn't care, she needed the bodyguard paying attention to what mattered.

Raziel's hand caught hers, his grip surprisingly strong given his condition. "Thank you," he said, his eyes meeting hers with an intensity that took her breath away. "For choosing me."

Before she could respond, his eyes rolled back, and he went limp in her arms.

Nadi stood there for a moment, his words echoing in her mind. Had she chosen him? Or had she simply made a tactical decision? She wasn't sure anymore.

Ivan's expression darkened as he took in Raziel's blood-soaked form. "What happened?" he demanded, already moving to help her load Raziel into the back seat.

"Braen was waiting for us," she said, carefully arranging Raziel's unconscious body. "He had silver bullets."

"And Braen?" Ivan arched an eyebrow.

"Dead." The word hung in the air, heavy with implication.

Braen Rosov wasn't just any vampire. His death would have consequences.

Ivan's jaw tightened as he slammed the car door and slid behind the wheel. "We can't go home," he said flatly as Nadi climbed into the back seat, cradling Raziel's head in her lap.

"What? Why not?" She pressed her hands against Raziel's wounds, trying to stem the bleeding.

"Don't think we can trust anybody." Ivan's eyes met hers in the rearview mirror, dark and serious. "Not like this."

Letting out a breath, she sighed. "Yeah." That made sense. Too much sense. Lana would have contingencies. If "Monica" couldn't finish the job, then Lana would make sure someone else would.

Ivan gunned the engine, the car lurching forward.

"Where are we going, then?"

"Somewhere safe." Ivan's focus returned to the road as he navigated the winding lanes leading away from the Rosov estate. "Somewhere Raziel goes when he needs to... get away."

The implication hung in the air. This wasn't the first time Raziel had been brought to the brink of death. It wasn't the first time Ivan had needed to hide him away.

"What happened?" Ivan asked, his voice low. "Raziel isn't careless."

Nadi hesitated, unsure how much to share. Ivan was Raziel's most loyal guard, but he was a Nostrom employee. Still, they needed his help.

Ivan grunted. "I know about them, Monica, if that's what's up."

Her jaw ticked. "It got personal. Braen started talking about their past. About Volencia turning them against each other." She left out the part where Raziel confessed his love for his "wife."

Ivan's hands tightened on the steering wheel until his knuckles whitened. "Shit." His eyes flicked to the rearview mirror, focusing on Raziel's unconscious form. "It nearly destroyed him."

Nadi looked down at Raziel, at the face that had once filled her with nothing but hatred. It was hard to reconcile the monster from her nightmares with the broken man in her lap.

"What happened between them?" she asked softly. "Braen said something about Volencia convincing him that Raziel had been manipulating his emotions."

"Not my place."

Nadi frowned. "Ivan, please. You said it almost destroyed him. And tonight, it almost killed him."

A heavy sigh. For a minute, she didn't think he was going to answer. But when Ivan finally spoke, his voice was distant, as if recalling events from another lifetime. "About a hundred 'n' fifty years ago, Raziel was different then—less, well. You see him. The Serpent reputation was still new. Volencia had him doing her dirty work, but he hadn't become what he is now." Ivan navigated a sharp turn, the car's headlights cutting through the darkness. "Then, he met Braen. They were both *broken* in their own way."

Nadi tried to imagine a less broken Raziel.

"Braen was the oldest Rosov, but he was always the black sheep," Ivan continued. "Too unpredictable. He had... tastes that his family found unseemly." A pause. "Though nothing like what he was doing with those fae in the basement of his club. That came later."

"And Raziel?" Nadi prompted, wanting to understand the man whose blood was staining her hands.

"Raziel was Volencia's dog, but he hadn't fully accepted that role yet. He still fought against it, still believed he could have some kind of life outside her control." Ivan's laugh was bitter. "Turns out he was wrong."

Beneath Nadi's hands, Raziel stirred slightly, his face

contorting in pain even in unconsciousness. She smoothed back his hair, the gesture automatic.

"Their uh... thing... was pretty intense." Ivan's hesitation in his words made her smile. He was treating her like she'd never had a boyfriend before Raziel. "It was—uh... volatile. But real. He seemed happy. Started talking about breaking away from Volencia, about building his own thing."

"And Volencia couldn't allow that," Nadi guessed, the pieces falling into place.

"Nope. She destroyed them, the way she destroys everything." Ivan sighed.

Nadi looked down at Raziel, trying to imagine what it must have been like. To have the one person you trusted, the one escape you thought you'd found, turned against you by your own mother.

"What did Braen do?" she asked, though she suspected she knew the answer.

"Betrayed him. Set him up. Ensured that a deal went wrong and had left him for dead in a back alley in the lower city." Ivan's voice was flat. "I found him there, nearly dead. Multiple stab wounds, a silver blade left in his chest."

"But he survived."

"Barely. Raziel went after Braen, said Braen had done it on purpose. Braen denied it all, and said that Raziel was the paranoid, delusional one. Raziel walked away. He was never the same after." Ivan's grip on the steering wheel tightened again. "Volencia told him it proved he could never trust anyone. That only she understood him." His laugh was hollow. "Raz believed her."

The car fell silent, save for the hum of the engine and Raziel's ragged breathing. Nadi tried to process everything she'd learned. It didn't excuse what Raziel had become—the monster who'd slaughtered her family—but it helped her at least *understand* how he'd gotten there.

The layers of manipulation, the systematic breaking of his spirit, the isolation from anyone who might offer an alternative path.

"So tonight, in the garden," she said slowly, "when Braen revealed that he knew Volencia had lied?"

"Dunno. How would you feel if your whole world was a lie?" Ivan finished for her. "Because he and Braen never..."

She thought back to the moment just before Braen had shot Raziel, the look of raw vulnerability that had crossed the Serpent's face.

She'd never seen him so unguarded, so... *human.*

"I know what you're thinking," Ivan said, his eyes finding hers in the mirror again. "You're wondering if the 'real' Raziel—the one beneath the Serpent—is someone worth saving." He shook his head. "It's not that simple. There isn't one."

"I know that." *More than I can tell you, Ivan.* More than the bodyguard could possibly understand, she truly, honestly, to her soul, knew there was no pulling the two apart. The thought had not ever crossed her mind.

There was no *real* Raziel hiding underneath the monster.

There was no monster to save him from. They were one and the same.

She had watched her entire family die at his hands. Her entire life had been spent plotting her revenge, learning to kill—honing her skills as an assassin. And what little she had, had been sacrificed to infiltrate his life for the sole purpose of destroying him and everything he held dear.

She had murdered her uncle Luciento in the name of the "greater good."

And yet, here she was, cradling his head in her lap, desperately trying to keep him alive.

If there was a monster in the car...

She was starting to believe it might not be Raziel.

"I'm not looking to redeem him, Ivan. I can promise you

that." She turned her gaze out the window. No, if he died, it would be because *she* decided he should. No one else. The words slipped out without her realizing it. "He'll die when I say he dies."

Ivan's eyes widened slightly in the mirror, and he barked out a surprised laugh. "Yeah. I think I get why he likes you."

Nadi didn't answer, not wanting to examine that statement too closely.

She was afraid of what she might find if she did.

FOURTEEN

Nadi watched the electric lights transition to gas as Ivan drove the car from the central city to the outer areas that were less advanced—less *polished*. Wherever he was taking them, it wasn't anywhere near Raziel's usual crawls.

It was dangerous, being this far away from Nostrom turf. The Rosovs controlled grounds near here, but this particular area was considered *no man's land*, where the building structure and topography weren't worth any major player holding onto it.

In fact, Ivan had taken them to a section of the old garrison wall. One of the ramparts that were meant to be the "last line of defense" against the Wild, before it was discovered that the Wild was *beneath* the city not just *around* the city. It stretched some fifty feet tall above them, and most of the stone structure, which was from around the same era as the Nostrom family estate, had long since crumbled away or had been taken down to make way for newer structures or buildings.

But some of it still remained, and this part was one of the old watchtowers. It looked in decent shape, all things considered, the windows all in their frames and no holes in the roof.

The bricks were stained dark from coal soot which wasn't uncommon in the area. Ivan pulled the car around to a wooden gate behind an iron one, both of them locked with several chains. Getting out, but leaving the car running, he unlocked the chains, and opened both sets of gates.

It revealed a small cobblestone courtyard that must have been used for carriages. Ivan pulled the car through and parked it before closing the gates and locking them with the chains now on the inside fastening everything shut.

Raziel's bodyguard said nothing to Nadi the entire time, just resolutely went through his tasks as though she weren't there. He put Raziel carefully over his shoulder and shut the car door before heading up the stairs to unlock the door and go inside.

The building was *ancient*, and it showed. The stone stairs that led up to a tiny door into the building were bowed in the middle, worn shallow from the sheer act of people walking on them over the centuries.

She shut the door behind them, her eyes instantly adjusting to the dim light from the windows. But Ivan flicked on an electric light. Pulling in a breath, Nadi couldn't help but stare.

The building was *gorgeous*. It was a blend of old and new. Ancient wood beams and iron supports mixed with the smooth marble countertops and luxurious leather sofas of an open-plan kitchen and living area. The watchtower was a single, circular space with stairs that spiraled up the middle. The only rooms were split by floors, it seemed, with doors she could see divvying up the more private areas on different levels.

Lush, thick blankets thrown over the arms of the sofas made her want to burrow into them by the enormous fireplace that dominated the wall of the watchtower. The face carved into the hearth was that of some sort of twisted monster. She wondered idly if it was meant to be a vampire or a fae.

Ivan was already walking up the spiral staircase, the

wrought-iron structure clunking under his heavy steps with the combined weight of him and Raziel.

She followed dutifully after. "No one knows about this place?"

"Just us." Ivan sniffed. "And he's the only one who comes here." He gestured dismissively up toward the top of the tower. "He flies in... as bats."

That made a lot of sense. Nadi used to lose track of Raziel sometimes for weeks at a time before all this insanity started, and she never could figure out *where* the bastard would disappear to in the metropolis. Now she knew. He had a secret little hideaway on the far edge of the city. "It's beautiful."

Ivan only grunted.

She almost laughed. She would have if she were in a better mood. "We'll need to feed him." Practical matters first. "Once we get the bullets out."

"I'll go get him someone. Something tells me you've got more delicate fingers for the bullets. Or you can transform into someone who does."

Yeah. That was a good bet.

It wasn't long before Ivan got to the fourth floor. It had a hallway with two open doors. A bedroom on one side and a bathroom on the other. The bedroom resembled the one Raziel had in his main home, except the walls were brick and the ceilings higher. She honestly preferred it, all things considered. Its more industrial harsh surfaces mixed with its lush bedding and upholstery seemed to somehow suit him more.

A creature of extremes.

Of disparate moments that could be true at the same time. A complex and tangled individual.

Ivan put Raziel down on the bed, as gently as a man that big was capable of putting down another man that big. "I'll leave you to, well." He gestured at the mess that was the Serpent. "Do what you gotta. Medical supplies are in the bathroom. Everything you'll need."

The bodyguard tramped down the metal stairs, leaving her to it.

Nadi was exhausted. But her night was only getting started. If she didn't get the silver bullets out soon, Raziel would never be able to start healing. She headed to the bathroom and started rooting through the drawers. She found long tweezers, bandages, and even what she'd need to stitch up the wounds—though they'd probably heal up fairly quickly on their own once he was able to feed.

Smirking at how annoyed he'd be at having to cut his stitches out, she headed back to the bed. Tucking towels underneath him, she pulled open his shirt. The bullets hadn't gone through. A silencer muffled the sound of a pistol, but it also slowed the impact of a bullet. And silver didn't fly as well as lead—that meant she had to dig out three slugs of silver, imbedded *somewhere* in his body.

Great.

Just great.

With a sigh, she went to work.

The most important one was the one in his chest, so she focused on that first. It was also the most shallow of the bunch. She went in with the tweezers, but realized that while that had the precision, she couldn't *feel* what she was doing. She needed to use her fingers.

Gritting her teeth, she scooted closer to him on the bed, and rolling up her sleeve, put her finger into the bullet wound.

His eyes shot open as he hissed in pain, baring his fangs at her. His hand grabbed her arm, digging his nails into her skin. There was no one home, save a feral animal. It was purely self-defense.

"It's me, Raziel—it's *me*." She dropped her glamor, meeting his animalistic form with her own. Crimson eyes to her black opal ones. "It's Nadi. I need to get the bullets out. *Stand down.*"

Those jagged fangs retracted into his jaw as he threw his head back into the pillow. The sound he made wasn't human. It was barely even a sound she recognized as vampiric. It was pure *pain.*

But his hand released from her arm.

And he slipped back into unconsciousness.

Her heart pounded in her ears as her finger touched the bullet in his chest. Working quickly, she pulled it out and tossed it onto the nightstand. The ones in his stomach were easier—it was fleshier material. But something about him was changing.

The blood that was leaving him was *changing.* It wasn't red anymore. It was turning darker. Black. Thicker. *Sludgy.*

This was bad. Very, very bad.

Three silver bullets removed. Now, all she could do was clean him up. Do her best to stop the bleeding and hope that Ivan returned quickly with blood for Raziel. Hopefully, in bottled form, and not a *person.* She knew they were killers. She knew how vampires fed. But a corpse seemed like an inconvenience they didn't need right now.

She gathered a collection of washcloths from the bathroom and a bin to put them in, and went to work. They'd likely be ruined when she was done. But that was the nature of his life, she supposed. Raziel likely generated a lot of bloody linen.

She started by gently wiping the blood from his face and his lips. For a moment, a memory snapped into place. Suddenly, she was wiping the blood from her mother's face. Cleaning the corpse of her father. Of her brother. Readying them for burial in the Wild.

Biting back the tears, it was a useless fight that time.

She let them fall down her cheeks. Clenching the cloth in her fist, she let out a noise that she couldn't describe, halfway through a choke and a sob. Damn the Nostrom clan to the *void.*

Damn them all to the worst kinds of torture she could dream up.

And Volencia worst of all. For if it weren't for her, maybe Raziel wouldn't have been sent to murder her family.

Maybe she wouldn't have been forced to clean the corpses of the people she loved.

Maybe then, he wouldn't have been turned into a monster.

Maybe then, neither would she.

And maybe then, she wouldn't be seated at the bedside of the same creature of death, of revenge, of *slaughter*, cleaning blood from his body...

Angry. Furious.

But not at him.

No.

At the ones who *made* him. She felt like she was going to lose her mind. Utterly snap like a twig under the weight of everything that had transpired that day.

"You better have been lying when you told him you loved your wife." She began to clean the blood from his chest. "Or I swear I *will* cut out your heart, Raziel Nostrom. Because I—" Her voice choked off.

She was so glad he couldn't hear her. So very glad.

But even then, she couldn't risk it. She couldn't even say the words to herself. She didn't even dare to think them. She couldn't give them that kind of power.

Leaning down, she kissed his cold lips. "Damn you, Raziel Nostrom. *Damn you* to whatever torment they make for souls like ours."

Nadi must have dozed off. She had curled up on the sofa near the wall, wanting to give Raziel space. Sleeping in the same bed with him was one thing.

Sleeping in the same bed with a veritable *corpse* of him was another.

She was woken up by a crash and the sound of breaking glass.

Instantly, she was on her feet, adrenaline rampaging through her system as she held a pistol aloft. She'd found it in a drawer in Raziel's nightstand and put it in reach before lying down to sleep.

Searching for the source of the noise, she quickly found it. Her heart dropped.

It was Raziel.

He was half-collapsed onto the nightstand. The crash had been the lamp hitting the ground, the glass shade shattering on the old, lacquered wood floor.

Still shirtless, his skin was ashen and gray. She could count his ribs from the back. It was like he had... decayed, in the time she had been asleep on the sofa. She'd never seen a vampire starved for blood.

Now she wished she hadn't.

"Raziel?" She crept closer to him, keeping the gun tight in her hand, but pointed downward.

He stood, slowly, as if it pained him. Head lowered, his dark hair, usually so smooth and perfect, was still stringy from the dried blood, serving as a veil to hide his face. Wavering on his feet, he swayed from side to side as if he were simply sleep-walking.

"Raziel...?" She kept her distance, some ten feet away, figuring that was probably how far he could jump at her if he attacked. She had dealt with deadly snakes in the Wild, and she had a pretty good instinct for how far a cornered animal could lash out when pressed.

Circling around slowly, she tried to see his face. His shoulders were curled. His hands limp at his sides, fingers occasionally twitching.

"Raziel, look at me."

She shouldn't have asked for that. She really, really shouldn't have.

Because he listened. He lifted his head. And those crimson eyes were not the ones she knew. They were the eyes of a feral, mad animal. His lips were pulled back from his teeth, making his fangs look longer and more vicious than before.

The snarl that left him wasn't human. It was the same noise he'd made before, when she'd touched the bullet in his chest. Only now, it was louder. It was *desperate*.

And it was *hungry*.

She fired off two bullets into his chest and jumped backward, trying to put as much distance between them as possible. He staggered, but ignored the wounds in his chest like they weren't even there.

These bullets weren't silver.

And nothing oozed from the holes they made.

He fell against the wall, smashing into a bookcase, sending much of its contents crashing to the floor. Weakly, as if every movement was agony, he started pulling himself back up to his feet.

And those red eyes never left her.

He was going to consume her. Every drop.

The gun wasn't going to stop him. Not unless she put a bullet in his skull. And that would kill him.

Fuck. Fuck—fuck—*fuck!* "Ivan!"

No one answered. He wasn't back yet. "*Ivan!*" she screamed again, desperately hoping the bodyguard was within earshot. But she was on her own. On her own with a feral, blood-starved vampire.

Raziel threw himself at her again, but more weakly this time than the first. His knees gave out and he fell to the ground with a painful *thud*.

A ragged wheeze left him, his nails digging into the wood

floor as he clawed at the ground in a pathetic attempt to crawl closer to her.

And that was when it hit her.

Raziel... was dying.

He'd been bled dry. And she'd just put two new holes in him.

Raziel was dying in front of her eyes.

This was what she wanted all her life.

To watch her most hated enemy, the man she had vowed revenge upon all those years ago, suffering in agony and slowly, painfully, coming to an end. And she would be the last thing he saw.

It was supposed to be the happiest moment of her life. When the ghosts of her family could be at peace.

So, why was she shaking?

Why did it feel... wrong?

Maybe it was because it wasn't by her hand that he was dying. It wasn't because of her that he was suffering. She hadn't been the one to get revenge, it'd been his mother.

Maybe it was because he was probably lost in the haze of whatever blood-starved madness had consumed him. He couldn't understand or appreciate what was happening to him.

Both of those things could be true.

But if they were? Neither of them would explain why she was crying.

"Ivan!" One last hope. One last chance.

Silence.

Nothing except the ragged gasps of a dying vampire, and the scrape of his nails against the wood floor. Raziel was going to die...

... if she didn't feed him.

But if she let him feed from her? *He would kill her.* He wouldn't be able to stop. He was a wild animal. He'd rip her to pieces, tear her open, and drink *her* dry.

One of them would die in the next fifteen minutes.

Shutting her eyes, she let the tears run down her cheeks, unchecked. It'd be a mercy to him to put a bullet in his head and end his suffering. How many people had he killed in the same way? How many people had *she* killed in her life? He deserved to die.

And she wanted to kill him.

But not like this.

So... she would let him starve to death in front of her? That was *better*? To let an animal with a leg caught in a hunter's trap bleat, and cry, and scream until it died, rather than just snap its neck and end its suffering?

No. No, he had to die.

This wasn't revenge, this was a kindness.

She lifted the gun and pointed it at Raziel's head with a trembling hand.

The expression on his face shifted. Just slightly. Just a flicker of something that might have been recognition in those rabid, crimson, glassy eyes.

He lowered his head. And the clawing stopped. The animal was accepting its death at her hand...

Then, she heard it. The noise. Through the gasping, dying rattle of air in his chest... he was crying. But vampire cried blood, didn't they? And he had no blood to weep.

She couldn't. She just *couldn't*. Flicking the safety back on the gun, she placed it down on a nearby table.

She couldn't kill him.

She hadn't been able to kill him back at Braen's estate.

And she couldn't let him die now.

Staring down at her palms through the hazy blur of her tears, she wondered what had become of her. What he'd done to her. She should have listened to Luciento—she should have escaped into the Wild with her uncle the moment she had the chance.

But she'd chosen the path of revenge. She'd chosen to stay in the metropolis and hunt the Nostroms. She'd chosen not to disappear into the Wild and find a new life.

She'd chosen death.

And she had let him *in*. She had let him get into her soul and twist something around his fingers. She had let him poison her in a way she didn't know was possible.

Yet... here she was.

Unable to scratch the name that had been at the top of her list for over eighty years. *The* name. The whole reason she was still *alive*. The whole reason she was still in the metropolis. The reason she had left a trail of corpses in her wake as an assassin.

Who was she, if she wasn't Nadi, the fae who wanted the Serpent dead?

What did she have to live for, if she didn't have that to drive her forward?

Nothing.

Absolutely *nothing*.

Pulling in a breath, it hitched halfway and she choked out a sob. No. No, this was all right. She could only hope that the gods would be kind and simply commit her soul to the endless oblivion. That they didn't leave her to wander as a ghost.

She supposed she was about to find out.

Taking another deep breath, she readied herself, and muttered a quiet prayer to the moons and the lords of the deep. To her family, she prayed for forgiveness.

And to Luciento, most of all.

Slowly walking up to Raziel, she knelt down beside him. "Raz..."

The noise he made was a strangled, unintelligible thing at first. The hand closest to her twisted into a claw and jerked toward her before he pounded it into the floor.

He was trying to fight it.

"*Run...*" He pulled in a hollow, rasping breath. His voice sounded like the wind escaping from a tomb. Cold. Empty. Death itself. "*Run... from... me...*" He sank his nails into the floor, leaving white scratches in the dark wood.

"It's okay. This is how it was meant to end between us." She gently urged him to roll onto his side facing her.

His eyes were sunken, his cheeks hollow. He was fading away as she watched. Like a corpse decaying. "*Run...*"

"You told me to run, once, long ago." She ran her hand down his cheek. He hissed, his mouth open, seeking the pulse of her wrist. "I'm not going to listen to you this time."

"*Na... di...*" Her name, as best as he could manage it.

"Ssh..." Gently, she picked him up, grunting under his weight at first. But as she slung an arm underneath him to pull him close, his own arm, which felt so weak at first, snapped around her like an iron girder.

"*Run...*" He was still telling her to run. Sharp nails scraped her scalp as fingers tangled in her hair and fisted it, yanking her head to the side.

Suddenly, she was in *his* lap—a burst of strength from the last desperate attempts of an animal to survive. And she knew there was no escaping now.

Taking a deep breath, she settled into his grasp, tilting her head away from his already opening mouth. "I'm going nowhere. I vowed to follow you straight into the void, Serpent. One way or another. So I need you alive."

It was then that the strange purr began in his chest. Rasping and broken, but there all the same. Shutting her eyes, she let the sound of it take her away. Let it soothe her, let it wipe away all the fear of what was about to come.

She felt the bite more as a jolt of her body as he sank his teeth into her. Then felt that *pull*. That glorious, wonderful bliss as he began to consume her.

He moaned, clutching at her, deepening the bite. She stroked his hair, holding onto him as she let herself simply disappear into the pleasure of him. Of his kiss.

The world began to fade away, and she could pretend she was simply falling asleep in the arms of her lover.

At least this was a good way to die.

FIFTEEN

Raziel held Nadi in his arms.

A drop of blood hit her pale cheek.

It had fallen from his eye. He was crying. He didn't care. He clutched her to his chest. He was too weak to stand. Too exhausted to move. Too dizzy to even *think* straight.

Everything was a blur.

He remembered Braen. The bullet wounds. He remembered Nadi pulling silver from his chest.

Darkness.

Pain.

Starvation. A burning need.

Then... honey. Salvation like nothing he had ever tasted before had filled him. He had been about to die. He knew that much. He had felt it, somewhere, in the back of his mind—calling to him.

But he was alive.

His room was in shambles. The bookcase had been emptied mostly onto the floor. A broken lamp. An overturned table. He had two bleeding bullet holes in his chest that had not been there before.

And in his arms... a dying fae siren. Her long, dark-scaled tail stretched out beside them. Beautiful and foreign, a creature so out of place in his watchtower loft. Her neck was covered in teeth wounds, as if gnawed on by a rabid animal.

One that should have been put down.

She had *tried* to put him down.

Clearly, he had overpowered her. There was a struggle. He had mauled her and ripped open her throat.

Nadi was still alive. But barely. He didn't know if she would survive. He knew nothing about how to tend to her. What did she need? How could he help her?

Or was it already too late?

Had he killed her?

Had he fallen in love with a woman only to destroy her? Had his family been right? How perfect would that be? How utterly and wonderfully poetic.

"You can't—you can't leave me," he murmured to her, his words still slurring and messy. He was weak. Healing. He had been on the brink of death. "Don't go, don't..."

His ears pricked at the sound of the door downstairs opening and shutting. "*Ivan!*" The shout was broken and sounded more like a cry from a child than anything else. But it was the best he could do. "Help—"

The sound of thudding footsteps told him that his bodyguard took it seriously. It meant that Nadi's secret was about to be shared with someone else... but if it meant that she would live, he couldn't care less.

Ivan burst into the room, carrying a case of glass bottles filled with crimson liquid in his hands. The bodyguard stared down at the scene in front of him with wide eyes. "What the *fuck*—"

"No time to expl—" He coughed. It hurt to speak. It hurt to do anything. "Monica. Help her."

Raziel didn't have friends in this world. But he had something better. He had Ivan. Because his bodyguard quickly set the bottles of blood on the ground with a *thud* and immediately scooped up the fae siren without a single hesitation—struggling a bit to offset the weight of the woman's long tail.

"I don't know wh—where to even start to—" Ivan was already heading to the bathroom with her.

"Try." Raziel bowed his head, pressing his palms over his eyes, wishing he could curl into a hole and stay there.

And, if she died, perhaps he would. His words were a whisper, more to himself, than anything else. "I can't do this without her."

* * *

"Drink this, laeiga. You'll feel better."

Nadi turned her head away from the cup pressed to her lips, muttering back in fae. *"Ni, ni'ha, laetesh."* She hated the taste of the boiled roots and herbs. She always did. Mother told her it was supposed to taste good. Nadi suspected it was a lie. It tasted like soap to her.

"Drink it, Nadi. Please."

A hand underneath her neck lifted her head. The cup met her lips again. This time, she had no choice. The disgusting soapy flavor entered her mouth and she swallowed it.

Coughing, she whined, sinking into the warm water around her. At least there was that. It was too close around her, too tight —there were walls near her. But she was warm.

"Laetesh, ni..."

"What is she saying?" A deep voice. She could barely process it.

"I don't know." That first voice. A man's voice. Not her mother's. But one she knew. She just couldn't remember from where.

A hand stroked her hair.

Everything faded away.

Waking up in a bathtub was a fascinating and unpleasant experience.

Nadi groaned. Moons, everything *hurt*.

"Boss—" Movement to her right.

Her head spun when she tried to look to see who had spoken. She felt feverish. She felt weak. Like she was still half asleep. What had happened...?

Where was she?

How did she—

A shadow in the doorframe, dimly outlined by the ambient light in the hallway behind him. A silhouette she knew.

Raziel Nostrom.

For a moment, instinctual fear took over, and she jerked. The adrenaline shock to her system was exactly what she needed, however.

"Fuck—" she groaned and sank into the water. At least it was hot water. With a shaking hand, she reached for her neck.

"Don't. It's still healing." Raziel knelt beside the tub. It was one of those old-fashioned, claw-footed things. Big enough for a human to stretch out comfortably.

But not someone with an eight-foot fish tail. Her tail was draped over the lip of the tub and onto the floor. They'd... thrown a blanket over it. To keep it from getting *cold*.

That was so oddly *thoughtful* that her focus got stuck on that and she didn't realize Raziel was talking to her for a solid few seconds.

"Nadi?" He gently placed his hand on her shoulder.

"Hm?" She turned her head weakly to look at him. "Sorry."

"I'm just—" He cupped her cheek in his palm. He still looked like shit himself, dark bruised circles under his eyes. His lips were chapped. He looked as though he had been walking across the plains in the blazing sun for a week with no food or water. "I'm glad you're awake."

"Relatively... speaking." She felt like her head wasn't attached to her shoulders. "Why'm..." She furrowed her brow. "Why'm in a tub?"

"I... I didn't know what to do." He frowned. "You always seemed to like to be in the water, and with your tail and all, I—"

Nadi began to laugh.

It wasn't much of a laugh. It was weak, it was dry, and it kind of hurt her, but she couldn't help it. That was the funniest moons-damned thing she'd heard in a long, long time.

And probably one of the sweetest.

"I don't need to be in the tub, Raz." She smiled at him. Just barely, he smiled back. "But I appreciate it."

"Good. It was getting annoying, constantly having to drain it and refill it to keep it warm. Ivan was starting to complain." He sighed.

"Ivan—You mean he saw me like this?" Another wave of adrenaline rushed over her. The other voice. "No. No, no, *no*." Struggling to move, she sat up, sloshing water over the edge of the tub and onto the floor.

"Nadi, don't, you're still too—"

Like *fuck* if she was going to listen to him. Forcing her glamor back over herself to summon her legs, she half clambered, half climbed out of the tub.

Raziel caught her before she fell and ate the floor. It seemed her legs, while they obeyed her summons, did not want to work properly. Her head spun, and she forced herself to slow her breathing down. She was going to black out if she didn't. She couldn't have that.

She had a bodyguard to murder.

Violently.

Quickly.

Immediately.

"Moons' sake, calm down, Nadi."

"He can't—he can't know, Raz. He can't—" She tried to squirm out of his grasp, but it was pointless. She was a wet noodle. And one that was *also* entirely naked.

"Can we discuss this when you're able to stand and breathe under your own power?" Raziel kept her up with one arm as he reached over to a hook on the wall and pulled a thick, plush dressing gown from it. He helped her put it on.

She couldn't even put on a damn dressing gown without his help. The moment he took his arm out from around her, she nearly fell to the floor, and had to lean against the counter to keep from toppling.

He had a point. She *hated* when he had a point. Letting out a sigh, she shut her eyes. "Fine."

"Good. Now. Come on." Without giving her a moment to protest, he scooped her up in his arms. "Let's get some food in you."

"Why did you tell him?" She glared at the side of his face as he carried her down the stairs toward the kitchen area. She'd be angry at him for carrying her around, but he was right to assume that her and a spiral staircase would be a recipe for a very painful fall.

"I didn't." His expression smoothed into a hard one. "After I attacked you, I... snapped out of it, just before killing you. Ivan found me with you. As you truly are, tail and all. There was no point denying any of it at that point."

He believed he attacked her. He didn't remember?

She didn't know how to feel about that. Relieved. Ashamed, weirdly. Like she had gotten away with something. "It wasn't your fault, what happened."

Raziel didn't speak as he set her down on the sofa in his living room. Ivan was standing in the kitchen over the stove, stirring something that smelled phenomenal. Something that smelled very much like home.

"What are you making?" She very, *very* much wanted Ivan dead. But she wouldn't stand a chance against the enormous vampire when she couldn't stand. No, she'd have to wait. Or talk Raziel into it. But for the moment, a more pressing mystery was in front of her.

"Weird stew," was all Ivan replied with.

Raziel rolled his eyes as he headed over to the kitchen and started rustling around for a bowl and a spoon. "I sent him down to the gray zone, near the Wild. Sent him to meet with some of your people. Asked them what would heal you."

The tea. "You made *an'ahnaka*." She snorted and then lost it again laughing. "That wasn't a dream. Oh, Mother moon—how much did you pay them?"

"It's not important." Raziel's back was to her as he nudged Ivan out of the way to ladle stew into a bowl.

"A lot," Ivan interjected as he left his post by the stove to go stand by the wall, his arms crossed over his massive chest. "Said it was all *fae magic*."

"You got played." She laughed again. "Oh, that's *hysterical*. Magic. It's literally—it's just one of those home recipes your mother made for you when you had the flu."

Raziel handed her the bowl of stew, a troubled look on his face as he moved to sit down in the plush chair across from the sofa.

"Your mother didn't make you anything when you were sick? I'm not surprised." She smelled the soup. The herbs in it came from the Wild. She hadn't had anything like it in almost a century, and it almost made her want to cry. The meat in it was from the Wild as well, she could tell from the gaminess of it. It wasn't grown on a farm like the human cows or chickens. It just *smelled* better. And it would taste the same.

"Vampires don't get sick." Raziel shook his head. "I don't really have anything to compare to what you're describing."

Odd. She'd never considered that. On one hand, that must

be useful—to not have to worry about children getting sick and dying. On the other hand, why did she feel *bad* for him? Like he'd missed out on something crucial, like having his mother make a bowl of meat stew for him?

"It's not magic. But it's appreciated." Nadi started eating the stew. It wasn't as good as she remembered—she figured neither Ivan nor Raziel were terribly great cooks—but she'd cut them some slack. "Now, can we talk about the three-hundred-pound *hyi'n* in the room?"

"I filled him in on everything." Raziel laced his fingers in front of him as he sat back in his chair. "No need."

"Everything." She stared at Raziel flatly. "Now he *really* needs to die. Are you insane?"

"I trust Ivan more than I trust myself, Nadi. He won't betray us." Raziel shook his head.

"If that were true, you would have included him from the beginning!" She paused, taking a breath. She really had to avoid shouting right now, she'd pass out into her soup.

"I knew how you'd react. And at the time, it wasn't necessary."

"Wasn't—" She really had to calm down. She took a long moment to steady herself and work on getting her heart rate under control. "This is a risk we can't afford. I vote that we kill him."

"You want to do this democratically? Very well. Let's vote. I vote that we *don't* kill him." Raziel smiled. "Ivan?"

"I vote for not killing me."

"Lords below." She pinched the bridge of her nose. She was going to scream. She was dealing with children. "He's a liability. How do you know he's not working for your brother? Or your sister?"

"I trust Ivan's loyalty to me far more than I trust yours, Nadi. And I have plenty of proof to back up that statement. Would you like me to elaborate?" Raziel arched a dark eyebrow. She found it deeply irritating that someone who had clearly been through the wringer like him could also still look so *put together* at the same time.

"No. I don't need you to *elaborate*, Raziel. But the fact of the matter is, we don't need more variables. Especially not at this stage, when we're so close to failure."

"So close to failure? How do you figure? I think this turn of events works perfectly for us." Raziel grinned. A flash of the Serpent returned to his features.

He'd been scheming while she was unconscious.

Lowering the bowl of stew to her lap, she found herself a little too intrigued by the wicked glint in those crimson eyes of his. "Raziel Nostrom, what are you planning?"

* * *

Fae were resilient creatures, Raziel would have to give them that. His mother often spoke of them like cockroaches—insects that were seemingly impossible to kill.

He'd never been more grateful for their pernicious nature. If Nadi were a different woman, she would still be in bed. In fact, he wished she would listen to reason and rest. But he knew she wouldn't, so he didn't waste his words.

At least she didn't try to claw at Ivan in her current state. She was smart enough to know when to bide her time. But if he didn't get her assurances that Ivan was *safe*, he would have to worry about protecting his bodyguard from his... whatever she was.

Nemesis? Lover?

Both were true.

But the question remained what she had become.

He knew that she was a ghost that would haunt him for the rest of his days, however long they lasted, and in whatever form she might take. And if anyone could die and haunt him from beyond the grave, it would be her, he was certain of it.

What else?

He knew what burned in his heart.

But what about hers?

She'd spared his life. Chosen to save it. *Twice.* That was no act of conscience. No mere moment of pity or mercy. And his siblings had granted her leverage that was greater than his own—so it wasn't about his position of power either.

It had to be something more. But what else was it tangled up in? What else was threatening to drag it down into the depths of the void like it had with Braen?

Raziel pushed those thoughts away to the corners of his mind. He had to focus on the matter at hand.

She had gone back to eating her stew. Good. She needed it. Her body was healing quickly, despite the amount of blood he had drained from her—but he would need her on her feet.

He cracked his neck from one side to the other. Every fiber of his body ached. "From the family's point of view, we were successful in our task. We slaughtered Braen, as we were commanded. While we must be very careful to watch our backs, we can't be invisible either. Whatever games my brother and sister wished to play, I suggest you keep stringing them along. Continued information from them will be crucial."

"How long was I out?" She touched her neck gently. It was bandaged.

He noted that she did not wish to elaborate on his siblings' *games.* Interesting. He couldn't say that he blamed her. "Thirty-six hours."

She hummed. "Too much time."

"No use mourning it." He would far rather mourn the lost hours than be mourning her. "Lana marries Zabriel in a week."

Nadi sighed. "Not much time to plan... whatever it is you're planning. I hope it's more foolproof than our *Braen* scheme." She shot him a look.

Raziel grimaced. "I bore the brunt of that misstep, not you."

She arched an eyebrow at him, clearly questioning that statement. But she said nothing.

He grunted. He was nearly mended, but he was still feeling the effects of being drained entirely of blood. "The wedding will provide us decent cover for an attack. But in the meanwhile, we'll need to make our appearances. Kiss the ring. Play the dutiful, obedient, subservient, and repentant children."

She snorted. "We have to keep it believable, Raz."

Ivan chuckled.

She shot him a look.

The bodyguard shrugged. "What? S'funny."

Nadi's expression was one of such absolutely beleaguered exhaustion, it was Raziel's turn to chuckle. And when had Nadi begun to refer to him as *Raz*? He had earned a nickname. He was honestly flattered. "Mael will be our target."

"Counterpoint." Nadi tilted her head to the side and scratched at the edge of her bandage on her throat. "I think Volencia should be the first to die, not Mael. Cut off the heads of the *issha*."

Raziel had no idea what an *issha* was, or why it had more than one head, but he understood the gist well enough. "I want her dead just as much as you do, believe me. There is no one in this world who harbors more hate for that whore than I do. But this needs to be done in sequence. Mael is more dangerous than you think. Without him, she will be rendered toothless."

"Don't slander whores like that." She sipped her water. "I know plenty of wonderful whores..." Would she fight him? Or would she listen? Tension hung in the air for a long moment, as dark opal eyes met his. "Your plans get me in a lot of trouble. But, fine. However—if I see a chance to take her out, clean? I'm doing it."

That, he knew he wasn't going to be able to argue his way out of. But perhaps he could still get another bargain from their negotiation. "All right. In exchange, you will have to give me your word that you won't attempt to murder Ivan."

"I don't like him knowing my secret." Nadi grimaced, baring her teeth. Her canines were much shorter than a vampire's—but were still sharper than a human's were capable of being. "He shouldn't be allowed to live. This is a stupid risk."

"Or, we need to admit that we can't do this with just the two of us. We'll need someone watching our backs. And having him know the truth will make this *much* easier." Raziel sat forward, leaning his elbows on his knees. He was still starving. He'd have to go out and feed soon, but he wanted to ensure that Nadi was asleep in bed before he did so. Bottles of blood were one thing, but he needed something—*someone*—fresh. "Do we have a deal, little fae?"

With a faint, frustrated growl, she tucked her knees up under her on the sofa and pulled a thick blanket around her shoulders. "Fine. Okay. *Deal.* But Ivan—if I even get a *whisper* of a *hint* that you *might* be working for someone else? I am going to cut off your balls, string them up with wire, and make you wear them as nipple tassels before I finish letting you die."

A grin split Ivan's face. "You're right, boss. I like her a *lot* more than Monica."

"Then, we have our next steps. We play our parts. And we plan to murder Mael at my sister's wedding." Reaching down, Raziel scooped Nadi up in his arms. She didn't make a fuss about it and looped her arm behind his neck. "Just another cheerful Nostrom family affair."

Everything was starting to feel dangerously like it might have a chance of working.

Which meant it was all more than likely going to come crashing down.

SIXTEEN

Nadi had never realized it before that day, but suddenly, she did.

She *despised* perfection.

In her experience, the more polished something appeared, the more rot festered beneath its surface. Either in its making, or in the mold it was simply covering up, like so much decay beneath layers of paint.

And nothing proved this theory more conclusively than the Nostrom family.

She stood beside Raziel in the foyer of Volencia's estate, wearing Monica's face once more. The dress she'd chosen was deliberately understated – a simple black sheath that fell just below her knees. Her hair was pulled back in a severe style that emphasized the sharp contours of her borrowed face. Just enough makeup to hide the lingering pallor from her near-death experience.

Her glamor hid the still-healing wounds on her throat.

Wounds that Raziel had given her.

Wounds she had offered herself up to receive.

The thought still made her dizzy. Three days had passed

since she had made that choice, and she still couldn't fully comprehend her own decision. Whatever tenuous thread had been forming between them had solidified into something she couldn't name—*refused* to name.

Something that terrified her more than any monster she'd encountered in the Wild, or any of the more mundanely shaped monsters that walked the metropolis.

"Ready?" Raziel murmured, his voice pitched low enough that only she could hear.

She met his gaze, taking in the perfect facade he'd constructed. His suit was impeccable, his posture relaxed but alert. No outward sign remained of the silver bullets that had torn through his flesh, or the blood starvation that had nearly killed him. Only she knew how much effort it took him to maintain the veneer of strength.

"Yeah. Sure. As I'll ever be," she replied, matching his quiet tone.

The grand doors to the main hall opened, revealing a gathering of Nostroms. Not the full council this time, but the inner circle—Volencia seated regally at the head of a long dining table, Mael at her right, Lana at her left. A handful of lesser family members filled the remaining seats, their expressions a careful blend of interest and wariness.

"The conquering heroes return," Volencia's voice cut through the room like a blade. The sarcasm was thick. "We were beginning to wonder if you'd joined Braen in the afterlife."

Nadi kept her expression fixed in the deferential mask she'd crafted for Monica—a blend of nervousness and determination that seemed to satisfy the Nostroms' expectations.

"My apologies for the delay, Mother." Raziel tucked his hands into his coat pockets. His tone was one that hovered perfectly between respect and confidence. "We thought it best to ensure we weren't followed by any of Braen's loyalists. He had no knowledge of the wedding, so we thought it prudent that our involvement wasn't traceable to the rest of the family and could just be blamed on my past history. We lay low in case we were caught."

"That was wise," Mael offered, his golden eyes studying them both with unsettling intensity. "The Rosovs are notoriously unforgiving, even to their own kind. And while his siblings asked us to be rid of him, the others were in the dark."

Lana's lips curved into a smile that never reached her eyes. "Do join us. We were just discussing the wedding preparations. Everything has gone exactly to plan." The sarcasm was so thick Nadi could almost have cut it with a knife. "Braen's death has left the city reeling, and the turmoil made Zabriel and I's wedding the *perfect* solution to make sure everyone came out of this stronger and richer."

Raziel guided Nadi to the two empty seats near the other end of the table—positioned just far enough from Volencia to emphasize their current standing in the family hierarchy. A servant immediately appeared, pouring bloodwine into crystal goblets before them.

"To successful ventures," Volencia raised her glass in a toast that felt more like a threat than a celebration. "And to Braen Rosov's long-overdue demise."

The gathered vampires echoed the sentiment, their voices a cold chorus that sent a chill down Nadi's spine. She lifted her glass and pretended to sip, careful not to actually consume the contents. The last thing she needed was to reveal her disgust for blood.

"Tell us, brother," Lana leaned forward, her magenta eyes gleaming with barely concealed excitement. "How did our dear friend Braen meet his end?"

Raziel's expression remained neutral, though Nadi caught the slight tension in his jaw. "Cleanly. As instructed."

"Cleanly?" Mael laughed, the sound echoing off the vaulted ceiling. "That's hardly your style, Serpent."

"I can be efficient when necessary." Raziel's voice was like cold iron.

Volencia tapped a long nail against her glass. "I'm told there was quite a mess in the gardens. That you were injured, Raziel." Her eyes narrowed. "That doesn't sound particularly 'clean' to me. Sounds terribly sloppy."

Nadi felt Raziel's leg press against hers underneath the table—a warning. They had anticipated this. The Nostroms had spies everywhere.

"I was badly wounded," Raziel admitted with practiced regret. "Braen was better prepared than your intelligence suggested."

"And yet," Volencia's gaze shifted to Nadi, "here you both are. Alive and well. How... fortunate."

The implication hung in the air like a guillotine blade. They weren't supposed to both return. One or both of them had been meant to die in that garden alongside Braen. That much was painfully obvious.

"Indeed." Raziel's voice betrayed nothing. "Monica proved herself quite valuable. Her abilities were instrumental to our escape."

All eyes turned to her, and Nadi channeled every ounce of Monica's personality as she lowered her gaze demurely. "I simply did what was needed, Lady Volencia."

"How modest!" Lana giggled, her voice dripping with false sweetness. "Perhaps you'll share the details with me later, sister. I do so love a good story."

"Of course." Nadi knew that refusal wasn't an option.

Volencia waved a hand dismissively. "The deed is done, regardless of the methods. Zabriel seems pleased with the outcome, which is what matters." Her cold eyes focused on Raziel again. "He speaks highly of your loyalty to family, my son. A quality I've sometimes questioned."

"Family is everything, Mother." Raziel's lie was so convincing that even Nadi almost believed it.

Volencia smiled, the expression never touching her eyes. "Indeed, it is." She turned her attention to the rest of the table. "Now, as to the wedding—"

The conversation shifted to preparations for Lana's upcoming nuptials. Guest lists, security measures, political considerations, who sat where, all discussed with the same cold calculation one might apply to a military campaign. Nadi contributed only when directly addressed—which was once, about how steak from the outer cities should be properly prepared—and she kept her response brief and said while she had her experience from home, she was certain Volencia's chefs very likely knew best.

Through it all, she observed. The way Mael watched her when he thought she wasn't looking. The knowing glances Lana cast toward her brother. The subtle ways Volencia undermined and controlled each interaction.

It was like watching spiders weave overlapping webs, each seeking to ensnare the others while avoiding entanglement themselves.

What she noticed most of all, however, was that Raziel was never addressed *once*.

After what felt like an eternity, Volencia rose from her seat. "I believe that covers everything of importance. Mael, you'll oversee the security arrangements as discussed. Lana, ensure your dress fittings are completed by tomorrow evening."

Her gaze swept over the gathered vampires, landing finally on Raziel and Nadi. "One last thing. *You two* will maintain a low profile until the wedding. The Rosovs are eager to make this alliance. I will not have you two risking this with any of your *antics*."

"Of course, Mother," Raziel inclined his head slightly.

"Monica," Lana's voice cut through the conversation,

"would you mind assisting me with something before you leave? Dress question. *Girl thing.* You understand, brother."

Nadi felt Raziel tense beside her. This was expected—one of his siblings would try to separate them. They had planned for it.

"Of course." Nadi rose from her seat.

Raziel's hand brushed against hers—a subtle reminder of their agreement. Play along. Gather information. Stay alive. But remember whose side she had chosen.

Lana led her from the dining room, not toward her personal chambers as Nadi expected, but to a small antechamber near the east wing of the estate. When they entered, Mael was already waiting, his massive frame seeming to fill the modest space.

The door closed behind them with an ominous click.

"Well," Lana smiled, dropping all pretense of warmth, "that was quite the performance in there. Mother almost seemed to believe you both survived through skill rather than design."

Nadi allowed the mask of *deferential Monica* to slip just slightly, revealing a hint of her true self. "I'm not sure what you mean."

"Please." Mael moved closer, his golden eyes studying her face intently. "We're alone now. There's no need for games."

"No games." Nadi maintained her harder expression. She was in a room with two of the most powerful vampires in Runne. She had to remember that. "Braen is dead, as required."

"Yes, and yet... Raziel is alive." Lana circled her slowly, like a *shinihe* assessing its prey. "And you were gone for three days. Three days, Monica. What happened during those *three days?*"

Nadi had prepared for this. Had rehearsed her lies carefully with Raziel until they were polished to a perfect shine. And they both knew that sometimes, the most convincing lies contained fragments of truth.

"I was injured," she said softly, allowing real vulnerability to enter her voice. "Badly."

Mael's expression shifted immediately, concern replacing suspicion. "How?"

Nadi lowered her eyes, one hand moving to her throat. She shifted the collar of her dress to show the false, purplish bruise she had let show through her glamor just for this occasion. "One of Braen's guards. He had a silver blade. He... slit my throat." She let her voice tremble slightly. "I've never... I've never felt pain like that before. It was meant for Raziel. I just happened to be wearing his face at the time."

"Silver?" Lana's eyebrows rose. "For any vampire, it's an almost guaranteed death sentence, let alone a fledgling."

"Yeah." Nadi let a shudder pass through her. "I learned that the hard way."

"And where was my brother during this attack?" Mael moved closer, his expression softening further. "Why didn't he protect you?"

Nadi hesitated, the perfect picture of a woman torn between loyalty, fear, and perhaps a little bit of temptation. "He... He was dealing with Braen. It happened so quickly."

"I see." Mael exchanged a glance with Lana. "And these injuries kept you hidden for three days?"

"Raziel didn't want to return until I could maintain my composure." She shrugged. "He said it would raise too many questions if I appeared... damaged."

"How considerate of him," Lana's voice dripped with disdain. "And where exactly did you recuperate? Not at his estate, surely."

"No." Nadi shook her head. And it was clear Lana already knew that from her spies, anyway. "Somewhere else. A property owned by Ivan, I think. I honestly don't know. I wasn't really awake when we got there or when we left. Everything has been a bit hazy."

Mael's massive hand settled on her shoulder, surprisingly gentle. "You poor thing. My brother has a habit of letting others suffer for his mistakes." His golden eyes searched hers. "You understand now, don't you? What I was trying to warn you about?"

Nadi allowed herself to lean into his touch, just slightly. Just enough to suggest vulnerability. "He did save me," she whispered, the half-truth easier to deliver than she expected. "He could have left me to die there."

"But at what cost?" Lana snarled with shocking vitriol. "What did he demand in return for this *salvation*?"

Nadi flinched, the reaction not entirely feigned. The memory of Raziel's fangs at her throat, of her life draining away, was still too fresh. "I... I don't know. But I feel myself being sucked in deeper and I don't know if I can ever escape." That was the moons' honest truth, wasn't it?

Lana looked like her heart broke in half. The woman took Nadi into her arms and held her in an embrace that felt *real*. Slowly, the blonde released her, but her pink eyes lingered on hers, searching for something. "I am so sorry."

Mael's expression darkened. "My brother never does anything without calculating the potential benefits for himself." His thumb stroked her shoulder in what was clearly meant to be a comforting gesture. "Did he hurt you, Monica? You can tell us."

The question hung in the air between them, weighted with implications. Nadi could see what they wanted—confirmation of Raziel's cruelty, evidence they could use against him. And part of her, the part that still burned with the need for vengeance, whispered that she should give it to them. Use their hatred of their brother to her advantage.

But the truth was, Raziel hadn't hurt her. Not deliberately. He had been lost in blood starvation, barely conscious of his actions. And she had offered herself willingly. And he had stopped himself from killing her.

She wondered what Mael would think if he knew the truth —that she had chosen to save Raziel's life at nearly the cost of her own. That in that moment of decision, her hatred had been overcome by something far more complicated and dangerous.

"Monica?" Mael prompted, his voice gentle but insistent.

Nadi let tears fill her eyes. Ones that weren't entirely fabricated. She was so tired of weaving lies within lies, of keeping track of which version of herself she was supposed to be in each moment. "I'm sorry. I can't..."

The pain wasn't feigned. The exhaustion was real. She was just carefully directing it toward the narrative they wanted to hear.

"It's all right." It was Mael's turn to pull her into an embrace, his massive frame enveloping her completely. "You don't have to say it. We understand. Believe us, we understand."

Over his shoulder, Nadi caught Lana's expression—a mixture of satisfaction and calculation that sent a chill down her spine. Whatever game the Sweetheart Mistress was playing, she wasn't motivated by concern for Monica's well-being.

"The important thing," Lana's tone was suddenly soft with manufactured sympathy, "is that you survived. And now you have choices, Monica. Real choices."

Mael released her, though his hands remained on her shoulders. "Remember what I told you. When the time comes, I can protect you from him. From *all* of this."

"We both can," Lana added. "After the wedding, everything will change. The question is, where will you stand when it does?"

The implication was clear. Their offers still stood—betrayal for protection. Raziel's life in exchange for a place in the family. The question was, *what were they planning?*

Nadi lowered her gaze, playing the part of the conflicted

victim once more. "I don't know what to do," she whispered. "I'm afraid."

"Fear is wise in this family," Mael said grimly. "But you don't have to decide anything now. Just... keep your eyes open. And remember that you have allies."

"Does your mother suspect anything?" Nadi asked, deliberately changing the subject. "About... about us taking so long to return?"

Lana's laugh was brittle. "Mother suspects everything and everyone. It's how she's survived this long." She touched Nadi's arm lightly. "But don't worry about her. Focus on keeping yourself alive until the wedding."

"And after?" She allowed herself once more to let real fear and vulnerability play on her voice. "Once you've... made whatever move it is you're making?"

"After," Mael replied, his golden eyes meeting hers with disturbing intensity, "you'll need to make your choice. And quickly. You'll know when the moment comes."

Lana glanced toward the door. "You should return to Raziel before he becomes suspicious. Remember—say nothing of our conversation."

Nadi nodded, straightening her posture and carefully reassembling the mask over the mask over the mask she wore every day to survive this stupid political nonsense. "Thank you. Both of you."

As she turned to leave, Mael caught her hand. "One more thing. Where is Raziel keeping the ledger from Braen's club? The one with the trafficking records?"

The question caught her off guard. She hadn't expected them to know about that. "I honestly don't know. He didn't tell me." She paused. "But I think I could get it."

Mael studied her face for a long moment, then released her hand. "Of course he didn't. My brother trusts no one, not even those closest to him. But if you *could* get it, Monica, that would be very valuable."

"I'll see what I can do."

After Nadi left the room, she paused in the corridor, taking a moment to steady her breathing. The conversation replayed in her mind, fragments of truth and lies twisting together until she could barely separate one from the other.

She found Raziel waiting for her in the main foyer, his expression neutral but his eyes alert. He offered her his arm as they descended the grand staircase, leaving Volencia's estate behind them.

It wasn't until they were sealed in the privacy of his car, Ivan at the wheel and the privacy partition raised, that either of them spoke.

"Well?" He didn't bother keeping his voice quiet. Ivan knew everything now. Nadi had to admit, unfortunately, that it was nice having someone "in" on the situation.

Nadi leaned back against the leather seat, suddenly exhausted. "They wanted to know where we've been for the past three days. I told them I was injured in the fight, but I left out your wounds."

"And they believed you?"

She turned to look at him, studying the blank expression he wore, one that revealed nothing of the violent, desperate creature she had seen in his tower. Nothing of the man who had wept as he held her dying body.

"Mael did," she finally replied. "He seemed genuinely concerned."

Raziel's expression hardened almost imperceptibly. "And Lana?"

"Lana is playing her own game." Nadi shifted her gaze to the window, watching the metropolis blur past them. "And Mael asked where Braen's ledger is."

Raziel's hands stilled in his lap. "That's... interesting. How would he know about that?"

"I don't know."

"And what did you tell them?"

"That I had no idea where you've hidden it." She sighed. And left it there. "Raziel, they're both still trying to turn me against you. They're convinced the wedding is going to change everything."

"They're not wrong about that," he murmured, almost to himself.

Nadi felt a chill at his words. The wedding would change everything—just not in the way Mael and Lana expected. Not if Raziel and Nadi's plan succeeded.

But as the car carried them back toward Raziel's estate, she couldn't shake the feeling that they were all dancing on the edge of a precipice. That the intricate web of lies and conspiracies they had woven was about to unravel, one delicate strand at a time. It was clear that theirs wasn't the only plan in play.

And she wasn't sure any of them would survive the fall.

SEVENTEEN

Raziel watched the metropolis from the window of his study, a glass of bloodwine untouched in his hand. The meeting with his family had gone as well as could be expected—false pleasantries masking deadly politics and loathing. A Nostrom family tradition.

Night had fallen, the two moons hanging in the sky like mismatched eyes watching the world below. The Father moon, full and bright; the Mother moon, a thin black crescent cutting through the darkness, only visible in its darker emptiness.

Behind him, the door opened. Without turning, he knew it was Nadi. He'd recognize her sound and scent anywhere now—the pattern of her steps, and that faint hint of sea salt and something else, something fae, that lingered beneath whatever perfume she wore as Monica.

"You've been quiet since we returned." Her footsteps were barely audible against the hardwood floor when she was herself. He wondered if that was because she was fae, or if that was because she was a practiced assassin.

Raziel turned, taking in the sight of her. She'd abandoned Monica's appearance within the privacy of his home, and her pale green-blue skin was nearly luminescent in the low light. He preferred her this way—real, unfettered by the lies they wore like armor everywhere else.

"I've been thinking," he replied, setting down his untouched glass. "About my siblings. About what they might have offered you. I know you're considering taking their offers and turning on me, even now."

Her expression tightened almost imperceptibly. Most wouldn't have noticed, but Raziel had spent centuries reading the tiny signs in the expressions of his enemies. And despite everything, despite whatever was growing between them, Nadi remained a potential threat. Perhaps the most dangerous he'd ever encountered.

Not undoubtably so.

"You've known all along." It wasn't a question.

"I suspected." He moved away from the window, circling his desk to stand before her. "Mael has always been transparent in his desires. And Lana..." He chuckled mirthlessly. "Lana has never seen a weapon she didn't want to wield herself."

Nadi held his gaze, unflinching. He could see the calculation behind those opalescent eyes—weighing what to tell him, what to conceal. Finally, the words hanging in the air like the daggers she loved to wield, she spoke. "They want me to kill you."

Despite having anticipated this, hearing it spoken aloud sent a cold sensation rippling through him. Not fear—he'd long since had that beaten out of him—but something else. Something almost like disappointment.

No. Worse than that.

Rejection.

"Both of them? Separately?" He kept his tone and his face neutral.

"Yes and no. I think they're working separately most of the time, but together for a single goal at the moment." She moved past him to pour herself a glass of alcohol, her movements fluid and precise. "Mael approached me first. He claims he wants to protect me from the monster he believes you to be." She turned back to face him, a sardonic smile playing at her lips. "Ironic, considering what I am."

"And Lana?"

"Lana is more direct. She offered me your seat at the table once you're gone." Nadi sipped her drink, watching him over the rim of the glass. "She thinks I'm a spy, though she doesn't know what kind. She finds it 'fantastic,' to use her word. I don't think she's told Mael her suspicions."

Raziel laughed, the sound echoing in the quiet room. "Of course she does. My sister has always appreciated audacity." He studied Nadi's face, searching for any sign of deception. "And how did you respond to these generous offers?"

"I played along." She set her glass down with a clink. "I let them believe I'm considering their proposals. That I'm afraid of you, that I might be willing to betray you if given enough incentive."

"And are you?" He asked the question before he could stop himself.

Something shifted in her expression—a flicker of surprise, perhaps even hurt. "If I were, would I be telling you about their offers now?"

"Maybe, maybe not." Slowly, he took a step closer to her. "If you thought it would gain my trust. Make me lower my guard. If it served a purpose for you."

She didn't back away. "Then why ask? If you'll only doubt my answer?"

It was a fair question. Why indeed? He'd spent centuries trusting no one, questioning every motive, seeing manipulation in every kindness. It had kept him alive. Why change that pattern now, for this fae assassin who had infiltrated his life with the express purpose of destroying him?

"Because I find myself wanting to believe you."

Nadi's eyes widened slightly, the only visible reaction to his admission. "Bullshit. You wouldn't be so reckless."

"It is reckless." He reached out, tracing the line of her jaw with his fingertips. "Nearly as reckless as sparing my life was for you."

She didn't flinch from his touch. "Yet here we are."

"Here we are," he agreed. "Both of us making choices that go very much against our... better natures."

Her hand caught his. She held it against her cheek for a moment before lowering it. "I'm not betraying you to your siblings, Raziel. Not now. We have a deal—your family falls, and then we settle our score."

It wasn't quite the declaration of loyalty he might have wanted, but it was honest. And honesty, he was beginning to realize, was a rare and precious thing in his world.

"Then, we're still allies." He stepped back to give her space.

"We're something." Her voice was softer than he was accustomed to hearing from her. "I'm not sure 'allies' fully captures it anymore."

The admission hung between them, neither of them willing to define that "something" more precisely. To name it would be to acknowledge it, and acknowledgment would make it real. Dangerous. Potentially fatal for them both.

"Tell me more about your conversation with my siblings." He proverbially retreated to safer ground. "What exactly does Mael claim he can offer you?"

Nadi followed his lead, her posture relaxing slightly. "Protection. If you do have to live, a place in the family hierarchy, positioned as the bridge between you and him. He seems to genuinely believe that keeping you alive but controlled is preferable to killing you."

"How magnanimous of him." Raziel's lip curled. "And what does my dear brother think would control me?"

"Me, of course." She huffed a laugh. "He thinks I'm your weakness."

The statement should have angered him. Throughout his long life, he'd systematically eliminated anything that could be used against him, any vulnerability that might be exploited. Weapons had no hearts to break.

Wincing, he turned his back to her to look out the window. He struggled to find the strength to deny the accusation. "He'll see that I've gone to considerable lengths to keep you alive now."

Silence stretched between them for a long minute, as a question burned through him like acid. "Do you trust me, Nadi?"

Her long pause before she answered was more of an answer than her response. "I'm not sure."

"Trust is a luxury neither of us can afford. Certainly something we haven't been able to enjoy in the past. But perhaps we can manage something adjacent to it. A mutual understanding."

"Based on what?"

"On the fact that we've both had opportunities to destroy each other and chosen not to take them." He moved to the sideboard, pouring himself a fresh glass of bloodwine. "On the fact that, despite everything, we keep choosing each other over alternatives that would objectively benefit us more."

She was studying him, half curious, half dubious. "That's not trust. That's... mutual insanity."

A smile tugged at his lips. "Is there a difference in our case?"

"Fair point." She almost smiled back. "So, what now? We continue our charade? Let your siblings believe they're turning me against you?"

"Yes." He sipped his drink, the rich flavor of blood barely registering. It was a distraction. And a poor substitute for what he really wanted—hers. "We use their arrogance against them.

Let them think they've found your price, that you're malleable, falling under their influence."

"While we plan their deaths."

"Precisely. Starting with Mael at the wedding."

Nadi nodded, her expression turning thoughtful. "Mael mentioned the ledger from Braen's club. I can use it as bait."

"It shouldn't matter to him. We need to find out why he needs it."

"There are only three reasons I can think of. Either he was involved, he plans to blackmail someone who was, or he plans to use it as a bargaining chip."

"Or some combination of the three." Raziel's mind raced with the implications. Her quick assessment of the situation was correct, but *which* of the options remained the question. "The ledger could be valuable leverage against more than just the Rosovs. If certain names appear in those records..."

"It could topple more than one powerful family," Nadi agreed. "Where is it?"

Raziel hesitated. This was the moment—to trust or not to trust. The ledger was one of the few pieces of concrete evidence they had, a potential weapon against multiple enemies. Sharing its location would be a significant risk.

"It's in a safe deposit box at the Mercantile Exchange Bank," he said finally. "Box number 227. Ivan has the key, but the security override code is 57-82-97. Even without the key, that will get you in."

The look of surprise on her face was genuine. "You're actually telling me?"

"If I were to die, you would need access to it." He finished his wine, setting the glass aside. "Consider it... a long overdue wedding gift."

She studied him, as if trying to decode some hidden meaning in his words. "This *mutual understanding* we're building really is insanity. I don't know if I like it."

"Imagine how I feel." He chuckled.

Silence settled between them, not uncomfortable but charged, all the same. He found himself watching the subtle changes in her expression, the way the moonlight played across her features. She was beautiful in a way that defied conventional understanding—alien and familiar all at once. Somehow *unreal.* He was surrounded by beauty every moment of his life. He had never had a shortage of it. Human or vampiric, it had always been within his reach. Whatever he had wanted, he could have it. But her? Something about her was ethereal. Like a ghost, stepping between rooms in the middle of the night.

Something he could not *take.* Something he might not ever truly have. Something that perhaps only ever visited him for a fleeting moment.

"I should rest," she said finally, turning toward the door. "Tomorrow will be another performance."

"Nadi." He couldn't help himself. Her name on his lips stopped her, and she glanced back at him. He shouldn't. But he did, anyway. "Stay."

Her pause was almost imperceptible. "That's not a good idea."

"Absolutely not," he conceded. "But I find I'm developing a taste for bad ideas lately."

A small smile touched her lips. Lips he hungered for. "Is that what I am? A bad idea?"

"The worst I've ever had." He stepped closer, drawn to her like a moth to flame. "Catastrophic."

She didn't move away. "And yet?"

"And yet," he reached for her, fingers trailing down her arm, "I can't seem to stop."

The contact sent a ripple of awareness through him. This wasn't like the other times between them—the raw, angry passion or the calculated seduction and control. This was something quieter. Almost tender.

Which made it all the more dangerous.

When she took his hand, lacing her fingers through his, it felt like surrender. Whose, he couldn't say.

"This is madness," she whispered, even as she moved closer.

"Undoubtedly." His free hand brushed her hair back from her face.

"We should stop."

"We should."

Neither of them moved away.

When their lips met, it wasn't with the desperate hunger of previous encounters. This kiss was slower, deeper, an exploration rather than a conquest. Her hands slid up his chest, coming to rest at the back of his neck, drawing him closer.

He felt the shift between them—something fundamentally changing in the gravity that drew them together. The volatility was still there, the history of blood and vengeance that could never be erased. But alongside it, something new had taken root. Something neither of them had anticipated or sought.

His hands traced the curve of her waist, the delicate line of her spine, memorizing her as if this might be the last time. As if tomorrow the world might end—which, given their plans, wasn't entirely implausible.

They moved together toward his bedroom, shedding layers of clothing and pretense with each step. By the time they reached his bed, they were stripped bare in more ways than one.

In the silver moonlight that spilled through the windows, he saw her true form—the pale green-blue of her skin, the opalescent shimmer of her eyes. No disguises, no facades. Just Nadi, the fae assassin who had come to kill him and had somehow become essential to his existence instead.

As they came together on the bed, skin against skin, breath mingling, Raziel found himself confronting a truth he'd been avoiding.

This wasn't just physical desire anymore.

It wasn't just manipulation or strategy or momentary weakness.

This was intimacy. Real, terrifying intimacy.

Her legs wrapped around his waist, drawing him closer as he entered her. The sound she made, a soft gasp of pleasure, affected him more deeply than he cared to admit. He moved slowly, savoring each moment, each sensation—the heat of her body, the rhythm of her heartbeat, the way her fingers pressed into his shoulders as if anchoring herself to him.

"Raziel," she breathed his name against his lips, and something in him broke.

He captured her mouth with his, deepening the kiss as they moved together. No power struggles, no domination. Not this time. For once, they were equals—both vulnerable, both surrendering something precious to the other.

And he felt as though he were *claiming* her in a way that he never could with all his collections of toys and chains and leather.

As they climbed toward release, bodies entwined and breaths synchronized, he knew he had to face the truth.

He had fallen in love with her.

He loved the woman who had sworn to destroy him.

More than anything else in his life, *he loved her.*

And he needed her.

And somehow, that felt like the truest thing he'd ever experienced.

When they finally shattered together, pleasure washing over them in waves, he held her close, unwilling to break the connection between them. For a moment—just a moment—the world beyond this room ceased to exist. No family plots, no vengeance, no inevitable reckoning.

Just this. Just them.

Afterward, as they lay tangled in the sheets and in each other, her head resting on his chest and his fingers tracing patterns on her skin, neither spoke. Words seemed inadequate, potentially ruinous to the fragile peace they'd found.

He knew this couldn't last. Knew that the path ahead was lined with blood and betrayal and consequences neither of them could fully predict. Knew that by all rights, one of them should be dead at the other's hand.

But for tonight, in the quiet darkness of his bedroom, with Nadi's breath warm against his skin and her heartbeat steady under his palm, he allowed himself something he hadn't permitted in centuries: hope.

Not for redemption—he was far beyond that. Not for forgiveness—some sins could never be absolved.

But for the possibility that amid all the death and destruction they had planned, something might survive. Something worth preserving.

Even if it destroyed them both.

EIGHTEEN

The morning light streaming through Raziel's bedroom windows felt different now. Nadi watched the specks of dust dance in the golden beams, her head resting on his chest. Something fundamental had changed during the night—a line crossed that couldn't be uncrossed.

She should have felt trapped. Should have been planning her escape. Not so long ago, that had been precisely what she had been doing. Instead, she found herself tracing lazy patterns on his skin, memorizing the feel of him.

He might be gone soon, after all.

And that feeling... hurt her.

Which was a whole different thing to reflect on.

"You're thinking too loudly." His voice was still rough with sleep. Slowly, he began combing his fingers through her hair, the gesture surprisingly gentle.

"Someone has to think in this relationship," she teased, immediately regretting the word choice. *Relationship.* As if that was what this was.

His hand stilled. "Is that what we're calling this now?"

She lifted her head to look at him, taking in the sharp angles of his face in the morning light. Even relaxed, he looked dangerous. A predator pretending to be domesticated. "I don't know what to call it."

"Neither do I." Red eyes studied her. "But whatever it is, we have more pressing concerns today."

Right. The wedding preparations. She would have to head over to Lana's for continued *essential feminine consultations* regarding the ceremony. Another performance to maintain, another layer of deception to navigate.

"What time am I expected?" Nadi sat up, immediately missing the feeling of his body against hers.

"Within the hour." Raziel's eyes tracked her movements as she rose from the bed. "Remember what we discussed. Gather intelligence about the security arrangements, but don't take unnecessary risks. And I *mean* that."

"Yeah, yeah... no murdering anyone, I get it." She nodded as she shifted into Monica's appearance. The transformation felt heavier now, like putting on armor. "And you'll be meeting with Mael?"

"Yes. He wants to discuss *security*. More likely, it's about my new role in the family hierarchy. Seeing as it's clear he views you as higher than me now." Raziel's smile was sharp as a blade. "I'm to be relegated to ceremonial duties only. A neutered attack dog, kept for show."

The bitterness in his voice made something twist in her chest. Whatever else Raziel was, he was brilliant—his intelligence wasted on his family's petty power games.

"Be careful," she said, surprising herself with the genuine concern in her voice. "Don't take unnecessary risks."

He smirked. "I will do what I can, my little assassin."

The endearment shouldn't have warmed her as much as it did.

. . .

The wedding was being held in Volencia's home. It was a hive of activity when Nadi arrived. Servants rushed about with flowers, fabric, and enough crystal to outfit a small palace. The scent of expensive perfume and bloodwine hung heavy in the air, mixed with the aromas of baking bread and roasting meat.

"Monica!" Lana swept toward her, resplendent in a dressing gown of midnight-blue silk. Her blonde hair was elaborately pinned with pearls, and her smile was radiant. "Thank the moons you're here. I'm positively *drowning* in last-minute decisions."

Nadi allowed herself to be drawn into the chaos, noting the unfamiliar faces among the usual staff. Caterers, florists, musicians—all vetted by family security, no doubt, but still potential vulnerabilities in the Nostrom defenses.

"The flowers alone are driving me to distraction," Lana continued, leading her through rooms filled with white roses, midnight-black orchids, and arrangements that probably cost more than most people earned in a *decade*. "Zabriel insists on incorporating Rosov family traditions, but I refuse to have anything that clashes with Mother's interminably specific demands. Everything with her has to be *crimson*. Ugh!"

They paused before an elaborate display of crimson roses interwoven with white jasmine. The symbolism wasn't lost on Nadi—blood and innocence, vampire and human, predator and prey.

"It's beautiful." Diplomacy first. Always. "Very... meaningful."

"Oh, you understand!" Lana clapped her hands together. "That's exactly what I was hoping for. Zabriel sees only the practical considerations—security, political implications, guest accommodations. But a wedding should be about more than mere alliance-building, don't you think?"

The genuine happiness in Lana's voice caught Nadi off guard. This wasn't the calculating Sweetheart Mistress she'd come to know. There was... *real excitement* in her voice. She studied Lana for a moment and there was actual—*oh*.

Oh.

"How long have you and Zabriel been together, Lana?" She had to tread carefully.

Lana's smile turned secretive, and she stepped in close to Nadi to lower her voice. "Longer than anyone suspects. Three years ago, at a gathering in the neutral territories, we got into a major row. He was supposed to be negotiating a trade agreement, and I was there representing Mother's interests in the textile markets."

Lana laughed, the sound perfectly girlish. "First, we were screaming at each other. Then, we nearly killed each other. Of course, *then,* we ended up having the most amazing sex of our lives. But what followed? It was amazing, Monica—we ended up talking until dawn, about everything except business." That time, her laugh was one of disbelief. As if the conversation was the truly unbelievable part. For her, it obviously was.

"And you've been seeing each other in secret since then?"

"Whenever we could manage it." Lana's expression grew wistful. "Stolen moments, clandestine meetings, coded letters. Terribly romantic, actually, though I wouldn't recommend conducting a courtship under such circumstances."

Oh, honey, if you only knew. Nadi figured she and Raziel probably had Lana and Zabriel beat. But she didn't offer that information.

As they moved through the estate, Nadi made mental notes of the security preparations. Guards at every entrance, additional patrols in the gardens, and what appeared to be new magical wards inscribed along the doorframes. The Nostroms were taking no chances with the most politically significant wedding in recent memory.

"Tell me honestly," Lana said as they entered what would

serve as the bridal preparation chamber, "what do you think of the dress?"

The gown hanging from an ornate stand was a masterpiece of vampire craftsmanship. Layers of ivory silk and black lace created a dramatic silhouette, while tiny garnets sewn throughout the bodice caught the light like drops of blood. It was beautiful and sinister in equal measure.

Nadi studied it for a long moment. "It's perfect for you." And it really was. "Zabriel won't be able to look away. Nor will anyone else, I imagine."

"That's rather the point." Lana's grin was predatory. "I intend to be *utterly* unforgettable."

A soft knock at the door interrupted them. "Come," Lana called.

A young woman entered, and Nadi almost instinctively froze. It was a seamstress. But Nadi recognized her... it was the woman from Braen's club. There was no mistaking her. The same woman with the nondescript appearance, dark hair, and same downcast eyes. Only this time, she was wearing a measuring tape draped around her neck and her smock had a sea of pins tucked into it.

"Begging your pardon, my lady," the seamstress said, her accent marking her as from the outer cities. "I need to make final adjustments to the bodice."

It took everything that Nadi had not to stare at the woman in wide-eyed shock. She had to turn her head to cough into her arm. Her whole body shook with adrenaline.

The fae were here.

The fae were *here*. At the wedding.

Fuck. Fuck! No, no, no. Not *now*. Not *now*.

"Of course," Lana gestured to the dress, then turned to Nadi with a thoughtful expression. "Monica, dear, would you mind helping me with something else first? I have a concern about tomorrow that requires your... unique perspective."

"Hm? Of course. Not at all." Nadi smiled, hoping she hid the panic well enough. But there was no telling if she was successful.

Lana led her from the preparation chamber to a smaller, more intimate sitting room. The walls were lined with portraits of Nostrom ancestors, their painted eyes seeming to follow their movements. "Please, sit." She gestured to an ornate settee.

"What can I help you with?" Nadi settled into the plush velvet cushions, her whole body on high alert.

"Well." Lana moved to a sideboard where crystal decanters caught the afternoon light. "I've been thinking about tomorrow's reception. There will be so many guests, so many... opportunities for things to go wrong." She lifted one of the decanters, the liquid inside dark and viscous. "I want to ensure that everyone in the family is at absolute peak performance. *Including* you."

Nadi's stomach clenched as she recognized what Lana was pouring. Fresh blood, still warm by the look of it.

"I know my brother has been negligent in ensuring you're properly fed," Lana continued, her tone light but her eyes sharp. "He loves to play his games. I'm sure he makes you suck his cock before he'll give you even a drop of blood. But newly turned vampires need consistent nourishment, especially during times of stress. And tomorrow will certainly be stressful." Lana approached with two crystal glasses, offering one to Nadi with a smile that never reached her magenta eyes. "To *family* solidarity."

The test was obvious.

Lana knew "Monica" wasn't really "Monica." They'd been through this before already. Now, the question she was trying to learn the answer to was—did Raziel turn a spy into a vampire?

Or was there a deeper deception at work?

If Nadi refused or couldn't drink blood, it would expose her immediately and reveal that she wasn't a vampire. And the only other thing she could possibly be was *fae*. And if she was fae? Well... then she'd be dead immediately, wouldn't she?

"He keeps me fed, and... mostly doesn't require sexual favors in return." Nadi managed to take the glass with steady hands. The metallic scent hit her immediately, making her stomach roil. She'd managed to avoid consuming straight blood since her arrival by claiming to still be adjusting to her new diet, but that excuse wouldn't work here. She'd had it diluted into wine, which made it easier to consume.

"I had it drawn fresh this morning." Lana settled beside her, raising her own glass. "Nothing but the finest for family, after all. I would prefer to watch you sink those pretty little fangs of yours into a throat but, you know. White carpets and all." She gestured at her home. "You younglings can be so *sloppy*."

Nadi lifted the glass to her lips, fighting every instinct that screamed against what she was about to do. The blood was warm, copper-sweet, and utterly revolting. She managed to take a small sip, the liquid coating her tongue like thick syrup. "Delicious," she forced herself to say, swallowing with considerable effort.

Her stomach immediately began to rebel, cramping painfully.

"Isn't it?" Lana's smile widened. "Such a lovely vintage. Young, healthy—the donor was particularly spirited. He screamed all morning until he died. I find that fear adds such a distinctive flavor, don't you?"

The casual cruelty in Lana's voice made Nadi's blood run cold. "I admit I haven't learned the difference yet." This time her stomach lurched violently, and she had to concentrate on breathing deeply to keep from vomiting.

Lana drained half her glass in one smooth motion. "Those of us who are born into vampirism, we don't know another life. But to see someone *blessed* with our gift? The hunger, the enhanced senses, the way it changes your experience of the world. That is why we vampires are gods. That is what makes us so much more superior to humans and fae. We can gift you with *ascension*."

Nadi realized at exactly that point in time that Lana was absolutely and undoubtedly *fucking insane*.

Lana leaned closer, her voice dropping to a conspiratorial whisper. "Tell me, what has surprised you most about your new existence?"

Another test. Nadi forced herself to ignore the revolt happening in her stomach and instead on what Monica would actually say. "The sounds. I can hear conversations three rooms away. Sometimes, it's overwhelming—all the heartbeats, all the whispered secrets. It's like the whole world is suddenly... *more*."

Lana nodded approvingly. "Excellent. Yes, the sensory enhancement can be quite disorienting. And the strength? Have you tested your new physical capabilities?"

"Some." Nadi took another sip, her body now actively fighting to keep the blood down. "The attack on Braen. I admit I'm the one who killed him." She smiled shyly.

Lana laughed. "Ooh, I knew it! I heard from Zabriel that someone had stabbed him several times from the back. Someone too small to be Raziel. I'm so proud of you!"

"Raziel... encourages me." By the moons, she wanted to puke all over Lana and her white furniture.

"How fortunate for you." Lana's tone carried a subtle edge. "My brother can be so unpredictable with his vampiric protégés. One never knows if he'll nurture them or destroy them on a whim. You aren't the first, of course. You won't be the last, unless you do something to ensure you are."

The implication hung in the air between them. Meanwhile, the blood felt like poison in her system, and her body was doing everything it could to reject it. And with Lana questioning if she was really a vampire—all Nadi wanted to do was disappear into bats like Raziel could. And suddenly she was very sad that wasn't part of her repertoire.

"I can see you're still struggling with acceptance." Lana's sickly sweet smile would have made Nadi ill if she weren't already well on her way. "Perhaps another glass would help? Exposure therapy, so to speak."

"That's very kind, but—" Nadi began, but Lana was already moving toward the sideboard.

"Nonsense. I insist." She returned with a fresh glass, this one fuller than the first. "To your continued education."

Nadi stared at the glass in veiled horror. There was no way she could consume more blood without her body completely rebelling. Already she could feel her control slipping, her stomach churning violently.

"Actually," she said carefully, "I should probably pace myself. Raziel mentioned that overfeeding could be problematic for new vampires."

"Did he?" Lana's eyes narrowed slightly. "How curious. In my experience, young vampires typically have difficulty stopping once they start. The hunger tends to be quite overwhelming. I'm impressed you know how to stop."

Another test. Nadi forced a weak smile. "Perhaps I'm an exception."

"Perhaps you are." Lana settled back into her seat, but her posture remained predatory. "Tell me about your home before you came here. Your family, your home in the outer cities. And please. *Drink.*"

The questions continued for another excruciating twenty minutes. Lana probed every aspect of Monica's fabricated history, watching Nadi's reactions with scientific interest. Through it all, Nadi clutched the glass of blood, taking sips when directly observed while fighting to keep her expression neutral.

By the time Lana finally dismissed her, claiming she needed

to attend to other wedding preparations, Nadi felt like she might collapse. She made her excuses and left the estate as quickly as politeness allowed, her stomach cramping with each step.

The moment she was safely in the car, she let out a pained groan and felt a cold sweat beading on her forehead.

Ivan looked at her with a furrowed brow. "Miss?"

"Just drive, Ivan. Just *drive*." She didn't trust they weren't being followed or observed. She needed to get somewhere she could retch in private. And that wasn't until she was back in Raziel's estate.

"What did she do?" Ivan muttered.

"Made me drink blood. A lot."

Ivan grunted. "You going to be okay?"

"I'll be fine. Just *fucking drive*," Nadi ground out between her teeth.

But she wasn't fine. Lana's test had been obvious, meant to expose her true nature. The question was whether she'd passed or failed—and what Lana planned to do with the information either way.

As Ivan drove her back to Raziel's estate, Nadi couldn't shake the feeling that she'd just painted a target on her back. Tomorrow's wedding was already dangerous enough without adding Lana's suspicions to the mix.

But there was no turning back now. For better or worse, they were committed to their course.

She only hoped they'd all survive to see the consequences.

NINETEEN

Raziel was getting ready to leave and meet with Mael as the door to his office swung open at an alarming speed.

Nadi, wearing Monica's face, stormed into his office, slammed the door behind her, and marched into his attached private bathroom.

Grinning, he couldn't help it. "How was my sis—"

"Shut the *fuck u*—" Nadi's glamor shimmered and faded as she collapsed to her knees in front of his toilet, retching violently.

Raziel was on his feet in a split second, moving before he even processed he had done so. Running to her side, he saw what was happening.

Blood. She was retching up blood into the toilet. He let out a long, ragged sigh. "This was bound to happen. Lana made you drink?"

The poor, haggard-looking fae nodded weakly, her head resting on the edge of the toilet as she reached up to flush the contents of the bowl.

Taking the tie from his hair, he gently pulled her long black strands into a ponytail at the base of her neck. Then, he ran the faucet and filled a cup of cold water as well as taking a wash-cloth and dampening it.

He had taken care of sick humans in his day. Yes, he had learned how to care for them because he had wanted to prolong their suffering—but that didn't mean he didn't know *how*.

"She was testing me." Nadi's voice was ragged. She was covered in a thin sheen of sweat. The poor thing had suffered for a long time, holding down that much blood for who knew how long. "To see if I was actually a v—"

Wincing, he rubbed her back as she retched a second time into the toilet. That time, he flushed it for her once she finished and sat down on the marble floor of the half-bath.

Pressing the damp, cool compress to the back of her neck, he handed her another one to wipe her lips with. "And?"

"I don't know if I passed. Lana's not an idiot." She let out a shaky breath. "Why couldn't *someone* in your family be stupid?"

"Trust me." Raziel chuckled. "I ask myself that question regularly." He handed her the cup of water, noting how her hands still trembled. "Small sips. Let your stomach settle first."

She accepted the cup, muttering thanks, and he found himself cataloging every detail of her condition—the pallor of her skin, the fine tremor in her fingers, the way she held herself as if her stomach still cramped. His sister had put her through hell, and for what? A test? A game?

"She had fresh blood, Raziel." Nadi's voice cracked with remembered revulsion. "She talked about how the donor was 'spirited,' how fear adds flavor. How he had screamed as he died. I had to sit there and pretend to enjoy it while she watched my reactions."

The rage in his chest crystallized into something sharper, more dangerous. Lana's casual cruelty was nothing new, in fact it was something he himself often enjoyed, but directing it at

Nadi felt like a personal violation. If anyone was going to make Nadi suffer, it was him, after all. "How much?"

"Three full glasses. Maybe more." She took another tentative sip of water. "She offered me a fourth glass when I couldn't finish the third fast enough. Said something about it *getting cold.*"

Raziel's hands clenched into fists before he could stop himself. The anger that rampaged through him was a surprise. When had his protective instincts toward Nadi become so pronounced? When had her suffering begun to bother him?

He loved her.

But that didn't *mean* anything to a creature like him. Surely.

"The worst part wasn't the blood," Nadi continued, leaning back against the cool bathroom wall. "It was the interrogation that came with it. She questioned everything—my feeding habits, my relationship with you, my memories of being human. Every answer felt like walking through a minefield. It's one thing to have to hold up an act. But she knows. She knows I'm not Monica, and she wants to know what I am. Whatever happens, after the wedding tomorrow, I think this act is over."

"What did you tell her?" He kept his voice level, though internally he was already calculating the damage, the potential exposure. But he felt the crushing suspicion that she was right.

"The truth, where I could. About the enhanced senses, the overwhelming nature of the transformation." Nadi closed her eyes, still looking pale and shaky. "But when she asked about... intimate feeding, about you and me..."

"Ah." Understanding dawned, along with a fresh wave of anger. "She was fishing for information about our bond."

Of course she was. Lana would want to know how deep the connection ran, whether it could be exploited or needed to be severed entirely. The thought of his sister probing into the most private aspects of his relationship with Nadi made his jaw clench.

Nadi opened her eyes to look at him, and he could see the exhaustion there, the strain of maintaining her deception under such pressure. "The question is, does she think I'm *just* a spy, a fae shapeshifter, or something else entirely?"

If Lana suspected that Nadi wasn't truly a vampire, there was no other option but for her to be fae. And if she was fae? Everything was over for *both* of them.

"We'll know soon enough. Survival requires adaptation. And if there is one thing you are good at, it's that." He helped her to her feet, steadying her when she swayed slightly. His hands lingered on her arms, reluctant to let go until he was certain she was stable. "I'm about to leave to find out where Mael stands in all this and what he wants me to do. The question all this raises is what Lana plans to do with her suspicions."

"She'll watch me more closely at the wedding, for one." Nadi leaned against the sink. "Test me again, probably. Maybe try to separate us to see how I react."

"Or she might decide you're too dangerous to keep alive." The words came out more matter-of-fact than he felt. The possibility of losing Nadi—of his sister deciding to eliminate her— sent a cold spike of fear through him that he couldn't entirely suppress. "If she suspects you are more of a threat to her than a potential weapon *for* her..."

"Then we move up our timeline on her death." Nadi straightened, some of her natural determination returning. "We can't wait for the perfect moment if there might not be one."

"No." The refusal was immediate, instinctive. He'd spent too many years planning this revenge to let fear derail it now. "We stick to the plan. Changing course now, when we're this close, is more dangerous than maintaining our position. Mael comes first."

"Even if Lana exposes me?"

"Especially then." He moved closer, his hands settling on her shoulders. Through the thin fabric of her dress, he could feel the warmth of her skin, the steady rhythm of her breathing. She was alive, safe, still with him. "Because if she tries to expose you publicly, it means she's confident in her position. Overconfident. And overconfidence creates opportunities."

He watched understanding dawn in her dark eyes, saw the moment she grasped what he was suggesting.

"You want her to make a move against me."

"I want her to reveal her hand," he corrected. The idea of using Nadi felt wrong, but strategically, it was sound. "Right now, we don't know who else is involved in her schemes, what resources she has, or how far she's willing to go. If she acts against you tomorrow, we'll learn all of that."

"You're using me as bait."

The accusation in her voice stung, though he couldn't deny its accuracy. "Using both of us as bait, because if she moves against you, she'll have to move against me as well. We're too closely associated for her to eliminate one without considering the other."

It was true, though not for the reasons his family would assume. They were bound together now by more than alliance or convenience. The thought of Nadi facing Lana's machinations alone made him want to abandon all subtlety and simply kill his sister tonight.

"If she corners me at the wedding, Raziel— I'm going to do what I have to do." Black, opalescent eyes met his. There was no deterring her.

It would ruin everything he'd worked toward. But it would keep her safe. "Do what you must do to survive, Nadi. I can't ask you to do anything else."

Nadi was quiet for a long moment, and he found himself studying her face, looking for signs of fear or doubt. When she spoke again, her voice was steadier. "There's something else. The seamstress who interrupted us—she is fae. Or from the Wild. I saw her at Braen's club when I was spying there."

"Are you positive?"

She nodded. "She had that... it's hard to describe, we *walk* differently, move differently, those of us who grew up in the Wild. Last I saw her, she was running toward the basement of captives with a gun. The ones you said were missing when you sent your men after them."

The revelation sent his mind racing. Fae infiltrators, Lana's suspicions, his family's political maneuvering—this was getting too complicated, even for his love of the game. "You're certain?"

"As certain as I can be without having questioned her." She pushed away from the sink, looking more like her normal self with each passing moment. "But who's she working for? Or do you think she's acting alone?"

"Tomorrow is going to be even more chaotic than we anticipated." Raziel ran a hand through his hair, scrambling to think of a way to adapt to the new variable. "Which could work to our advantage, if we play it correctly."

"Or get us all killed."

"There's always that risk." He smiled, though there was no humor in it. The stakes kept climbing, the potential for catastrophe growing with each revelation. "The question is whether you're willing to take it."

He watched her face as she considered, seeing the moment she made her choice. There was steel in her spine, fire in her eyes. "You think I'm backing out now, Serpent?"

Without thinking, he leaned down to kiss her forehead. "I have a feeling tomorrow is going to test us both in ways we haven't anticipated."

"More than tonight already has?"

"Tonight was just Lana being suspicious. Tomorrow..." He paused, his mind already turning to the countless variables they'd have to navigate. "Tomorrow, everyone will be playing for keeps."

Including him. Including them.

And despite the dangers ahead, despite the blood still staining his toilet and the tremor that occasionally ran through Nadi's hands, Raziel found himself looking forward to it.

After all, chaos had always been his preferred element.

The clock chimed. He swore. "I'll have to learn what else you know when I return. I need to go meet my brother. Are you all right on your own?"

"Go. Not the first time I've had food poisoning." Clearly exhausted, Nadi collapsed onto the bed, her glamor of Monica returning as she fell. He couldn't imagine what it was like to have to exist like that.

But now, it was time for him to meet Mael and to learn where the last and most important piece on the board was going to be set before Lana's wedding. Because if everything went to plan, his brother would be dead within twenty-four hours.

And damn him if that didn't bring a smile to his face.

Raziel sat in Mael's home study, projecting an image of subdued compliance while internally cataloging every weapon within reach. His brother's personal office was a study in controlled power—light-stained wood, leather-bound books, and artifacts from conquered territories displayed like trophies.

"I appreciate your understanding about the new arrangements." Mael perfectly feigned sympathy while pouring blood-wine into two crystal glasses. "Mother feels it's time for you to step back from active operations."

"Of course." Raziel accepted the glass. "The family's needs come first."

Mael studied him carefully. "You're taking this rather well. I expected more... resistance."

"Perhaps recent events have given me perspective." Raziel sipped his wine, maintaining his mask of resignation. "Braen's death was a reminder of the costs of this life. Maybe it's time I found other pursuits."

"Such as?"

"Monica, for one." The lie came easily. "I find myself deeply invested in her development. She has potential that goes beyond her current abilities. And if that means I need to take a back seat, so be it."

Something flickered in Mael's golden eyes. "She is remarkable, isn't she? Such adaptability, such strength." He paused. "I've been meaning to ask—her injuries from the Rosov estate. How severe were they really?"

Raziel's hand tightened almost imperceptibly around his glass. "Severe. Silver poisoning isn't something to be taken lightly, especially for a new vampire."

"Of course." Mael nodded sympathetically. "It must have been difficult, watching someone you care about suffer like that."

The word choice was pointed and significant. *Care.* Mael did not go so far as to claim that Raziel loved Monica. Nor did he suggest that Raziel held no feelings for her either. Interesting. He was waiting to see if Raziel would correct him.

"It was certainly educational." Raziel met his brother's gaze steadily. "I learned quite a bit about my own priorities during those three days."

"I'm sure you did." Mael moved to stand beside the window, looking out over the metropolis. "The city is changing, Raziel. Old powers are shifting, new alliances are forming. The question is whether we adapt or get swept aside."

"And where do I fit in this new order?"

"That depends entirely on you." Mael turned to face him. "Your talents haven't diminished, but perhaps they could be... redirected. Less emphasis on direct action, more on strategic consultation."

Strategic consultation. A euphemism for being kept like a

dangerous pet, fed scraps of information and occasionally unleashed under careful supervision.

"I'm honored by your confidence," Raziel said smoothly.

"Good." Mael smiled, but there was no warmth in it. "Because I have a special assignment for you regarding tomorrow's ceremony."

Raziel waited, readying himself to fight if he needed to.

"There have been... rumors," Mael continued. "Whispers of potential disruption to the wedding. Nothing concrete, you understand, but concerning enough that we're taking extra precautions."

"What kind of disruption?"

"The same *old* enemies who couldn't help but interrupt your wedding," Mael's voice dropped lower. "There are those who see our alliance with the Rosovs as a threat to the existing balance of power. We have reason to believe representatives of these factions may attempt to infiltrate the ceremony."

Fae. He was talking about fae infiltrators. Perhaps the same one that Nadi had seen? But how much did Mael actually know?

"What would you have me do?" Raziel asked.

"I want you to work with our security teams tomorrow. Your... particular gifts... make you uniquely suited to solving any particular issues quietly and quickly."

It was a test, Raziel realized. Mael suspected something—whether about Monica's true nature or Raziel's own loyalties, he couldn't be sure. But this assignment would put him exactly where he needed to be to protect Nadi while positioning himself for their planned strike.

"I'll be honored to serve." He sipped the drink.

"Excellent." Mael moved back to his desk, retrieving a folder thick with documents. "Here are the guest lists, security protocols, and intelligence reports. Study them carefully. I want you familiar with every face that will be in attendance tomorrow."

Raziel accepted the folder, his mind already racing. Among these documents would be valuable intelligence about security at the event—information that could make the difference between success and catastrophe for their mission.

Mael's eyes never left him as he studied the folder. "Keep a close eye on Monica tomorrow. Given her... unique abilities... she may be particularly attractive to those who would wish us harm."

The warning sent ice through Raziel's veins. "You think she's in danger?"

"I think she's valuable," Mael corrected. "And valuable things have a tendency to be stolen if they are not properly guarded."

"No one knows that more than me, brother."

"One more thing," Mael added as Raziel rose to leave. "The ledger. The one that Braen kept on all his... dealings." He grimaced. "Bring it tomorrow. I have need of it."

"Monica told me you asked for it. May I ask why?"

Mael's smile was picture-perfect. Jovial. Friendly. And couldn't have matched his voice less if it had belonged to one of the paintings on the wall. "No. You may not. Now, go."

Raziel's jaw ticked as he left the room.

Tomorrow would be an interesting day, indeed.

* * *

It was late that night before Raziel returned home. Nadi couldn't sleep. She was lying there in his nest of thick blankets and comforters, her mind churning with possibilities for the next day. Mapping out each possible outcome for their attempt on Mael's life.

There were too many variables. Too many possible

approaches. It made her nervous. They didn't even know *how* they were going to take him down yet. Only that they were going to "wait for the right opportunity."

She hated it. *Hated it.*

The door to his room opened as Raziel walked in. She didn't even need to look to know it was him. She recognized the sound of the way he moved, the way he smelled in the air. He clicked the door shut behind him and threw the deadbolts. He held a thick folder in his hand that he tossed onto the dresser.

It meant she could drop her glamor again, which she was more than eager to do so. "How did it go with Mael?" She turned her head on the pillow to watch him.

"You first." His expression was drawn tight. He was still lost in thought. "Lana. What else did you learn?"

Rolling onto her side, she stretched with a yawn. "Lana and Zabriel have been conducting a secret romance for three years. This isn't just a political marriage—they're genuinely in love."

That got his attention. He turned to face her as he unbuttoned his shirt, his crimson eyes sharp with interest. "Are you certain?"

"Absolutely. And it changes everything about tomorrow's power dynamics." She cracked her spine, glad to finally be out from under Monica's appearance. "If they've been planning this alliance for years rather than months, they've had time to build networks, establish loyalties, position themselves for what comes after."

"After they eliminate the current leadership..." Raziel murmured, tossing his shirt aside.

"What did you learn from Mael?"

"That we're not the only ones planning surprises for tomorrow." He gestured at the thick folder on the dresser. "You were right about that seamstress. Mael thinks that fae are trying to infiltrate the wedding."

Getting up, Nadi walked across the room to the folder, not

caring that she was stark naked. It was nothing Raziel hadn't seen or enjoyed many times already.

Flipping over the folder, she found the document she was interested in. Scanning it quickly, her blood went cold. The Nostroms had been monitoring increased fae activity in the outer cities for *weeks*.

Communication patterns suggesting coordination between normally isolationist clans. Reports of strangers asking questions about vampire security protocols. Smuggling routes.

Including putting *unsanctioned and uncontrolled escorts* in and out for the night of the wedding. "This is why he wanted Braen's ledger. He wants to know who is coming in and going out of the city, who is smuggling them, who is helping buy them."

"Which raises the question," his hand on her shoulder turned her to face him, "do you know anything about this?"

The question hung between them like a blade. Nadi met his gaze steadily, knowing that her answer would determine whether he still trusted her or began to see her as another threat to neutralize.

"No. I've had no business with any fae clans since I arrived in the metropolis. My people don't know where I am or what I'm doing." She glared up at him. "My last contact with my family was when I killed Luciento to get to you, unless you forgot."

"But if they *do* show up tomorrow," he shifted to trap her between him and the dresser, "where would your loyalties lie?"

It was the question she'd been dreading, the one that struck at the heart of her conflicted feelings. She'd spent decades planning revenge against the Nostroms, but now she was sleeping in her enemy's bed, sharing his secrets, protecting his life.

Killing her estranged uncle was one thing.

Betraying her *whole people* was another.

"I don't know." It was another honest answer. "But I know

this—the fae aren't organized. That's the only thing that's ever stopped them from coming together to overthrow the vampires. The clans are too divided, too insular. But if they ever *did* work together? If their hatred of each other was ever second to their hatred of the city? The walls around the metropolis would fall. The Wild would take over in a heartbeat."

"And all that we've worked for would dissolve, and all the humans would die. Vampire society would collapse." Raziel studied her for a long moment, then nodded slowly. "I can assume we have a common interest in ensuring that doesn't happen, then?"

She paused. "Yeah." Though, sometimes, she wasn't so sure that wasn't the ultimate right answer. Burn it all down. Start over. But it was a pipe dream. She changed the subject. "Mael has positioned you perfectly for tomorrow, hasn't he? Security detail means access to restricted areas, freedom to move throughout the venue."

"And authority to act on any identified threats as I see fit." He huffed a laugh, his hand settling on her naked hip. "Though I suspect he might be hoping I'll identify *you* as one of them."

"Or that's what Lana is telling him." Nadi furrowed her brow. "The question is, does Mael suspect me of anything?"

"Everyone in this family suspects everyone. The question is of what and how much." Raziel gathered the security documents into a neat pile. "He made a point of telling me to keep a close eye on you tomorrow. Said you might be 'particularly attractive to those who would wish us harm.'"

"Meaning?"

"Meaning he either suspects you're not what you seem, or he's *also* planning to use you as bait to draw out whoever is working against us." Raziel's expression darkened. "Either way, you'll be a target."

Nadi felt the familiar weight of being hunted, the sensation that had driven her for so many years. But this time, it was different. This time, she wasn't alone.

"Or, perhaps," a devilish grin tugged at the corners of Raziel's mouth, "he's simply hoping to interrogate you..."

Rolling her eyes, she shoved his chest, trying to nudge him backward. He didn't move. "If both Lana and Mael are watching us—or—" She froze. "Wait. *That's it.* They *know*, Raziel. Mael and Lana both know about the fae threat, they *have* to. That's why Mael is after the ledger. That's why Lana is questioning me."

Raziel tilted his head to the side slightly, thoughtfully. "It makes sense. Mael would want ammunition to bring to the table if he needed to broker peace with the fae tribes. Lana would want to know who would be in her direct sphere of influence if she suspected someone. And, most importantly, if Mael wants *you*, he would seek to drive us apart."

Shutting her eyes, she let out a breath. The board had too many players. This was precisely why she preferred being an assassin. Simple. Get in. Kill. Get out. "What do we do? They'll be watching us the entire time."

"Then we give them something to watch." He leaned forward, nuzzling into her hair, grasping her hips now with both hands. "We play to their expectations. Let them think they're controlling the situation while we position ourselves for the real strike."

"When do we move?" It was hard to focus with him digging his fingers into her skin, gripping her like that.

"Just after the ceremony. Everyone will be focused on Lana and Zabriel. No one will care about Mael, or you, or me. The moment Mael steps off stage, the moment after Lana and Zabriel kiss as husband and wife, we will take him in the shadows while everyone is distracted by the applause and music."

It was audacious, striking at the heart of the celebration

when defenses would be at their most complex but potentially most distracted. "And if the fae *do* attack?"

"Even better. Chaos has always been my preferred operating environment." He slid one of his hands slowly up her back, tracing the line of her spine. "But there's something we need to discuss."

The direness in his tone made her look up. "What?" And that was the trap she fell into.

His hand fisted in her hair. He pulled her head back hard enough that it sent a sting through her that had her gasping. "You. And whether or not I can trust you *not* to go rogue tomorrow, little murderer."

"I—" She was already moving. He dragged her to the bed, and before she could react, she was face-down on the plush, velvet surface, bent over with her feet on the ground.

His hand stroked her ass. It was the only warning she had before his palm fell against her skin with a hard *crack*.

She hissed, baring her teeth, her hands digging into the comforter. "Raziel, what're you—"

"I know you. And I know what you're going to do, my little fae." His voice was deep, already husky and thick from lust. His hand fell against her ass with a second hard strike.

She gasped, but when she went to struggle, he grabbed a handful of her skin and squeezed hard enough that it brought tears to her eyes.

"Ah-ah. Stay still, beautiful... accept your punishment."

"But I haven't done anything *wrong*."

"Oh, but I know you will." He chuckled, still pinning her head to the bed with her hair, his hand pressing to the sheets beside her. His hand stroked the burning skin on her ass. "Tomorrow will be abject chaos and I *know* you will misbehave."

His hand left her to deliver another hard *crack!*

This time, she bit her lip to keep from moaning. Why did

this do such terrible things to her? *Why?* She should be screaming, fighting, tearing his face off. But here she was, submitting to the Serpent—*her enemy*—and desperate for more.

"Fuck you, Raziel, you—*ahnh!*"

She hadn't heard him undo his pants. And he barely paused at her core before he rammed himself into her body, filling her in one smooth, brutal movement.

The pace he set was as unforgiving as how he began it. And it was *exactly* what she needed. What they both needed. She snarled, swearing at him in fae as he pinned her shoulders down with one hand, the other grasping her hips as he pounded into her like a machine.

And all he did was laugh. "That's it, my—*nnh*—little wild beast... fight me. I want to feel the moment you remember you're *mine.*"

Moons, it felt so damn *perfect.* Everything about it.

"Say it," he growled at her, lifting her torso from the bed. His thrusts became violent impacts into her, sending blinding flashes of ecstasy crashing through her. "Say you're *mine.* Now and always. And say you're *sorry* for what you're going to do. Beg me. *Beg me* for forgiveness."

At first, she resisted, swearing at him with every obscenity she knew, and there were plenty. But it only spurred him on, and she could only take so much.

Finally, with a half-sob, half-wail, she surrendered. "Please—"

Her cheek met the sheets again.

His tempo slowed, but it only seemed to allow him to bury himself harder, deeper into her body. Pausing only to speak. "Please *what?*"

Each thrust felt like it was going to drive her mind out of her body. "F—*ah*—forgive me—"

"Mm... not good enough... I want to hear you say it all at once, fae..." He leaned back to caress her ass again before slapping his palm down on the sensitive skin hard enough that she had to bite the sheets to muffle her moan. "Look at you. Look at how much you love this. What a perfect little thing you are. Now *say it*. Say you're mine, and *beg for forgiveness for whatever you're going to do tomorrow.*"

She couldn't take it anymore. She just couldn't. Her body was on the edge of release, and it was making her head spin. "Please—Raziel—I-I'm sorry, please forgive me—I-I'm yours, now and forever, *please—*"

Both his hands went to her hips as he unleashed himself on her, giving them both what they desperately needed. It was only moments before she was crashing over into oblivion, her body unable to handle much more of the onslaught. He doubled over her second later, clutching her to him, pleasure claiming him in turn.

When she could think straight again, she was under the sheets with him, nestled up against his chest. He was holding her gently. He placed a kiss to the top of her head. "You shouldn't walk around naked," he murmured.

"You shouldn't be such a bastard," she grumbled back at him.

He chuckled. She could feel his mood drop. "Tomorrow isn't just about eliminating Mael. It's about survival. All of us—you, me, even Ivan—we're all potential targets. And I need you to be careful."

They'd started this game thinking they were the hunters, but somehow, they'd become the prey. Multiple factions circling, each with their own agenda, each seeing the wedding as an opportunity to reshape the metropolis.

"Are we making a mistake?" she asked quietly. "Should we abort, find another way?"

Raziel was quiet for a long moment, his fingers tracing small circles along her lower back. "We've come too far to turn back now. And honestly? I'm looking forward to it. Let them all come. Let them all make their moves. When the dust settles, we'll be the ones left standing."

His confidence was infectious, reminding her why she'd chosen to trust him in the first place. Despite everything—the blood, the surveillance, the approaching storm—she found herself smiling.

"Then, we see this through."

"Together."

Nadi couldn't shake the feeling that they were walking toward the edge of a precipice. Tomorrow would bring the moment when all their careful preparations would either secure their victory or destroy them utterly.

Even with how complicated their current situation made everything.

But tonight, in the quiet sanctuary of Raziel's bedroom, she almost allowed herself to pretend that they were simply lovers planning their future together. Almost believed that the morning wouldn't bring another performance, another layer of deception, another dance on the edge of a knife.

Almost.

Because the wedding was going to change everything. Somehow. Everything would be transformed.

In the darkness of the night, surrounded by shadows and secrets, Nadi closed her eyes and tried not to think about how many ways tomorrow could end in disaster.

TWENTY

The afternoon of Lana's wedding dawned with deceptive serenity. Pale golden sunlight streamed through the windows of Raziel's estate, casting everything in soft, honeyed tones that belied the violence planned for the day ahead.

Nadi stood before the mirror in his dressing room, adjusting the deep burgundy gown she'd chosen for the occasion. The silk fell in elegant lines to just below her knees, the color complementing Monica's pale complexion while remaining appropriately subdued for a family event. She'd swept her borrowed dark brown hair into an elaborate updo, secured with pearl pins that glinted in the afternoon light.

"You look beautiful, even if I have come to prefer your real face." Raziel's reflection appeared behind hers in the mirror. He was already dressed in his formal attire—a dark charcoal suit that emphasized the breadth of his shoulders and the predatory grace of his movements. His long black hair was tied back with blood-red ribbon, and his crimson eyes seemed to glow in the soft light.

"I look like a woman about to attend her first Nostrom family wedding. Besides her own, of course, that went so *horribly* wrong." She turned to face him. "Nervous, excited, completely unaware that she's walking into a war zone."

His lips curved in that familiar, dangerous smile. "Perfect, then."

She studied his face, noting the subtle tension around his eyes. "Are you ready for this?" Her going after his family was one thing. He was killing his *brother*.

"I've been ready for this my entire life." He reached into his jacket and withdrew a small velvet box. "But first, there's something I want you to have."

Nadi's breath caught as he opened the box to reveal an intricate silver necklace. The pendant was shaped like a serpent, its body coiled in an elegant figure-eight, with tiny garnets for eyes that seemed to blink in the light.

"It is white gold."

"Raziel, I can't—"

"You can, and you will." He stepped behind her, lifting the necklace to drape it around her throat. His fingers brushed the nape of her neck as he fastened the clasp, sending a shiver through her. "It's not just jewelry. The pendant contains a small blade, dipped in a fast-acting poison—twist the head counter-clockwise and pull."

The weight of the gold against her skin was suddenly ominous. It was perfect for them, wasn't it? "Thank you."

"Don't thank me yet." His hands settled on her shoulders, his eyes meeting hers in the mirror. "I am going to ask you for a promise, Nadi, though I know I have no right to."

"What?"

"Whatever happens—whatever you see, whatever choices you have to make—remember why you came here in the first place. Don't try to protect me by sacrificing yourself. None of this has value if it means losing you." His grip tightened slightly. "Survive, Nadi. That is what I want you to promise me. That you will simply *survive*."

The vulnerability in his voice made her chest tight. Here was the Serpent, perhaps the most feared vampire in the metropolis, asking her to simply survive.

Not to be brave, not to save him, not to kill everyone, not to be heroic—just to *live*.

"I promise," she whispered, covering one of his hands with hers. "But the same goes for you. No martyrdom, no grand gestures. We both walk away from this."

"Together." He pressed a kiss to the top of her head, careful not to disturb her carefully arranged hair. "Now, let's go to a wedding."

The ride to Volencia's home was conducted in relative silence, each of them lost in their own thoughts. Ivan drove with his usual stoic competence, though Nadi caught him checking the rearview mirror more frequently than usual. The streets were busier than normal—guests arriving for what was being touted as the social event of the decade.

As their car approached the estate gates, Nadi felt her pulse quicken. The grounds had been transformed overnight into something resembling a fairy tale—if fairy tales involved blood-drinking monsters and political assassinations. White silk pavilions dotted the manicured lawns, their panels fluttering in the gentle breeze. Elaborate floral arrangements in deep crimson and pure white created dramatic focal points throughout the gardens.

"Security's been tripled." Raziel gestured idly toward the uniformed guards stationed at regular intervals. "Mael's taking no chances."

"Can you blame him?" Ivan glanced back through the partition. "Half the vampire nobility from three territories is going to be here. Plus however many *uninvited guests* decide to crash the party."

They were waved through the gates after a brief inspection of their invitation and identification.

The main house loomed before them, its white stone facade glowing in the afternoon sunlight. Servants in pristine uniforms directed arriving guests toward the garden pavilions, while others supervised the unloading of wedding gifts and floral arrangements.

"Remember," Raziel murmured as their car pulled to a stop, "the moment he gets off the stage. And not a moment sooner."

Nadi nodded, settling Monica's personality around herself like a familiar cloak. Excitement tinged with nervousness. Gratitude for being accepted into the family. Determination to prove herself worthy of their trust.

It wasn't entirely a lie. She was nervous, though not for the reasons anyone would expect.

They were handed champagne flutes the moment they stepped from the car—bloodwine mixed with something lighter, judging by the taste. Nadi accepted hers with a smile, taking the smallest sips possible while maintaining the appearance of enjoyment.

"Raziel! Monica!" Lana appeared as if summoned, resplendent in a morning gown of pale blue silk that complemented her blonde hair and magenta eyes. She looked radiant, practically glowing with happiness and anticipation. "I'm so glad you're here early. Raz, *darling*, I was hoping to steal Monica away for a few final preparations."

"Of course." Raziel's smile was perfectly calibrated—warm enough to seem genuine, distant enough to maintain appropriate boundaries. "I should check in with Mael about the security arrangements. See where I'm needed."

"Yes, Mother has him running around like a man possessed." Lana laughed, linking her arm through Nadi's. "Come, dear. I want to show you the bridal suite. And I have a special request."

As they walked away, Nadi caught Raziel's eye over her shoulder. His expression was carefully neutral, but she saw the flicker of concern there. They were being separated, just as they'd anticipated.

The question was whether this was standard wedding preparation or something else.

Lana led her through the main house and up a grand staircase to the second floor. The suite that had been converted into the bridal room was a vision in white and silver—silk hangings, crystal chandeliers, and enough fresh flowers to perfume the entire wing of the house. Cut flowers, of course—safe from the influence of the Wild.

"Isn't it perfect?" Lana spun in a circle, her arms outstretched, basking in the opulence around her. "Zabriel wanted something more traditional, but I insisted on elegance over convention."

"It's beautiful." It was a bit much for her own personal tastes, but Nadi meant it. "You must be so excited."

"I am." Lana's smile turned secretive. "More than you know. Today marks the beginning of a new era, Monica. For our family, for the metropolis, for all of us." She moved to an ornate dressing table and picked up an elaborate hair ornament—a thin, delicate crown of twisting silvered leaves and pearls that caught the light like captured starlight. "I was hoping you'd help me with this. It was my grandmother's. Be careful, it is *real* silver."

Nadi approached, accepting the piece as though it might shatter in her hands. It looked immensely old—an antique that long pre-dated the metropolis. It took her breath away. "It's... stunning, Lana."

"Isn't it? Grandmother Lilivra wore it at her own wedding, *centuries* ago. I don't even know to whom." She chuckled. "Records have been struck clean of who she married. But she gave me this to wear today. To think, a vampire being bold enough to wear actual silver." Lana settled into the chair before her vanity, meeting Nadi's eyes in the mirror. "Lilivra was quite remarkable, you know. Beautiful, powerful, absolutely ruthless when necessary. She understood that sometimes you have to destroy everything you know to build something better."

The words sent a chill down Nadi's spine. Was Lana speaking metaphorically about her marriage, or something more literal about her plans for the family?

Or the world?

Something told Nadi it was the latter.

"Tell me," Lana continued as Nadi carefully positioned the crown in her elaborately styled hair, "what do you think about change, Monica? Are you someone who embraces it, or do you prefer the comfort of the familiar?"

Another test. Nadi kept her hands steady as she secured the ornament with hidden pins. "Change is inevitable. The question is whether you guide it or let it happen to you."

"How very wise." Lana's reflection smiled. "And what about loyalty? How do you balance personal loyalty against larger principles?"

"I suppose it depends on the circumstances." Nadi stepped back to study her handiwork. "But I believe in honoring my commitments. If I give my word, I keep it."

"Even when those commitments conflict with each other?"

The probing was becoming more direct. Nadi met Lana's gaze in the mirror, allowing a hint of confusion to show. "I'm not sure I understand. Have I done something wrong?"

"Oh, no, no." Lana turned in her chair to face her directly. "Let me be more specific. What would you do if you discovered that someone you cared about—someone you'd made commitments to—was planning something that would hurt innocent people? Where would your loyalty lie then?"

The loaded question hung in the air between them. She was talking about Raziel, obviously. Nadi felt the weight of the serpent pendant against her throat, a reminder of the man who'd given it to her and what they were planning to do that day. "I would try to understand their reasons first and then decide what I could live with. And if not... then, I would act."

"What you could live with." Lana repeated the phrase thoughtfully. "That's interesting. Most people would say they'd try to stop them or report them to the authorities. But you'd consider their motivations."

"People rarely do terrible things without believing they have good reasons. Or justified ones." Nadi shrugged. "That doesn't make the things less terrible, it just makes things more complicated when you consider the person as a whole. In our context, if we ousted everyone whose actions brought around anything other than perfectly pure ends, we'd be standing in a very lonely field of headstones."

Lana studied her for a long moment, then laughed—a sound like breaking crystal. "You know, Monica, I think I may have misjudged you. You're far more sophisticated than I initially gave you credit for. I really do think you would be a perfect fit for our family. *Regardless* of where you're from."

Before Nadi could respond, a knock at the door interrupted them.

"Come in!" Lana's call was so chipper it almost made Nadi sick.

The door opened to reveal the same seamstress Nadi had noticed the day before—the one she'd seen in Braen's club. The fae. Or at least someone who had grown up in the Wild around the fae.

"Begging your pardon, my lady," the seamstress said with a curtsy, "but there's been a small issue with the train of your gown. Nothing serious, but it needs attention before the ceremony."

"Of course it does." Lana sighed dramatically. "Monica,

would you mind? I should probably rest for a few minutes before the chaos truly begins, anyway."

"Not at all." Nadi headed for the door, grateful for an excuse to leave before Lana's questions became more pointed.

As she passed the seamstress in the doorway, the woman's hand brushed against hers—a contact that lasted a fraction of a second longer than necessary. In that brief touch, Nadi felt something pressed into her palm. A small piece of paper, folded tight.

Her heart hammered, but she kept her expression neutral as she continued down the hallway. Only when she was safely in a powder room with the door locked behind her did she unfold the paper.

The message was brief, written in the flowing script of the fae language—*When the bells toll, escape while you can.*

Nadi stared at the words, her mind racing. The fae were not only here to disrupt the wedding...

They knew what she was. *Who she was.*

That wasn't possible. It wasn't—how? *How?*

Ripping up the paper into tiny shreds, she quickly ran to the restroom and flushed it down the drain. As she stood there, watching the evidence disappear, she felt the weight of impossible choices settling on her shoulders.

No, no, no, no, *no, no—*

Raziel and his family were planning their own internal destruction. The fae were here and they knew who she was.

And she was caught in the middle, bound by conflicting loyalties and impossible promises.

The sound of bells chiming in the distance made her freeze. Wedding bells, calling guests to take their places for the ceremony.

When the bells toll, escape while you can.

Whatever was about to happen, it was starting now.

Nadi took a deep breath, straightened her shoulders, and

walked back into the corridor. She had a wedding to attend, a family to help destroy, and her own people to face.

All while trying to keep the vampire she'd come to kill, that she'd grown to care for, alive.

The afternoon's deceptive serenity was about to shatter completely.

And she still wasn't sure which side she would choose when it did.

The bells continued to toll, their bronze voices carrying across the estate like a funeral dirge disguised as celebration. Guests began moving toward the garden pavilion where the ceremony would take place, their voices bright with anticipation.

Nadi moved with them, scanning faces for signs of recognition or threat. The seamstress had vanished, melted back into the crowd of servants and vendors who made such gatherings possible. But her message burned in Nadi's memory like a brand.

She spotted Raziel near the main pavilion, speaking with Mael and several other family members. Even from a distance, she could see the tension in his posture, the way his eyes moved constantly, cataloging threats and opportunities.

Their gazes met across the crowd, and she saw him nod almost imperceptibly. He'd received some kind of signal too—whether from his own sources or simply from reading the atmosphere, she couldn't tell.

But they were both ready.

An arm caught her wrist and jerked her around to face the scrutinizing face of Volencia Nostrom. "Get to your seat, *girl*. Before you make an ass of us all." And with that, the matriarch pushed her forward with a dismissive gesture that held more strength to it than should have been possible.

Mother moon, she *hated* that woman. Fire seethed in her blood. And if she had her way, the dusty old hag would not leave the wedding alive, no matter what Raziel had made her promise. He had said they were only here to kill Mael, but if she saw an opportunity to take out Volencia *or* Lana—they were going to die. Especially the bitch of the old woman.

The bells fell silent, and in that sudden quiet, Nadi heard the rustle of fabric, the whisper of steel, the collective intake of breath that preceded violence.

And she still didn't know if she was a soldier, a spy, or simply another casualty waiting to happen.

* * *

Raziel positioned himself near the main pavilion, his eyes constantly scanning the assembled guests while maintaining the appearance of casual conversation with the security detail. The setting sun had nearly finished its journey below the horizon. It cast long shadows across the manicured grounds, like hungry, grasping fingers.

He had a glass of wine in his hand, swirling it idly between his sips. It gave him something to do. He was told toying with his usual gold coins or smoking a cigarette was absolutely out of the question.

"Raziel." Mael's voice cut through his focus, drawing his attention to his brother's approach. The massive vampire moved with surprising grace through the crowd, his golden eyes bright with what might have been anticipation. Or calculation. "I trust everything is in order?"

"As much as it can be with these many variables in play." Raziel withdrew the leather-bound ledger from inside his jacket, noting how Mael's gaze immediately fixed on it with hungry intensity. "The item you requested."

Mael accepted the ledger with careful hands, as if it contained something far more precious than mere trafficking records. "Excellent. This will prove quite useful for our purposes."

"Will it?" Raziel stepped closer, lowering his voice so their conversation wouldn't carry to nearby guests. "I'm curious, brother. What exactly do you plan to do with Braen's client list? Most of those names are already known to us—minor nobles with unsavory reputations, merchants seeking exotic pleasures. Hardly earth-shattering intelligence."

"You'd be surprised what patterns emerge when you have the complete picture." Mael's smile was enigmatic as he tucked the ledger away. "Sometimes, the most valuable information isn't what's written down, but what connects the dots between seemingly unrelated events."

Something in his brother's tone set Raziel's nerves on edge. There was a smugness there, a satisfaction that went beyond simply acquiring useful blackmail material. "Enlighten me."

"Have you ever wondered," Mael began, his voice taking on the cadence of someone settling in to tell a story, "about the deeper implications of fae trafficking? Not just the immediate horror of it, but the... ripple effects it creates in their communities? Or even *why* our kind desires to keep them as pets?"

Raziel's hand stilled on his wine glass. "What exactly are you getting at?"

"Oh, just thinking about cause and effect. Actions and consequences." Mael's golden eyes gleamed with something that made Raziel's skin crawl. "Tell me, do you remember every family you've destroyed over the years? Every life you've snuffed out in service to our mother's ambitions?"

"Get to the point, Mael." He rolled his eyes. "Unless you're about to confess you have a personal taste for fae flesh, you're boring me."

"The point?" Mael chuckled, the sound carrying an edge of cruelty that Raziel recognized from their childhood. His brother rarely brought it out in public. "Very well. Once upon a time, long ago, there was a young fae girl who watched her whole family get murdered by a serpent. A tragedy, certainly, but hardly an uncommon one."

Ice began forming in Raziel's veins. He kept his expression carefully neutral, but internally, alarms were screaming.

"But this particular young girl," Mael continued, his voice dropping to barely above a whisper, "was *very* special. A shapeshifter, you see. The Rosovs were in conversations with her family to buy her a long, long time ago, but she disappeared the moment her family died. You can imagine how useful a fae with the gift to become anyone would be, if she could be broken and tamed. That is, unless, she had instead decided to exact the most exquisite revenge on those who had wronged her."

Raziel's mind raced through the implications, the terrible mathematics of what his brother was suggesting. "That's a fascinating story, Mael. But I fail to see—"

"Oh, but you do see, don't you?" Mael's smile turned predatory. "You see it perfectly clearly. Because you, my dear brother, have been sleeping with the enemy, haven't you? Quite literally."

The words hit like physical blows. Raziel fought to keep his breathing steady, his expression unchanged, but inside he felt something fundamental shifting. His brother knew. He knew *everything*.

How?

"I have no idea what you're talking about."

"Don't you?" Mael leaned closer, his voice barely audible over the growing chatter of arriving guests. "This ledger isn't for me, Raziel. It's for my new business partners. They want to expand their own... operations. This is the key to their own rise to power. One of my new fae associates grew up with little Nadi in the Wild. Remembers her quite well, actually. Sweet child, apparently, before you turned her into a killer. It wasn't hard to put two and two together once I had that piece of information."

Raziel's hand moved instinctively toward the knife concealed in his jacket.

Mael caught the motion and laughed. "Please. We're at a wedding, surrounded by hundreds of witnesses. Besides, you're hardly in a position to threaten me now, are you? Not when your precious Monica—or should I say, your precious *Nadi*—is somewhere in this crowd, completely unaware that her cover has been blown."

The implications crashed over Raziel like a tidal wave. If Mael knew about Nadi, how many others knew? Was this why Lana had been testing her so aggressively? Had they been trying to convert her to their side earlier by forcing her to reveal her true nature? Had the entire family been playing *him* from the beginning? Or were they playing them both?

"What do you want?" The words came out rougher than he intended.

"Want?" Mael's eyebrows rose in mock surprise. "I want exactly what I've always wanted, brother. Order. Stability. A family that serves its interests rather than its obsessions." His expression hardened. "I want you to stop destroying everything you touch out of some misguided need for revenge."

"And Nadi?"

"Ah, yes. Your little assassin." Mael's smile turned almost gentle, which somehow made it more terrifying. "She presents a fascinating dilemma, doesn't she? On one hand, she's exactly what she appears to be—a weapon pointed at our family's heart. On the other hand, you've clearly developed... feelings for her."

The way Mael said the word *feelings* made it sound like a disease.

"So tell me, Raziel," Mael continued, "when the moment comes—and it will come very soon—which will you choose? Your family, or your fae pet?"

Before Raziel could formulate a response, the first wedding bells began to toll across the estate grounds. The clear, bronze voices rang out in a pattern that was both celebration and summons, calling all guests to witness the union of Lana Nostrom and Zabriel Rosov.

"Ah." Mael straightened, his demeanor shifting back to that of the dutiful brother. "The ceremony begins. We should take our places, don't you think?"

As if nothing earth-shattering had just been revealed. As if Raziel's entire world hadn't just been turned inside out with a few carefully chosen words.

Around them, the crowd began moving toward the main pavilion where white silk chairs had been arranged in perfect rows. Vampires in their finest attire, human dignitaries, and—if Mael was to be believed—fae infiltrators disguised among the servants and guests.

Raziel found himself scanning faces with new intensity, looking for signs of deception, for the subtle tells that might reveal interlopers among them. His mind raced with contingencies and calculations, trying to adapt their carefully laid plans to this new reality.

Mael knew about Nadi. Which meant others likely knew as well. Which meant their window for action was closing rapidly —if it hadn't already slammed shut.

The bells continued and guests filtered toward their seats with the excited murmur of spectators gathering for a grand performance. But Raziel could hear something else beneath the surface chatter now—a tension, an undercurrent of anticipation that had nothing to do with weddings and everything to do with violence.

"Before I forget, brother," Mael said quietly as they began walking toward the pavilion. "When this all begins—remember that I gave you a choice. Remember that I tried to offer you a way out."

"A way out of what?"

But Mael was already moving away, his massive frame

cutting through the crowd like a ship through calm waters. Leaving Raziel standing there with questions burning in his throat and the terrible certainty that everything they had planned was about to go catastrophically wrong.

The bells reached their crescendo and fell silent, leaving behind a sudden, expectant quiet that felt like the breath held before a scream.

In that silence, Raziel caught sight of Nadi across the crowd, her borrowed face composed and serene as she took her seat among the other family members. She looked so perfect in her deception, so completely convincing as Monica Valan. But it was all a lie.

A lie that had long since fallen apart. How many knew about it, and what they planned to do about it, was what Raziel didn't know. The ceremony was about to begin. And with it, whatever chaos Mael had been planning would finally be unleashed.

Slowly, carefully, as to not raise suspicion, he began to make his way to her. He had to reach her. Warn her. Get her out of there safely—somehow. They had to escape. To where, he didn't know. But their cover was blown. He had to reach her before Mael did. Before everything went to the void.

Because now, all they had was their lives. And each other.

For however many precious seconds all that might last.

TWENTY-ONE

The setting sun had finally given way to night as the wedding guests had settled into their silk-draped chairs like jeweled birds perching in an elaborate aviary. All the while, Nadi's thoughts spun.

What was she supposed to *do*? The fae knew she was here. Knew what she *was*. Knew who she was *playing*. That required a level of knowledge and infiltration where the knock-on effects were staggering.

Either Raziel had told them, or Ivan had, or a third party—or parties—knew her secret. Option one wasn't impossible. Raziel might sell her out to save face with his siblings if he was trapped in a corner. Option two, she would *like* to believe, but as much as she would loathe to admit it, she had grown to appreciate the bodyguard. He wasn't the kind to double-cross someone.

Option three, however? Option three was the most likely. Someone else knew. And that *someone* was a dangerous scenario. Because it was likely one of their would-be targets. And that meant... everything was over.

And it had been over before they had walked into the wedding.

Which meant they had walked into a trap.

Nadi was seated in the front row, next to an empty chair meant for Raziel as she picked at the edge of the program for the wedding. Raziel wasn't meant to take his seat in the audience—he would simply wait backstage for Mael to slip the knife between his ribs.

Or at least, that had been the plan. Before everything had gone wrong.

Her assignment had been to make sure that Mael wouldn't be able to leave from the front aisle instead.

But now everything was fucked, and she didn't know what to do. Except sit there and panic and try to think.

She should run. But not with Volencia watching her. All eyes would see her get up and make a hasty retreat. The other voice in her head told her it didn't matter—she should head for the nearest exit, change her face, and disappear back into the Wild where she belonged. She'd be alive, and that was better than nothing.

The two moons hung in the darkening sky like mismatched eyes. Father moon full and bright, and Mother moon a darker black against a purple-blue backdrop of stars.

Torches had been lit around the perimeter of the pavilion, their flames dancing in the gentle evening breeze and casting shifting shadows across the white silk panels overhead.

Looking up, she caught sight of Raziel. He was trying to make his way to her. But he couldn't just *march through the rows*, not without causing a scene. Their eyes met briefly across the crowd, and she caught the tension in his expression. Something had changed during his conversation with Mael—she could read it in the rigid set of his shoulders, the way his hand rested just inside his jacket.

Shit. He knew too. He was trying to get to her to warn her.

Their shared expressions were brief but said it all to each other.

We're dead, aren't we? Nadi started to stand, ready to say *Fuck it* to all the pomp and circumstance and just run for the horizon. But she never got a chance.

"Sit down, you *hussy*," Volencia hissed at her between her teeth. "Or I will have you shot here and now and finish the job that worthless son of mine couldn't."

Regardless of whatever might come of this debacle, Nadi deeply hoped she got the chance to murder that bitch. Biting back the deeply inappropriate slew of obscenities she wanted to call the woman, Nadi slowly settled back into her chair.

The string quartet began tuning their instruments in preparation for the processional, when a commotion near the main entrance drew everyone's attention. Murmurs rippled through the assembled guests as an ornate litter appeared, carried by four vampires in ceremonial dress, with golden masks concealing their faces.

The litter itself was a masterwork of craftsmanship from a bygone era—ebony wood inlaid with gold and garnets, its sides draped with heavy black silk that completely concealed its occupant. The carriers moved with supernatural grace, their faces solemn as they approached the pavilion.

"By the moons," whispered an elderly vampire seated nearby. "Is that...?"

"It can't be," another guest breathed. "She hasn't appeared in public for *centuries*."

But Nadi could feel the weight of ancient power emanating from the veiled litter, a presence so old and potent that it made everything in her want to hiss like a feral *yupui* and crawl under the furniture. Whoever was inside that conveyance was no ordinary vampire.

The carriers brought the litter to a halt near the altar, positioning it so that its hidden occupant would have a perfect view of the ceremony. The gathered guests had fallen into complete silence, even the children clearly sensing the gravity of this unexpected arrival.

With practiced motions, the carriers drew back the heavy black silk drapes to reveal sheer ones that did nothing to reveal anything but a silhouette of a figure within, seated on a chaise longue.

Nadi couldn't make out any details except that the woman had long hair and was thin in frame.

A voice emerged from within the litter—female, melodious, but carrying an undertone of such authority that it seemed to resonate in Nadi's bones. It had the cadence of someone accustomed to absolute obedience.

"My children," the voice said, and despite the fabric barriers, every word carried clearly through the evening air. "How lovely to see you all gathered for such a joyous occasion."

Volencia rose from her seat in the front row, her face a mask of shocked reverence. "Mother. You honor us with your presence."

Mother. Nadi's blood turned cold as understanding dawned. *Lilivra.* The ancient vampire matriarch, the one whose portrait dominated the chapel at the ruined estate.

The woman who forged the alliance that drove the fae into exile.

The *original* vampire.

"The honor is mine, dearest Volencia," Lilivra's voice continued. "It has been far too long since I witnessed such a momentous union. Today will indeed be historic for all of Runne—a day that will be remembered for generations to come."

Her words carried weight beyond their surface meaning, as if she possessed knowledge of events yet to unfold. Nadi felt a chill that had nothing to do with the evening air.

"Raziel, my child," Lilivra's voice called out, and every head turned toward where he stood among the security detail. "Come closer. I would speak with you, my grandson."

A murmur went through the crowd. Nadi didn't miss how Mael glanced at Raziel with thinly concealed rage.

Nadi watched as Raziel approached the litter, his movements careful and controlled. Even from a distance, she could see the tension in his frame as he drew near to his legendary ancestor.

"You have grown strong, grandson," Lilivra said, her voice carrying a note of what might have been approval. "The trials you have endured have forged you into exactly what you were meant to be."

"Thank you, Grandmother." Raziel's voice was steady, but Nadi caught the underlying current of unease.

"Do you remember," Lilivra continued, "the words I spoke to you on the first day you came to see me? When you were still a frightened child, seeking answers about your destiny?"

A long pause. "I remember."

"Good. Today, your true path will finally begin." The silk panels rustled as if their hidden occupant had shifted position. "The serpent must shed its skin to become something greater. Remember that, when the pain begins."

The cryptic exchange left Nadi's mind racing. What had Lilivra told Raziel all those years ago? And why did her presence here feel less like a blessing and more like the tolling of a funeral bell?

"Now then," Lilivra's voice returned to its earlier warmth, "let us witness this beautiful union. The joining of our house with the Rosovs marks the beginning of a new age."

Volencia returned to her seat, though Nadi noticed her hands trembling slightly as she smoothed her dark skirts. Around the pavilion, guests exchanged nervous glances, clearly unsettled by the ancient vampire's unexpected appearance and ominous words.

The quartet began their processional melody, signaling that the ceremony was about to begin despite the disruption. A hush fell over the assembled guests as all attention turned toward the main pavilion entrance where the bridal party would emerge.

"Nervous, beautiful?"

The voice came from directly behind her, and Nadi's blood turned to ice. She knew that voice, but it wasn't Lana's sweet tones. This was deeper, more resonant—Mael's distinctive rumble pitched low for her ears alone.

"The ceremony is beautiful," Nadi corrected, not turning to look at him. "Lana looks radiant."

"She does indeed." Mael moved to sit in the chair beside her, the one meant for Raziel, his massive frame blocking her view of the nearest exit. "Though I suspect you appreciate the significance of tonight more than most of our guests do."

Something in his tone made Nadi's skin crawl. "I'm not sure what you mean."

"Oh, but I think you do, *Nadi*."

The name hit like a punch to the gut. Nadi's hands clenched in her lap, fighting every instinct that screamed at her to run, to fight, to do anything except sit there like a trapped animal.

"I'm sorry?" she whispered, her voice carefully modulated to sound confused rather than terrified.

"Please." Mael's hand settled on her knee. His thumb began to run a slow circle along her skin over the sheer fabric of her stockings. "We're past the point of pretense now, aren't we? I know exactly who you are. Nadi of the Iltani clan. Shapeshifter. Assassin. The woman who's been sleeping in my brother's bed while plotting his death. You killed your own uncle to get to us. I'm not upset. Anything but. I'm in awe."

The words were delivered with such casual certainty that Nadi felt her carefully constructed world crumbling around her. She forced herself to remain still, to keep breathing, even as panic clawed at her chest.

"In fact, I must say," Mael continued, his voice pitched so low that only she could hear it over the music, "you've done *remarkable* work. The deception was flawless. If it weren't for some very specific intelligence from someone who used to know you, I would never have suspected anything at all." His hand slid just a little bit higher.

Around them, other guests continued their polite conversation, completely unaware of the deadly revelation taking place in their midst. The quartet played on, their melody sweet and haunting in the torchlight.

"What do you want?" Nadi asked, abandoning the lie. If Mael knew, there was no point in maintaining the charade.

"What I've always wanted." Mael's hand on her leg tightened just slightly. "Order. Stability. A future that serves the interests of all our people rather than the obsessions of a few." He paused. "And you, of course..."

"I don't understand." She sighed.

Chuckling, he leaned forward, his breath warm against her ear. "Don't you? You came here for revenge against the family that destroyed yours. But Lana and I had nothing to do with it, and revenge is such a limited goal. So much effort, so much sacrifice, all for the satisfaction of ending a few lives. Think *bigger*, Nadi. Think about how much more change we could do together in this world."

Nadi felt trapped, hyperaware of how easily he could snap her neck before she could even attempt to shift forms.

His hand slid just the slightest, little bit higher, angling between her legs. Her cheeks went warm despite herself at the strength in his touch. "I'm offering you something better. Safer, *kinder*," Mael continued. "Something that could benefit both our peoples in ways you've never imagined."

"Which is?"

"Partnership. Alliance. A true joining of vampire and fae bloodlines." His voice carried genuine passion. "Imagine it, Nadi. No more hiding in the Wild, no more cowering behind walls. No more wearing this false face of yours. A new order where your people have not just a voice, but *real* power."

The proposal was so audacious that Nadi found herself momentarily speechless. "You're talking about... integration? Freedom?"

"I'm talking about *evolution*, Nadi. My mother's ways are dying—we both know it. The walls between our peoples, the ancient hatreds, the senseless conflicts—they serve no one anymore." Mael's golden eyes gleamed in the torchlight as he squeezed her thigh, just a little harder. She would be lying if she said her heart didn't quicken at his touch. "But together, we could build something the likes of which this world has never seen."

Despite herself, Nadi felt a flicker of something that might have been hope. How many times had she wondered what the world might look like if the fae reclaimed their rightful place? How many nights had she dreamed of her people walking free under the open sky? "And what would this partnership entail?" she asked carefully.

"Marriage, of course." The word was delivered simply, matter-of-factly. "A union between the eldest Nostrom heir and a representative of the fae clans. A symbol of the new age we're building."

Nadi's breath caught. "You want me to marry you. As... as *myself*?"

"I want you to help me create a future worth living in." Mael's hand moved to cup her face gently, his thumb tracing her cheekbone. "You're remarkable, Nadi. Intelligent, resourceful, deadly when necessary but capable of restraint. You could be so much more than just another assassin. Besides... it's clear you don't have a problem with vampires…" He smirked. "I am so much better than my brother."

The touch should have repulsed her, but there was something tempting in it, a gentleness that belied his massive frame and fearsome reputation.

"And what about your brother?" she asked quietly.

Mael's expression grew sad. "Raziel is… damaged, you know that. Beyond repair. Mother made sure of that." He paused, studying her face carefully. "What was done to him was beyond cruel. But I see how you look at him. There's genuine feeling there, isn't there? Despite everything he's done, everything he represents. You have a big heart, Nadi."

The observation was too accurate, too perceptive. Nadi felt exposed under his knowing gaze.

"He doesn't have to die," Mael continued softly. "If something unfortunate were to happen to him during tonight's festivities… well, accidents do occur during times of chaos. But you would be protected. Cherished. Given the power to make real changes for your people."

"You're asking me to let him die."

"I'm asking you to choose a future over the past. To choose hope over vengeance." Mael leaned back slightly. "Because if you continue down this path of revenge, if you refuse the hand I'm extending? Well. Let's just say that tonight will end very badly for everyone involved."

The processional music swelled, and Mael straightened, his politician's mask sliding back into place. "Think about what I've said. When the moment comes, you'll have a choice."

With that, he moved away to take his position near the altar, leaving Nadi sitting frozen in her chair. Around her, guests leaned forward in anticipation as the bridal party began to appear at the pavilion entrance.

Nadi's mind raced through the implications of everything Mael had revealed. They knew who she was. Lana and Mael both. They knew why she was here. But instead of exposing or eliminating her, they were offering her something she'd never dared to imagine—a chance to be part of something larger than revenge.

The offer was seductive. Partnership instead of domination. Integration instead of war. A future where the fae could reclaim their place in the world without having to destroy it first.

But it would mean betraying Raziel. The man who had become... what? Her ally? Her lover? Something more complicated and dangerous than either of those simple terms could encompass?

She caught sight of him across the pavilion, still standing near Lilivra's mysterious litter. Their eyes met, and she saw the question there—tense, furious, on the edge of panic—was everything all right? She managed a slight nod, though her stomach churned with the lie.

Raziel's gaze flicked to Mael, then to her. Then, he headed toward the backstage entrance. Wait. What was he *thinking*?

Oh, no... he had seen Mael touch her. And now he was going to double down on the attempt on his brother's life, when the rational choice was to simply run.

Fuck.

And there she was, trapped in her seat like a total moron.

Nadi wanted to scream.

The processional music shifted to the bridal march, and all attention turned to the pavilion entrance. Lana appeared like a vision in the torchlight, her ivory silk and black lace gown flowing behind her as she began her slow walk down the white-carpeted aisle.

Zabriel waited at the altar, his face radiant with a genuine happiness that seemed to glow even brighter than his bride's.

For a moment, watching them approach each other with such obvious love and joy, Nadi could almost believe in Mael's vision of a better world. A world where vampire and fae could stand together as equals, where ancient hatreds could be set aside in favor of something new and hopeful.

The ceremony proceeded with ancient ritual and modern touches. Honestly, Nadi couldn't focus on a blessed second of it. All the while, she was screaming in her head about what was happening.

Mael knew. Lana knew. That meant Zabriel knew.

Did Volencia know?

No, probably not.

Raziel was going to try to murder his brother now out of spite for her sake. And she had to try to... what, stop him? To save Raziel's life? Or Mael's?

This was all so damnably complicated it was going to give her a migraine. Lana and Zabriel exchanged vows that spoke of love transcending political necessity, of two souls finding each other across the divide of family loyalties. Nadi wished she could pay more attention, as she had never actually seen a vampiric wedding besides her own before. And that one hadn't actually focused on formality—it had been to a *human,* after all.

But she was still sitting there rigid as a statue, every nerve in her body about to explode because she was ready to snap and murder someone if they moved too suddenly.

When Lana and Zabriel kissed to seal their union, the assembled guests erupted in applause that echoed across the estate grounds.

And finally, she could breathe. For better or worse.

Because that was when the first explosion shattered the evening's joy.

The blast came from somewhere beyond the main pavilion, a deep rumbling boom that sent shock waves through the ground and extinguished several of the torches. Guests screamed and dove for cover as a second explosion followed, closer this time, accompanied by the sharp crack of gunfire.

Chaos erupted instantly. Vampires moved with inhuman

speed toward exits and cover, while humans struggled to process what was happening. Security guards shouted orders that were lost in the pandemonium as more explosions echoed across the estate grounds.

Nadi waited for a split second, watching Lana and Zabriel at the altar.

Instead of fear, she saw grim satisfaction on both their faces —*this wasn't a surprise attack.*

This was expected.

Planned.

Part of whatever larger game the Nostrom siblings had been playing.

Fuck.

Well. There went the plan to assassinate Mael. He was working with Lana, which she had been starting to suspect. But now it was confirmed they were working *with* the fae in attendance. But to what ends? *Why attack their own wedding...?*

A figure burst through the eastern entrance of the pavilion —one of the estate guards, but moving wrong, too fluid, too wild. More figures poured in behind him, no longer bothering to maintain their human disguises.

Gunfire erupted from multiple directions as the infiltrators engaged the Nostrom security forces. Guests scattered in all directions, some seeking shelter behind overturned chairs, others rushing toward what they hoped were exits. The white silk pavilion became a battlefield, its pristine beauty torn and stained by violence.

Lilivra's guards, ancient-looking things, quickly disposed of anyone who wandered too close—friend or foe—and began to carry out the litter that carried her toward the exit. They seemed entirely unconcerned with the chaos as if it were something they dealt with regularly.

Turning toward the stage, Nadi tried to make it to the front of the room but instantly stopped. It was pandemonium in that direction. Bodies and bullets criss-crossing between all parties. She wasn't going to make it to Raziel. She had to retreat. Ducking outside of the pavilion, she drew her knives and did her best to gather her wits and get a sense of her bearings.

Through the mayhem, she spotted a familiar figure trying to reach the main house—Volencia Nostrom, her dark gown billowing as she moved with surprising speed for someone of her apparent age. The lesser matriarch was heading for what had to be a secure room, somewhere she could wait out the attack in safety.

This was it. The opportunity she'd been waiting for.

All the planning, all the sacrifice, all the months of deception.

Mael was off the table. So was Lana.

Raziel was a complicated mess.

But that bitch?

That bitch could die. Right now.

Nadi pushed through the panicking crowd, using her smaller size to slip between guests and around security forces engaged with the attackers. A fae warrior appeared in her path, wild-eyed and bloodied, raising what looked like a silver blade.

"*Ui quala vuampi, fi'ti!*" Nadi dropped her glamor to her own face, swearing at the fae warrior that she wasn't a vampire, and calling him a colorful name to boot.

The fae warrior blinked, his silver sword freezing in midswing. He didn't even apologize before moving on to cut down his next target.

Swearing again to herself, she shifted back to the vampiric Monica and ran toward the house. It had cost her precious seconds.

The main house loomed ahead, its white walls now scarred by bullet holes and scorch marks. Volencia had disappeared inside, but Nadi had seen the direction she'd taken. The east wing, where the family kept their private offices and secure rooms.

Behind her, the battle raged on. She could hear Raziel's voice cutting through the chaos, shouting her name, and part of her wanted to turn back. To find him, to stand beside him, to face whatever came next together.

But this was her mission. Her purpose. The reason she'd sacrificed everything to get here.

The matriarch who had ordered her family's death was finally within reach.

And Nadi intended to make her pay for every drop of blood she'd spilled.

She reached the main house and slipped through a side entrance, leaving the bloodshed of the wedding behind. The interior was eerily quiet after the violence outside, her footsteps muffled by thick carpets as she followed the route she'd seen Volencia take.

Somewhere in this house was the woman responsible for everything—the deaths, the suffering, the decades of hatred that had shaped Nadi's entire existence.

Today, that debt would finally be paid in full.

TWENTY-TWO

The interior of the Nostrom estate felt like stepping into a tomb after the chaos of the garden battle. Nadi's footsteps were muffled by thick antique carpets as she moved through corridors lined with portraits of long-dead vampires, their painted eyes seeming to track her movement through the shadows.

The sounds of gunfire and explosions continued outside, but here the violence felt distant, almost dreamlike. She followed the route she'd seen Volencia take—past the grand staircase, through a sitting room filled with antique furniture, toward the family's private wing.

Her hand found the serpent pendant at her throat, thumb running over the hidden blade mechanism Raziel had shown her. The weight of it was both comforting and thrilling—a reminder of the man who'd given it to her, and the moment she'd been building toward for eighty years.

Focus, she told herself. *This is what you came here for.*

She turned the silver dagger over in her other hand. Now, its weight was a familiar comfort, like greeting an old friend.

A soft click ahead made her freeze. Through an open doorway, she could see into what appeared to be a private study—

rich mahogany paneling, floor-to-ceiling bookshelves, and Volencia Nostrom standing before a wall safe, her fingers flying over a complex combination lock.

The vampire matriarch was pulling her silver-streaked hair from its formal hairstyle into a severe bun, transforming her from elegant society hostess to something far more dangerous. She had kicked off her heels and donned a pair of slip-on flat shoes that were easier to run in. Nadi was impressed at the hag's practicality.

Nadi slipped closer, staying in the shadows of the doorway. The safe clicked open, revealing stacks of documents, several small weapons, and what appeared to be vials of dark liquid. Volencia began stuffing items into a leather satchel with practiced efficiency.

A predator's smile curved Nadi's lips as she watched. How fitting that Volencia would be packing for an escape she'd never make.

"Going somewhere?" Nadi stepped into the room.

"Good, you can help me get my things together and you'll finally be useful—" Volencia rolled her eyes in annoyance at her.

Cracking her neck, Nadi let Monica's appearance drop away like a discarded mask. She felt a savage kind of satisfaction at how Volencia's expression shifted from annoyance to shock.

"You," Volencia breathed, her amber eyes taking in Nadi's true form with rapid assessment. "I knew there was something off about you. But this..." She gestured at Nadi's obvious non-human nature and her pale, green-blue skin. She laughed. "I admit, this is unexpected."

"Is it?" Nadi moved farther into the room, her movements fluid. She was savoring this—the fear beginning to creep into Volencia's eyes, the way the vampire's breath had quickened slightly. "Your family has made a career of underestimating the fae. I suppose it runs in the blood."

Volencia's hand drifted toward the satchel, where Nadi could see the grip of a gold-inlaid pistol protruding from the leather. "A *fae* shapeshifter. Of course. How resourceful, to make that part of your cover. May I ask which clan you represent? The terms of your employment? I'm always interested in acquiring new talent."

The casual assumption that Nadi could be bought made her smile widen. "Oh, lady. I'm not for hire. At least, not by you."

"Everyone has a price." Volencia's voice took on that hypnotic quality Nadi had noticed at family dinners, the same commanding tone that suffered no disobedience. "Name yours. Wealth? Territory? The lives of your enemies? I can provide all of that and more."

For a moment, Nadi felt the pull of her vampiric influence, the way it tried to wrap around her mind like silk threads. It seemed Raziel got it from somewhere, his was just a far more impressive manifestation. But her fae nature provided protection, just like with him.

"You're right." She took another step closer, letting Volencia see the hunger in her eyes. "Everyone does have a price. In this instance, however, you're already in debt to me. A debt that you accrued eighty years ago."

Something flickered in Volencia's eyes—perhaps the first hint of genuine concern. "Eighty years? I don't recall any... you'll have to be more specific."

Nadi tilted her head, considering. She was in no hurry now. This moment—this perfect, singular moment when Volencia still didn't accept what was about to happen to her—was to be *preserved.*

"The Iltani warehouse. Seventh district. A family of fae smugglers who thought they could operate in your territory without paying proper tribute." Nadi's voice remained conversational, almost friendly. "Ring any bells?"

Recognition dawned slowly across Volencia's features,

followed by what might have been amusement. "Ah. That unfortunate business. Yes, I remember now. Talien Iltani and his little enterprise. Such a shame. He showed promise."

The casual dismissal of her father's death made something dark and joyful unfurl in Nadi's chest. Perfect. She wanted Volencia to be exactly this callous, this dismissive. It would make what came next so much sweeter. "We were just trying to survive." Nadi kept her tone deceptively mild.

"Yes, well, one has to be careful when one is dealing with Luciento. Oh! But you killed him, didn't you?" Volencia grinned, her perfectly painted red lips curling in pure disdain. "How utterly wonderful. Now, tell me—that useless runt Raziel. Does he even know what you are?"

Nadi laughed quietly. "My mother's name was Essira. My brother Kaen was sixteen. My younger sisters, Meri and Lissa, were twins." She turned the knife over in her palm, admiring how the blade caught the lamplight. "Would you like to hear how they died? I have such vivid memories."

"How touching," Volencia's tone dripped with false sympathy, but Nadi could see the unease creeping into her posture. "Though I fail to see how ancient history is relevant to our current situation."

"Oh, but it is." Nadi took another step closer, close enough now that she could smell Volencia's expensive perfume, could see the slight tremor in the vampire's hands. "You see, I watched my entire family die, then spent the next eighty years learning to kill. Learning to hunt. Learning to become the kind of monster that could infiltrate your city and get close enough to your precious trained Serpent." She paused, letting her smile turn genuinely warm. "But most importantly, I learned to enjoy my work."

"But you didn't kill him, did you?" Volencia's political instincts were reasserting themselves, her voice taking on a calculating edge. "My son still lives. In fact, unless I'm very much mistaken, you've grown rather fond of him."

"That doesn't change what he did. What you ordered him to do." Nadi's grip on the knife tightened, her pulse quickening with anticipation.

"Doesn't it?" Volencia smiled—an expression both knowing and desperate now. "Tell me, child, when you look at Raziel now, do you still see the monster who destroyed your family? Or do you see the broken boy who was shaped by forces beyond his control?"

"Both," Nadi answered honestly.

"Both," Volencia repeated, confusion flickering across her features. "How complicated. You know, I think I'm beginning to understand why my son has been behaving so strangely lately. You've given him something he's never had before—someone who sees all of him and chooses to stay anyway."

"Oh, I didn't stay for him." Nadi's eyes glittered with dark joy. "I stayed for this moment. Right here. Right now. You see, killing your son would have been too easy. Too quick. But killing you?" She sighed in contentment. "This is going to be *so* much better."

Volencia's composure was cracking now, fear finally breaking through her aristocratic mask. "You're stalling, aren't you? Trying to work up the courage to do what you came here for."

"Stalling?" Nadi laughed again, she couldn't help it. The woman was scrambling for options and failing. "I'm savoring the moment. I wanted to make sure you knew who I was. The names of the lives you took that are now ending your own. I wanted to see that fear in your eyes. I wanted to watch you realize that all your power, all your influence, all your centuries of cruelty have led to this—dying alone on the floor at the hands of a 'savage' fae."

"Killing me won't bring them back," Volencia tried once

more, her voice gentle now, almost motherly. "It won't undo the pain or fill the emptiness inside you. All it will do is make you a murderer."

"With all due respect, I'm already a murderer. You made more than one monster in your life." She turned the knife over in her palm one final time. "I've killed dozens of your people over the years. Guards, enforcers... anyone who served your interests."

"Ah, but those were soldiers in a war. Combatants who knew the risks." Volencia spread her hands in a gesture of openness, but Nadi could see her muscles tensing, preparing to lunge for the gun. "I'm just an old woman trying to protect her family and maintain order in a chaotic world. Killing me would be different. It would be personal. Petty. Beneath someone of your obvious intelligence and skill."

"You're right. This *is* personal. This *is* petty. This *is* beneath me." Nadi let her smile turn radiant. Indulgent. "And I'm going to enjoy every single second of it."

Volencia finally made her move, lunging for the pistol in her satchel, but Nadi was already there. The blade flashed in the lamplight as it found a space between Volencia's ribs, sliding up and in with the precision of someone who'd spent decades practicing for this exact moment.

The vampire matriarch's eyes went wide with shock, her mouth opening as if to speak. But no words came—only blood, dark and thick, spilling over her lips to stain the pristine white of her blouse.

"This is for Talien," Nadi whispered, her voice filled with savage joy as she twisted the silver blade deeper into the matriarch's heart. "And Essira. And Kaen, and Meri, and Lissa. And every other fae whose life you destroyed."

Volencia's legs gave out, and she crumpled to the floor, her aristocratic features slack with approaching death. Her amber eyes fixed on Nadi's face, and for a moment there was something that might have been respect there. "Raziel... chose well."

"Yes." Nadi watched the light fade from those inhuman eyes with deep satisfaction. "He did."

Volencia Nostrom—matriarch of one of the most powerful vampire families in Runne, orchestrator of countless deaths, architect of fae suffering—died on the antique carpet of her own study.

Nadi stood over her for a long moment, feeling the warm glow of completion spreading through her chest. This was what justice felt like. This was what eight decades of planning and sacrifice had been building toward. The woman who had ordered her family's death was finally, permanently silenced.

Taking the iron poker from the fireplace, she stuck it through the woman's skull. Vampires were notoriously hard to kill and keep dead. And even though the knife was silver, she wanted to make absolutely certain the bitch stayed down.

The sound of approaching footsteps in the corridor finally snapped her back to reality. She quickly cleaned the blade and returned it to the pendant, then began moving toward the study's secondary exit. She needed to find Raziel, to share this moment with him, to figure out what they were going to do now that—

The door burst open, revealing three vampires in dark clothing. They moved with inhuman speed and coordination, spreading out to surround her before she could fully process their presence.

"The shapeshifter," one of them said. "Grab her."

Nadi shifted into Ivan's form, hoping the added mass and strength would give her an advantage, but she was outnumbered. One of them hit her hard in the back of the head, and she went down to her knees. She cried out, fighting as hard as she could, but soon it was three versus one, and she was restrained.

Someone pressed a cloth over her nose and mouth—something that smelled sweet and cloying and made her thoughts swim like thick honey.

Through the haze of whatever drug they were using, she saw them drag another figure into the room. Tall, broad-shouldered, with long black hair and familiar crimson eyes that were glazed with the same chemical confusion affecting her.

Raziel. They had Raziel too.

She tried to call out to him, to fight harder against her captors, but the drug was pulling her down into darkness. The last thing she saw before consciousness fled was his face turning toward hers, recognition and something like desperation flickering in his eyes before they both succumbed to oblivion.

After that there was nothing but darkness, and the distant sound of someone laughing with cold satisfaction.

But even as consciousness faded, Nadi held onto one bright, perfect truth—Volencia Nostrom was dead, and she had been the one to kill her.

Whatever came next, that victory could never be taken away.

Even if their souls would follow Volencia's into the void before long.

TWENTY-THREE

Nadi didn't know where she was being taken. A bag had been put over her head. No one was speaking to her. She had no clue which end was up. No one was hurting her either—so at least there was that.

It was clear who was to blame for this. Mael and Lana. She tried to piece everything together in her head. It had all happened so quickly. They had hired the fae to crash her own wedding. But *why*? To what end? It was obvious their goal was to remake the politics of Runne in the name of some new world order, but—

Oh.

Fuck.

The men storming into the room hadn't been after her, had they?

They had been after *Volencia*.

She started to laugh underneath the hood. And she laughed hard. The whole thing had been a setup to murder their mother to get her out of the way. And Nadi had gone and done their job for them.

And they had Raziel. But he had been alive, last she'd seen. Why? What purpose did he serve?

Either way, she was alive. And that meant she might have a chance at escape. She had a chance to get out of this alive, somehow. But getting out *with* Raziel? That would be much harder, if not impossible.

Part of her should be fine with that. Willing to say *Fuck it, good, let the bastards sort their own shit out.* But the other part of her wasn't willing to let him go. Especially not now, after realizing she had foolishly...

Did she even *want* to escape with him anymore? Mael's offer was still on the table. And it was tempting. Raziel was now very clearly the losing side. Mael and Lana had won. They had the fae working with them, and they had played everyone—including her and Raziel—like chumps. It would be suicidal to side with Raziel.

But...

No. Now wasn't the time to start thinking about how she did or did not feel.

She was sitting in the back of a car. At least she hadn't been crammed into the trunk this time. They had taken her somewhere, then loaded her into a building, then loaded her into another car, then another building, and then into another car. She had been allowed to sleep for a little while—and then another car.

How many hours had passed, she had no idea. She was just told to "Get up." "Get in the car." "Sit down." And she silently obeyed. Now wasn't the time for games. Now was the time for waiting. And listening.

When they pulled her out of the car that last time, she heard something interesting.

Water.

More specifically—the *ocean.* They were at the docks. But... *why?*

She'd been asking herself that a lot lately.

When someone pushed her up onto a surface that clomped under her feet, and angled upward, she realized she was on a gangway. She was boarding a ship. She could hear an engine idling. A boat. A large boat.

The Nostrom yacht, maybe? Why in the name of the moons were they bringing her on the *yacht?*

To take her back to the family estate, maybe. To sacrifice her and throw her into the pit where Monica should have gone in the first place. It'd be a fitting place to hide the body of the woman she was still pretending to be, even if Mael—and therefore, she assumed Lana—knew her secret.

But she was only guessing at all of those things. The person gripping her by the upper arm dragged her along the deck of the boat—it was definitely large judging by how long it took to bring her to where they were going. They shoved her down into a chair.

Finally, they ripped the bag off her head.

Blinking, she tried to focus her eyes. She hadn't seen light in who knew how long.

"Sorry for the treatment, beautiful." It was Mael. He was seated in another chair across from her. She *was* on the Nostrom yacht, she was right. "We had to get Raziel and 'Monica' out of there before our people and the Rosovs demanded proof of both of your heads on pikes. They'll follow us to the ends of Runne now, but not with that mad dog and his new wife in tow. There were conditions. I'm sure you understand."

She studied him curiously for a moment. Sitting next to him on a three-seater were Zabriel and Lana. She furrowed her brow at them. "I..."

"First, can we drop the pretenses?" Mael smiled. "I would love to see your real face, Nadi."

She glanced at the men and vampires standing around the

deck, all heavily armed, and hesitated. "Well, that answers the question on whether or not Lana knows."

"I was the first one to suspect. You think my dear dunderhead of a brother put it together on his own?" Lana chuckled and snuggled in closer to Zabriel's side. The other vampire draped an arm around her, kissing her temple. Lana had changed out of her wedding dress into a less ornate affair. "But he was the one who figured out from one of his associates that you were *fae*."

Leaning back in the chair, Nadi turned her attention back to Mael. "This associate. Who are they?"

"A young man who you used to know, when you were young." He reached into the pocket of his suit coat and pulled out Braen's leather ledger. He flipped back through several pages. "Kalo Lohti, to be specific. Remember him?" Finding the page he was looking for, he placed the book down in front of her. There, clearly written, was Kalo's name. As having sold six fae into Braen's... *care*.

Nadi's heart lurched in her chest. For two reasons.

The first was the simplest. She did remember Kalo. She had pretty much grown up with him. The Lohtis and the Iltanis were clans that met frequently to trade, and often intermarried. He had been a bossy, older boy who had teased her about her tail and she had threatened to drown him a few times. Her mother had always warned her that the teasing meant Kalo would ask for her hand someday. Nadi would just laugh and repeat her threat of drowning.

The second reason she had a pang of pain that made her visibly wince, however, was far more complex. Raziel had given the ledger to Mael.

It *hadn't* been locked up in a safety deposit box like he had told her. A stabbing pain made her wince as she realized this was precisely why she had always worked alone. He'd *lied* to her.

And Lana was too perceptive to miss the flash of emotion that crossed her borrowed face. "Oh, you didn't know that Raziel gave us the ledger?"

It seemed Mael was quick enough to put it together on his own. "What did you think he was going to do with it, love?" He frowned. "Use it to find your people and free them? Keep it safely tucked away? Trust *you* with it?"

Trust.

That was the issue, wasn't it?

She had just been starting to trust him.

Her jaw ticked, and she stayed silent. "Kalo told you about me."

"When I asked him about anyone he knew who might be able to shapeshift between faces, he offered the whole story to me for free." Mael shook his head. "That alcohol you lot drink is *something else*. How do you pronounce it? Ghripsa?"

Nadi smirked despite herself. "*Ghri'sa.*"

"I had already given my word I wasn't going to kill you. He just seemed happy you were alive. I think he might be harboring a bit of an old crush." Mael closed the ledger and tucked it back into his coat, sitting back in his chair. "Lana and I had nothing to do with the death of your family. That was Volencia and Raziel. And you already got your revenge on one of them today."

"Good job with that, by the way." Lana laughed. "Crushing the skull! You really did *hate* her, didn't you?"

"We have taken the precaution of severing her head from the neck. They have already been cremated separately and the remains will be scattered on opposite ends of Runne." He gestured at the boat.

Ah. That explained the yacht. Though she was still suspicious.

"Now... can we please see the real you?" Mael smiled

gently. "I find I'm deeply curious. And seeing this dead woman —the real Monica—I assume she's dead?"

"Raziel killed her." Nadi didn't know why she was offering up the information. Maybe part of her was reminding herself of the hard truth of the situation. "I switched places with Monica when she first arrived at the metropolis. I paid her off. But when Raziel went to 'sacrifice' Monica, I learned... well, I hadn't been fooling him as well as I'd thought."

"You had been playing him for *that long*?" Lana's eyes went wide. "Oh, you *are* good. I thought the swap came later."

"Not good enough," Nadi sighed and shrugged. "Because here I am."

"You got caught because there are how many of us, and how many of you?" Mael shook his head. "You also let yourself be compromised. If you had just taken out Raziel and vanished, then tried again for any one of us, and gone for us one at a time? You might have succeeded."

The truth of his statement hit her harder than any kind of torture could have. She knew he was right. It was the same thing she'd been repeating to herself over and over again. But she kept arguing herself out of it—saying *No, she had to stay, it was her only choice.*

But it hadn't been.

Shutting her eyes, she let her glamor fall. What was the point? She kept her legs, however. When she opened her eyes again, Mael and Lana were looking at her with shockingly similar expressions.

Both a mix of hunger, fascination, and... lust.

Even Zabriel was eyeing her like he was wondering how she might taste.

Vampires.

"I..." Mael's golden eyes flicked between hers. "I can see why my brother has become so smitten with you. If anyone could crack the heart of that madman..."

"Of course, he loves her! She's a broken thing because of him. An assassin of *his making*. So much blood on his hands, but all of it *his* fault?" Lana chuckled. "So wonderfully narcissistic, isn't it?"

She'd never thought of it that way.

"If he asked you to wear his face while he fucked you, I wouldn't be surprised." Lana rolled her eyes. "You represent every life he's ever ruined, all the carnage he's left in his wake—and the thought that he had fashioned you in his image? A little work of art? He fell in love with you because, in his mind, you're *him*."

It churned her stomach. Raziel didn't love her. That wasn't possible. And everything Lana was saying was just a manipulation to get into her head. It had to be. "It doesn't matter anymore, does it?"

"It does." Mael stood from his chair, straightening out his suit coat. "If you still have feelings for him, it does. What were you two plotting?"

"To kill you." No harm in telling the truth. They knew. That much was already clear from the way he asked the question. It was just a test to see if she would answer. "The moment you stepped off stage, Raziel was going to kill you in the shadows. I was to cover the exits in case you took a different direction—get you somewhere alone. If that didn't work, we knew the fae were going to attack, and we'd hoped in the chaos no one would notice one more corpse."

Lana's grin was positively gleeful. "I love how just—*how matter-of-fact she says it*, don't you?" She was basically in Zabriel's lap. "Ugh, I could eat her up."

"I have always wondered what fae blood is like." Zabriel tilted his head to the side slightly. "I never believed that old lie of it being a poison to us."

"It's worse than poison." Mael shook his head. "It's extremely addictive. One of the most potent drugs available to a vampire. You'd do well to stay away from it, Zabriel. I'm damn sure it's what sent Braen half-mad. It may be another reason why Raziel is smitten with her, if he wasn't aware of its effects."

More reasons to doubt. More fuel for the fire. They were doing a very good job at putting a rift between her and Raziel. She just had to judge for herself whether or not it was legitimate. And she knew she had to judge *fast*.

"Why attack your own wedding?" Nadi had to ask. They had no reason to answer her—she certainly wasn't in a position of power. "Just to get Volencia out of the way?"

"You say 'just' like it isn't something we've worked toward for decades. Some of us are too well positioned to simply breeze in, murder someone, and vanish." Zabriel grimaced. "It took the careful planning of nearly half a century to be rid of her. Even if you just waltzed into the room to do the deed like it was nothing, it was because *we* provided the setup for you to do so."

"A very fair point." Nadi paused. "I at least managed to eke out some revenge for my family. And for that, I... admit I'm grateful." She pulled against the restraints that kept her hands behind her back. There was no budging them. Even if she shifted to Ivan's form, she would just break all the bones in both her wrists.

This was a bad, *bad* situation. She couldn't see a way out of this.

Unless she decided to change sides.

Mael paced a few steps away from her, staring out over the ocean, black against a barely brighter night sky. "Raziel is a madman, Nadi. He plans to destroy the metropolis. Burn it all down and rule over the ashes. He's had this dream since he was a child."

"I know."

"He told you, then." Mael turned to watch her, his golden eyes glinting in the darkness, reflecting the light back at her. "And you were willing to go along with it?"

"You only have to hitch yourself to a train to get to the next station. I wasn't planning on following it off a cliff. I knew it was something I would have to deal with eventually, but our chances of making it that far were slim enough I figured it wasn't a problem. I was right." She shrugged, tugging on the restraints to prove her point. "My goal has always been to take out as many Nostroms as possible. I never expected to get out of this alive."

"You realize... he was *always* doomed to fail. In all of it. Killing us. Ruling this world. He was never going to win." Mael crossed the deck to her chair to kneel at her feet. He placed his hands on her knees.

His touch was warm. Sincere. He was so much kinder, gentler, than his younger brother. She searched his face for any sign of cruelty. Any sign of a lie. Any sign of a monster, lurking beneath the surface, waiting to burst through the waves and clamp its jaws down around her throat.

She wondered who he really was, deep down—was he really the smiling, gentle vampire? The one who dealt drugs because he had to? Because it was a necessary evil?

Or was he the inverse of Raziel? Was Raziel cruel on the exterior, with a kindness buried within, while Mael had cruelty hidden deep within?

At least with Raziel, she knew what she was getting.

With Mael, it was a gamble. A risk. Turning over cards in a deck until she came up short.

"When he killed Monica, I had a choice. Return to the Wild or join with him to work with killing all of you." She shook her head. "I had already sacrificed so much to get that far. It... felt so *wrong* to run away."

Mael lifted a hand to her cheek and stroked it gently. "You aren't a coward, Nadi. You followed your heart, not your head. And you are *loyal*. To *Raziel*, of all people." He laughed in quiet, stunned disbelief. "That is to be lauded, not shamed. He's my brother. He will always be my brother. I love him. But I have to make sure he can't hurt anyone else, ever again."

He stood, walking behind her. "I am going to trust you, Nadi. Our family hurt you in ways I can't even begin to imagine. And you took one part of your revenge tonight." He unlocked the cuffs at her wrists. "Which does not begin to right the wrongs we have done, I understand that."

Pulling her hands in front of her, she rubbed her wrists, stunned at the fact that he'd just simply released her. But... what could she really *do*? She was surrounded by vampires with guns. She was one, unarmed fae.

But they likely didn't know that her true form was that of a creature who could swim and breathe underwater. Otherwise, Mael likely never would have released her wrists.

Kalo had presumably left *that* part out of his story. Small favors from a childhood pseudo-bully, pseudo-friend, she supposed.

Ten steps and a jump and she would be free.

She glanced between Mael, Lana, and Zabriel. "None of you had a hand in what happened to my father and my family. At least, not that my research has turned up. It was Volencia who ordered it and Raziel who did the deed."

Her goal had been to wipe the Nostrom plague from the face of Runne. But now? Everything had been cast in such a different light.

"Tonight, I am going to deal with Raziel, once and for all." Mael's expression was grim. "You may take part or recuse yourself. Then, you will have a choice. Join us—stand at my side as Nadi Iltani, wearing *your own face*, and help me reshape the metropolis for vampires and fae alike. Or... we will bring you anywhere you like. And you live your life however you like, or you may disappear. The same offer my brother gave you."

Nadi considered his words for a long moment. "What's... happened to him?"

"Nothing. Yet. We wanted you to witness it. Because you should have this chance to choose your next step." He held out his enormous hand to her. "We've decided enough of your life."

Swallowing the rock in her throat, she put her hand in his and let him help her up to her feet.

Another choice lay before her.

Only this time, it wasn't just the direction of her life that would be determined.

It wasn't just Raziel's.

It was all of Runne.

TWENTY-FOUR

Raziel was impressed, quite honestly.

Organizing the fae to attack their own extravagant party, all to stage a situation where Volencia could be murdered and he himself could be taken out of play?

Masterfully done.

He'd told his siblings as much, as Mael had punched him in the jaw. The single hit had knocked him unconscious. The next day and change had been ones of confinement and solitude. No one spoke to him. Nor did he particularly care.

Tonight, however, that changed.

He was dragged out to the family yacht. He would know the rumble of the engine anywhere. He was forced to his knees, his hands cuffed in front of him to a loop in the deck usually reserved for tying down furniture.

The bag was pulled from his head. And he watched as Lana, Zabriel Rosov, Mael... and Nadi, wearing her own face, approached.

She was unrestrained. But by the way she was rubbing her wrists, and her uncertain, unhappy expression, it hadn't been for very long.

Betrayal burned in his chest. If he had cut him open, gutted him like a fish, it might have hurt less. No, it *would* have hurt less.

But something bothered him more. Something that pushed through the realization that Nadi had turned on him to side with his siblings.

They were going out to sea. Why?

"You didn't have to go through this kind of effort to hide my body, brother. They will celebrate my death. It'll hardly be a crime." He tugged on the handcuffs that tethered him to the deck. No. They wouldn't budge. And they were edged in silver—which meant he couldn't change his form into a swarm of bats. *Fantastic.*

"This isn't about hiding evidence. This is about punishment." Lana smiled, hugging Zabriel's arm. "Besides, we have to dump Mother's ashes *somewhere*. I don't want that dusty cunt wafting around Runne."

In a strange way, Raziel was honestly relieved that Lana and Zabriel were truly in love. He wanted his sister dead. He *hated* her. But in the same breath, he wanted her to be happy.

Families were complicated.

"We figured that since you've spent so many decades creatively making your victims suffer, it only made sense to ensure that you suffered creatively in return." Mael walked over to an object on the deck that Raziel hadn't noticed before. It looked like a couple of crates covered with a canvas tarp. As he pulled the covering away, however, Raziel understood.

He began to laugh.

It was a coffin.

A *silver* coffin, with *silver* chains. One with a decorative R.N. emblazoned on the lid.

"Oh brother... you truly have outdone yourself." He tilted his head back, grinning his best, most sadistic expression. "I am truly flattered. Mother would be so proud of you. How did you have it made? No one in our circles would have done it without alerting my men."

"I commissioned it." Zabriel Rosov's tone was surprisingly cold and level. "I told my men it was for Braen. He was no more loved by me than you are by your siblings."

Raziel was also impressed with the middle Rosov sibling. He was clearly the calculating one. Good. Mael and Lana would need someone who could handle logistics.

"Take care of her, Zabriel. Keep her bloodlust contained." Raziel leaned forward slightly. "I am not the mad dog in the family. *She is.* You'll learn that soon enough."

"Shut *up*." Lana spat at him. "You don't get to talk!"

"You're—" Nadi was staring at the coffin, quietly interrupting. "You're going to... chain him in the coffin, and... throw him... overboard?"

Mael opened the lid. "He will drown. Forever. The blood in his body will not be consumed, as he'll enter a sort of stasis. But it will be agony. It will shatter whatever is left of his twisted mind. If anyone is ever unlucky enough to dredge him up, there will be nothing left of him but a raving madman."

"Mother did it to several of his bursars who betrayed him. Raziel will have good company!" Lana sounded downright pleased with herself.

"And this is where you have your first choice to make, Nadi." Mael turned to face her. "The coffin is big enough for two. Will you let this happen? Or will you join him?"

Nadi was unrestrained. She could shift forms. Take the shape of Ivan, himself, or even Mael. Cause total chaos. They could escape. She had the opportunity to upend everything.

All he needed was a distraction. If she could get the cuffs off him, his hypnotism could work on the few humans that were on the deck.

But then he did the math. Even with the humans, they would lose. They were outnumbered. The moment Nadi's form began to shift, she would be riddled with bullets. And so would he.

Raziel grimaced, lowering his head. "Remember your promise, Nadi." Survive. That was what he had made her vow to him. *Survive.*

Nadi walked up to him, gently lifting his head in her palms to make him look at her. If he wasn't mistaken, he might be about to cry. "Tell me something, Serpent... What is there between us? Can you name it?"

He gazed into those dark, opalescent eyes and said the word in his mind.

Love.

He loved her.

Moons, he loved her.

And he wanted to whisper the word to her. He wanted to tell her how much he loved her. How she was the only one he had *ever* loved. That he hadn't even known what it was *to* love until her.

But he had made her make a promise. That she would survive.

And if he said those words? If he told her that he loved her?

It would throw it all into question.

So he shut his eyes. And felt a warm, bloody tear run from his cheek.

As he said nothing at all.

Leaning down, she kissed him. Slowly. Clearly savoring the embrace. Knowing that this would be the last time she ever felt the shape of his lips against hers.

It was all right. This was how it should be. She deserved his death. She deserved to watch him die. She never should have cared for him. This was simpler. Easier. Cleaner.

The universe had a funny way of correcting its mistakes, didn't it. After she broke the kiss, he felt her breath wash against his ear.

"I've already told you what you need to know."

That had him blinking his eyes back open as she stepped away from him. What did she mean?

She pulled the wedding ring from her finger that she wore as Monica and slipped it into the lapel of his suit coat. "Goodbye, Raziel."

Mael jerked his head. Two men standing nearby came forward. One unclipped Raziel's handcuffs from the loop in the deck. Both forced him toward the silver coffin.

Fear—*terror*—instinctual and raw came over him in a wave. "No—! *No! Brother!*" He screamed and began to kick at the men. Baring his fangs, he thrashed. "Don't do this—*don't!*" But it was too late. A punch to the stomach, another to the head, and he was down.

Panic overcame him. He was a feral animal. Teeth. Nails. Anything he could use to defend himself. Anything he could summon.

Another punch to the jaw, and he was in the coffin. The gas lamps of the ship went dark. "*No!*" He screamed and beat his fists against the lid, the handcuffs still holding them together. "Let me *out! Lana!* Mael! *Mael!*" His screams were deafening in the small space. He didn't care. "Please, no! *No!*"

He still had air with which to shout. For now. The sound of the lid locking shut. The sound of chains feeding through loops.

"*No!*"

He wailed.

"*Please! No! Please!*"

Darkness. Movement.

He screamed. He begged. Gravity ceased to exist for a split second.

And then it came crashing back.

For a moment... nothing.

And then the cold began to seep in.

It triggered a memory, buried deep in his soul. One that

woke him up at night when he least expected it. An image burned in his mind of lying at the bottom of a fountain, gazing up at the ripples of the surface of the water. Feeling the water in his lungs. The ache of the desperate need for air that would not come. Seeing the distorted faces of his family above him.

Judging.

Celebrating.

Laughing.

Water began to fill the coffin. "No, no, no—" he moaned. "Please, no—please—*please*—" Maybe it was all just a joke.

A prank.

Like they used to play on each other as children. That was all it was. That was all it had to be. Mael was just playing one of his cruel tricks. That was it. This was just like the times he spent at the bottom of the fountain.

They had attached a chain to the coffin, surely.

They wouldn't do this to him.

He pounded on the lid. "Let me out! Anyone! Please! *Mael!*"

The water reached his chin. It was coming in fast. It was so cold. He lifted his head, trying to hold onto what little air he could in the pitch-black space.

"Nadi! Lana!"

Clawing at the lid with his nails in desperation, he wept. "Please, *someone—anyone—!*"

He pulled in his last gasp of air before water filled the space.

It wasn't a prank.

It wasn't a game.

Panic welled in his body. He thrashed, kicking violently in the coffin, punching at the lid, the sides, trying to destroy the silver box in any way he could.

But it was hopeless.

Utterly hopeless.

His lungs began to burn.

He thought they might explode.

When he could not hold onto the air any longer, it left him in a rush.

And what took its place was so much worse.

It was so very cold.

It reached a tiny hand out to him, broken wrist bones jutting from a child's arm. *"It's not so bad, look—"* He reset them back *into his arm with a sickening crunch. "You see? Just like that. I don't know why he's screaming so badly. Raziel is such a baby. Mael didn't mean to push him from the tree. Raziel's just so much smaller than he is. But off he goes, crying to Daddy, like he always does."*

A shattered memory. He pushed it away. But another one came to take its place.

"What have I done, Mother? What did I do wrong?" He stared down at the silver shackles that bound his wrists. They ran through loops buried in the stone blocks at the bottom of the fountain in the garden.

Terror. No, horror flooded him. His body shook with adrenaline. Tears stung his eyes. He did not understand.

For a moment, his mother didn't answer as she finished ratcheting the silver restraints shut. The sound of it like the slamming of a prison gate. He had heard that noise plenty in his life, as well.

"Nothing, my dear, weak little boy." Volencia patted his cheek. "Nothing at all. And once you learn that? You will truly be free." She motioned her hand to the vampires holding the other ends of the chains.

It would take all their combined strength to pull his struggling form beneath the surface of the water. He screamed and fought as hard as he could.

It had been useless to try. As were all his attempts to fight the lessons his mother had been trying to teach him. In the end, he so neatly fit the mold she had made for him.

Monster. Murderer. Killer. Torturer. Enforcer. Mad dog. Serpent.

He was all of those things. Gladly.

But wasn't he something more...?

A new memory came to touch his mind. To hold his hand.

The feeling of lips upon his.

Kill them all, Nadi.

Kill them because I couldn't.

* * *

Nadi stood on the deck and watched the coffin sink beneath the waves. Mael's hand settled on her shoulder, heavy and warm. "Let's get you a drink."

"Yeah." She turned from the railing and headed to the bar with him. Maybe she'd drink herself stupid.

With what she was about to do tonight...

She was really, *really* going to need a few drinks in her system.

Gathering around the bar, she was handed a perfect metropolis by Lana, who pulled her into a hug shortly after and placed a kiss on her cheek.

Mael was next, turning her to face him. His kiss was far more personal. He crooked a finger under her chin, stepped in close, and caught her lips with his. She shut her eyes... and returned the gesture.

He tasted like daylight. Like the summer sun. He was nothing like his brother. Firm, but unassuming. There was nothing demanding. Nothing that *took*. In his kiss, she felt protected. Honored. Treasured.

He smiled down at her, running his thumb tenderly along her cheek.

"Welcome to the family, Nadi Iltani. We are going to *change the world.*"

* * *

Nadi.

He loved her.

And he had never told her.

Now he never would.

"We are the Nostrom family."

Raziel watched his father with keen interest. The man was a towering figure, though he could not recall now what he actually looked like. The sword he held in his hand shone with wet blood that dripped from the tip onto the floor.

Blood that had recently come from the fool who had decided that he was not going to obey his father's simple rule.

Which was to obey all his rules.

He had few memories of his father. But the ones he had, he coveted. There were some things his mother could not be allowed to poison. And the knowledge of what vampires should be, and how they were meant to rule, was one of them.

Volencia had corrupted their way. If his father had been alive... none of this travesty would have ever happened. The world could have been made right if only Raziel had won.

If only.

If only.

If only.

Two words that meant nothing in the end.

In his memory, Raziel's father held the blade aloft, pointing it at the others who stood in attendance. "We are vampires. And we are to be feared."

Nadi.

He loved her.

And he had never told her.

Now he never would.

His grandmother Lilivra. A shadow behind a curtain. Never appearing in full, always just a silhouette, seated in bed. Her voice was strong, but somehow... even as a child, Raziel was worried the old woman was frail.

Something was wrong with her.

"Your grandchildren, Mother." Volencia stood behind them, her head bowed. Mael, Lana, Raziel. The first time they had ever seen their grandmother. They were told not to speak. Lana was shaking in fear.

The silhouette of the woman sitting up in bed didn't seem like an old lady. She looked young to Raziel. Or at least, she wasn't hunched and withered. But it was hard to tell.

"One is destined to rule. The others to die. One is a mad dog, who delights in the kill. Another a golden beast, with honor in his heart." Lilivra lifted her hands, palms up in front of her, as if cupping water. "The third, will change this world forever. Come closer, Raziel, second grandson. I have words meant only for you."

Volencia sputtered. As a child, the moment had seemed strange to him. As an adult, Raziel knew how angry that had made his mother.

"Silence, Volencia."

Raziel had crept forward, his hands clutched together in front of him. He hovered close to the edge of the gauze curtains.

A hand darted out from behind the curtain and snatched his wrist, yanking him close. The hand wasn't skeletal—wasn't wrinkled—it was youthful and the grasp was impossibly strong.

Grandmother Lilivra's whispered words were seared into his soul that day.

"Tear down the walls. Burn the metropolis to the ground. What they have built is a mockery to what we vampires are meant to be. Only you understand our true nature."

She had pushed him away violently then, sending him sprawling onto the ground.

His destiny. Laid out before him when he was nothing more than a child. All their destinies, in fact—and their mother had seen to it that they would fulfill them, whether they liked it or not.

Raziel had always wondered if Lilivra had never spoken those words, how much of his life would have played out the way it had.

Would he have ever learned to delight in murder the way he had? Would he ever have become the bastard that he was now? Would he ever have been trapped inside his own mind, dying forever?

A flash of the real world. Of where he was. Of darkness. Of a coffin. He wondered if he was still sinking. He wondered if it mattered. Of drowning.

Nadi.

He loved her.

And he had never told her.

Now he never would.

The memories were better than the pain of drowning.

He remembered his first kill. A human that had raised a hand and struck some of his sister's "merchandise." And bruised merchandise earned less on the market.

So there he was... asked to not only deal with the man, but to make an example of him. He easily picked the lock of the man's apartment when he wasn't home and relocked the door behind him. Perusing the man's sad, pathetic little space for ten minutes, he became quickly bored with it.

It didn't shock him that a person who paid for a night's company only to strike the woman in frustration was a miserable sack of shit.

Sitting down on the cleanest piece of furniture in the man's living room, Raziel took out a coin from his pocket and began walking it across his knuckles. He waited.

The man returned home a half an hour later from work. He'd been to the bar already and stank of cheap alcohol. Damn. It meant he'd feel Raziel's efforts all the less.

Whatever.

Once, a man walked into the kitchen and got himself a beer from the icebox without even noticing Raziel sitting in his living room. That had made Raziel smile.

It had turned into a game after that night. He would sit in a person's home and just quietly wait to see how long it took them to figure out they weren't alone.

Some people figured it out instantaneously.

Some people took embarrassingly long.

A different time, someone had made dinner, eaten it, taken a shower, and was about to go to bed before Raziel had finally made his presence known. Or else he would have had to sit there all damn night.

But this particular man noticed, finally, when he walked into the living room, intending to likely drink his beer on the sofa. He froze.

"Who the fu—"

"Sit down." Raziel kept the faint smile on his face.

The man sat on the floor right where he was standing. Right. Yes. He was still adjusting to how extremely literally people took his instructions. He had to learn to be very specific with what he told them. "Why did you strike the woman you spent last night with?"

"Huh?" The man made a face as if his question made no sense. "You're here about a whore?"

"I am here—" Raziel sighed. "Because I was told to be. Now. I'm asking you a question, and you're going to answer me. Why did you strike the woman?"

The man paused. "She wouldn't put my dick down her throat."

"Why?"

"Claims it made her choke. Bullshit excuse for a whore. So I smacked her once or twice, then made her take it anyway."

"Hm. Well." He despised the man. He was going to be rather glad to kill him. "Did she choke?"

"Yeah. Felt good. And?" The man furrowed his brow. "Why can't I move?"

Standing, Raziel brushed off his pants. "Listen to me very carefully. Once I leave your apartment, you are going to swallow that beer bottle, neck first."

"But I'll—I can't—"

Raziel walked toward the door, patting the man on the shoulder as he slipped his coin back into his other pocket. "Who knows. Maybe it'll feel good. Have a lovely night." Opening the door to the hallway, he shut the door behind him with a click.

At first, he'd made sure the punishments fit the crimes. At first, he tried to care. But little by little, it chipped away. It wasn't about the person he was killing anymore. The part of him that felt remorse for taking lives was gone.

If it had ever existed in the first place.

Honestly, he doubted it ever did. At least, not human lives. Or fac. Or those he was simply told to kill. When he knew the people he had to end, cared about them, of course he felt remorse.

Like when someone in their ranks turned traitor—someone he knew, someone he had laughed with, drank with, shared stories with.

Those deaths hurt.

Those deaths stung him.

Which was why he chose not to have friends after a while. It just made life easier. The only people he trusted to never betray him were the ones he would choose to keep around. Which was precisely one. Ivan.

He thought it would be two. Nadi.

But here he was.

Nadi.

He loved her.

And he had never told her.

Now he never would.

He dreamed of her atop him. Of her beside him in bed. Of the sight of her sleeping. Of her in the bath. Of the sound of her laughter.

Of the flash of her dark-scaled tail as she swam in his pool.

He had never seen this. But he had imagined it. And he had wanted to see it, so very badly. Her, in her natural form. In her true environment.

It came to him in a rush.

He felt himself crawling along the floor of his watchtower apartment. The wound in his stomach was still an open gash. His tongue was missing. He was dying. Standing before him—Nadi.

Nadi.

He loved her.

And he had never told her.

Now he never would.

Her blood was singing to him. And he was crying for it. For her.

Digging his nails into the wood, he needed her. Needed what ran through her veins.

Or he would die.

He didn't attack her... he didn't overpower her... did he?

She knelt at his side. "Raz..."

No. No, no, no. He remembered now. He hadn't before. Weakly, desperately, he had begged her to run.

He remembered the girl in the alleyway now too.

Pressed against the wall. Her family dead on the street behind him. Tears streaking down a face that wasn't hers.

He'd told her to run.

That night she'd listened.

But the night he'd been dying? She'd stayed.

"I'm going nowhere," she had said, as she picked him up into her lap. Instinct had taken over. The last strength in his body demanding he feed. "I vowed to follow you straight into the void, Serpent. One way or another. So I need you alive."

He'd torn her neck open like an animal.

She had been willing to die to save his life. But why?

Nadi.

He loved her.

And he had never told her.

Now he never would.

He hoped he would dream of her more. If the moons were kind, he would dream *only* of her.

Moonlight overhead. The silhouette of a siren, a tail, like tattered black lace.

Lips pressed to his.

Air filled his lungs.

And his mind went blissfully empty.

Raziel woke up, retching water from his lungs.

Someone held his hair back, their other hand gently on his shoulder. They were talking to him, though he wasn't listening.

He was too busy attempting to breathe.

Collapsing onto his side, he coughed a few more times, wheezing, before finally his lungs seemed to want to obey him. Air.

Air.

Blessed, underrated, undervalued *air*.

Opening his eyes, he stared at his hand in front of his face.

His wrist had the handcuff still attached to it. The linkage that was meant to run to the other was severed. The coffin.

He was—

Where was—

What had—

He tried to sit up. And failed spectacularly. He wound up sprawled on his back with a groan, his vision spinning.

Someone laughed quietly beside him. "Be smart and stay down for a minute, will you?"

He knew the voice. He reached for them, needing to know that they weren't a figment of his imagination. Needed to touch them.

She caught his hand and placed his palm to her cheek.

"I told you, I'm following you into the void. You don't get to die until I say so. Leaving you chained up at the bottom of the ocean wasn't an option."

"Nadi—" he choked out between gasping, shuddering inhales.

"Focus on breathing. I'm here. You're all right."

All right was a matter of opinion. He hurt everywhere. His whole body ached. It was a familiar pain—he had experienced it many times in his life as a child. But that didn't make it any less horrible. Even nearly starving to death didn't hurt quite like he did at the moment. Feeling his stomach gurgle, he struggled to roll onto his side. She helped him before he retched out the watery contents of his stomach one more time.

The noise he made afterward was hardly dignified. He didn't particularly care.

She stroked his hair. "I know... trust me, I know." She'd thrown up all that blood that night. She did have recent experience. "Here. Let's sit you up a bit. Maybe that will help."

Carefully, she helped get him up vertical. It did help ease his breathing, even if it did nothing to help his swirling head for a few moments. He clung to her until the world settled its reeling.

Once everything seemed calmer, he took a slow, deep breath, testing his lungs. Good. He didn't immediately vomit up more water. Or cough. A second breath, and his head felt a little clearer.

Blinking, he finally tried to focus on where he was.

And realized the bottom of the ocean might have been safer.

"Nadi..."

They were sitting on the edge of a lake. But they weren't outdoors—not precisely. They were *underground*. A great cavern stretched around them in all directions, soaring overhead some hundred or two hundred feet. The rock walls shone in shades of blue and green. Every surface was covered in plants and trees, and the space seemed alive with the movement of *animals*. Even in the air of the great chamber, creatures with wings and feathers flitted from place to place.

The silver coffin was dragged half ashore, the chains sliced off. Nadi sat beside it, her long fish tail draped in the water, a set of bolt cutters in her hand.

Everything in the enormous cavern was illuminated by the glow of gigantic vines. Some of the vines were as thick as trains. And all of them glowed an eerie shade of purple that seemed to set off the world around them in every other color imaginable.

Nadi shifted her tail into legs and stood. She held out a hand to him to help him up. With a smirk, she confirmed his worst fear.

"Welcome to the Wild, Raziel Nostrom."

A LETTER FROM KATHRYN

Dear Reader,

Thank you for reading *The Serpent's Sin*, the second installment in the *Bloodlines* trilogy. I hope you enjoyed this continuation of Raziel and Nadi's murderous story. I cannot wait to show you all how the story concludes in part three.

If you enjoyed reading it as much as I enjoyed writing it and want to keep up to date with all my latest releases, just sign up at the following link! Your email address will never be shared, and you can unsubscribe at any time.

www.secondskybooks.com/kathryn-ann-kingsley

Some authors can write books and leave them in a drawer, never caring how people engage with them. I am not one of those authors. I love to hear from you, and how the book made you feel. Did it make you laugh? Cry? Did I surprise you? Stop by and let me know or leave a review.

If you like my style of writing and want to see more of what I have to offer, check out my links on the next page. Thanks again.

Wishing you the sweetest nightmares,

Kathryn

KEEP IN TOUCH WITH KATHRYN

www.kathrynkingsley.com

discord.gg/kathrynkingsley

facebook.com/KathrynAnnKingsley

bsky.app/profile/KathrynKingsley

ACKNOWLEDGMENTS

I would like to thank Jack, my editor, and Noelle, the social media marketing manager, for Second Sky.

I would also like to thank the copyeditors, proofers, formatters, finance and accounting people, project managers, interns, audio book producers, narrators, cover designers—all the people who work behind the scenes of making a book "a thing" beyond simply putting words down on paper.

I'm what's been deemed a "hybrid" author—releasing self-published works and working with companies in the more traditional publishing space—so I know precisely how much work it requires to take a book from soup to nuts with the level of polish that Second Sky is capable of. (And one could argue that polish can make or break a series at the end of the day.)

So, to all those whose name doesn't make it onto the cover?

Thank you.

You're a huge part of this too.

PUBLISHING TEAM

Turning a manuscript into a book requires the efforts of many people. The publishing team at Bookouture would like to acknowledge everyone who contributed to this publication.

Audio
Alba Proko
Melissa Tran
Sinead O'Connor

Commercial
Lauren Morrissette
Hannah Richmond
Imogen Allport

Cover design
Damonza

Data and analysis
Mark Alder
Mohamed Bussuri

Editorial
Jack Renninson
Melissa Tran

Copyeditor
Rhian McKay

Proofreader
Catherine Lenderi

Marketing
Alex Crow
Melanie Price
Occy Carr
Cíara Rosney
Martyna Młynarska

Operations and distribution
Marina Valles
Stephanie Straub
Joe Morris

Production
Hannah Snetsinger
Mandy Kullar
Nadia Michael
Charlotte Hegley

Publicity
Kim Nash
Noelle Holten
Jess Readett
Sarah Hardy

Rights and contracts
Peta Nightingale
Richard King
Saidah Graham

Dear Reader,

We'd love your attention for one more page to tell you about the crisis in children's reading, and what we can all do.

Studies have shown that reading for fun is the **single biggest predictor of a child's future life chances** – more than family circumstance, parents' educational background or income. It improves academic results, mental health, wealth, communication skills, ambition and happiness.

The number of children reading for fun is in rapid decline. Young people have a lot of competition for their time, and a worryingly high number do not have a single book at home.

Hachette works extensively with schools, libraries and literacy charities, but here are some ways we can all raise more readers:

- Reading to children for just 10 minutes a day makes a difference
- Don't give up if children aren't regular readers – there will be books for them!

- Visit bookshops and libraries to get recommendations
- Encourage them to listen to audiobooks
- Support school libraries
- Give books as gifts

There's a lot more information about how to encourage children to read on our websites: **www.RaisingReaders.co.uk** and **www.JoinRaisingReaders.com**.

Thank you for reading.